THE COMPLETE CASES OF
MALACHI MANATEE

THE COMPLETE CASES OF

MALACHI MANATEE ™

WILLIAM R. COX

INTRODUCTION BY
WILLIAM LAMPKIN

POPULAR PUBLICATIONS • 2025

PUBLISHING HISTORY

Introduction copyright © 2025 William Lampkin. All rights reserved.

"Malachi Comes Home" originally appeared in the August 1944 issue of *Dime Detective* magazine. Copyright 1944 by Popular Publications, Inc. Copyright renewed 1971 and assigned to Steeger Properties, LLC. All rights reserved.

"Malachi Butts In" originally appeared in the January 1945 issue of *Dime Detective* magazine. Copyright 1945 by Popular Publications, Inc. Copyright renewed 1972 and assigned to Steeger Properties, LLC. All rights reserved.

"Malachi Attends a Party" originally appeared in the May 1945 issue of *Dime Detective* magazine. Copyright 1945 by Popular Publications, Inc. Copyright renewed 1973 and assigned to Steeger Properties, LLC. All rights reserved.

"Shame on Malachi!" originally appeared in the July 1945 issue of *Dime Detective* magazine. Copyright 1945 by Popular Publications, Inc. Copyright renewed 1973 and assigned to Steeger Properties, LLC. All rights reserved.

"Slay-Belle" originally appeared in the October 1945 issue of *Dime Detective* magazine. Copyright 1945 by Popular Publications, Inc. Copyright renewed 1973 and assigned to Steeger Properties, LLC. All rights reserved.

"Vacation—With Slay" originally appeared in the January 1946 issue of *Dime Detective* magazine. Copyright 1946 by Popular Publications, Inc. Copyright renewed 1973 and assigned to Steeger Properties, LLC. All rights reserved.

"Objective—Murder!" originally appeared in the March 1946 issue of *Dime Detective* magazine. Copyright 1946 by Popular Publications, Inc. Copyright renewed 1974 and assigned to Steeger Properties, LLC. All rights reserved.

"Death Wins an Oscar" originally appeared in the June 1946 issue of *Dime Detective* magazine. Copyright 1946 by Popular Publications, Inc. Copyright renewed 1974 and assigned to Steeger Properties, LLC. All rights reserved.

"Game, Set and Murder" originally appeared in the September 1946 issue of *Dime Detective* magazine. Copyright 1946 by Popular Publications, Inc. Copyright renewed 1974 and assigned to Steeger Properties, LLC. All rights reserved.

TABLE OF CONTENTS

MEET MALACHI MANATEE

by William Lampkin

"This is my hometown. There is an election going on. That man over there with the white hair is running for office. He wants to clean out the crooks who have been infesting Bay City for twelve years."

WITH THAT straightforward, to-the-point quote, William R. Cox introduces us to amateur detective Malachi Manatee in "Malachi Comes Home" *(Dime Detective,* August 1944).

Twenty years before John D. MacDonald made Florida the stomping grounds of Travis McGee, in 1964's *The Deep Blue Good-by,* Cox's Manatee began cleaning up corrupt cops, politicians, and businessmen along the Sunshine State's west coast beaches.

"Malachi is a weird one, one of a kind because we had to write of oddballs," Cox tells James L. Traylor in an interview published in *The Armchair Detective* (Vol. 15, No. 3; 1982) and reprinted in *Dime Detective Companion* (Altus Press, 2011). "The competition was keener in crime than in westerns, and I have never been a John Dickson Carr and had to depend upon characterization. Kenneth White, a tough editor for *Dime Detective,* the top book at Popular, ... liked Malachi and bought a string of them."

Cox's amateur detective prowled Florida's fictional "Bay City" and nearby resort towns through nine stories in *Dime Detective* between August 1944 and September 1946. He's accompanied by his pal, Tack Hinton, and his ex-fiancée, Ilene Carver.

Malachi, one of pulp magazine's many "defective detectives," and Tack are recently discharged for injuries suffered as Marines, fighting in the bloody battle for Tarawa Island nine months earlier. A Japanese soldier stabbed Malachi, a lieutenant, in the knee with a bayonet. Initially, Tack, a sergeant and the narrator of the series, suffers from "spots on my lung" caused by malaria, followed by pneumonia, which leaves him short-winded. (In later stories, he blames the enemy: "When they got Malachi in the left leg, they got me through the lungs, and the resulting scar tissue had not healed" ["Death Wins an Oscar," June 1946].)

In either case, both men are back in Malachi's hometown, Bay City, after months of rehabilitation. Tack recalls, "We made the rounds of private hospitals, clinics, good docs, trying to get his leg and my scar tissue fixed."

The pair turns to adventure as a cure-all, to help them put memories of the war out of their minds. "Since the Pacific war days, Malachi and I, both somewhat crippled, needed stimulation to keep our minds from ourselves and our ills," Tack says ("Vacation — With Slay," January 1946).

They can do that thanks to Malachi's millions. Malachi inherited much of his fortune from his father (but the fortune seems to grow from $1 million in the first story to $6 million to $12 million by the end of the series). Both had athletic pasts. Tack played for the New York Giants, boxed, and worked six months as a private eye on divorce cases. But, unlike Malachi, Tack is penniless.

In the first story, Malachi offers Tack a job:

Malachi turned his full attention upon me. He said: "I know who you are." He has eyes which can be very tender and good when he wants. He is a bad character in lots of ways, this Malachi Manatee. He is tough and he just plain don't give a damn when he gets started on something. But he is a good one in a pinch, believe me. He said: "This is hard to get out. We've been together for two years. Lots of people didn't like us. You suit me and I want you to stay with me."

He had never let go of me since we were discharged. We made the rounds of private hospitals, clinics, good docs, trying to get his leg and my scar tissue fixed. Lots of times I thought I was doing it on my own, because I paid my bills as long as the cash held out. But now I realized that he had tooled me along with that persuasive manner of his.

He said: "You know how I am, Tack. Erratic. Neither of us feels very good about — things. I want to offer you a job as my secretary … hell, to take the raps in the jaw I collect — like you know about."

The pair runs into Malachi's ex-fiancée, Ilene, at a small nightclub near Bay City. After her uncle and ward is murdered, she takes up with Malachi and Tack on their adventures.

Whereas Travis McGee was a hired "salvage consultant," Malachi feels it is his obligation to root out corruption, but not as a paid investigator. He does it because he wants to.

That feeling of obligation leads the three — Malachi, Tack, and Ilene — to politics, business, and murder. "Corruption in public office was (Malachi's) particular interest and the carelessness of the American public in this respect was his despair" ("Malachi Butts In," January 1945).

Tack describes his pal in the opening story:

Malachi stretched his bad leg. He is six-feet-four, tops me by one inch, and although at that time he had not regained his normal poundage, he was a noticeable figure every place we went. He has blond, satanic good looks and a certain magnetism which springs from his brooding slant on life and from an unorthodox and speedy mind.

We later learn that Malachi's family took its curious surname from the Manatee River (which runs just north of the Bradenton/Sarasota area and empties into Tampa Bay) at "a time when their own name would have proved embarrassing."

In the stories, good guys often end up dead. One example is Dave Acton, a citrus grower who ends up stabbed in a fit of passion:

> Dave Acton had never done a lick of work in his life, owned almost as many shekels as Malachi, had been 4F in the war — and no wonder, the liquor he drank. Not that the booze showed any effects on him. He was a two-fisted guzzler, but liquor only made him more amiable and friendly. He never said a cross word, nor did a mean thought ever seem to cross his mind. He wasn't pretty, but he was kindly and people liked him. ("Objective — Murder," March 1946)

It's not the underprivileged — jealous of the wealthy — who take nefarious action. It's the wealthy themselves — jealous of each other's power, money, land, and women. The crime Malachi uncovers revolves around greed and lust.

Cox's Malachi Manatee stories follow a basic formula: The characters are introduced; a murder is discovered; a second murder occurs despite Malachi, Tack, or Ilene being able to do anything about it; then Malachi puts the clues together to reveal the killer.

The last four stories clock in at over 8,500 words (the final one totals over 11,700, divided into three chapters), giving Cox more space for character development. The later stories are better written, too.

They are all tight tales with terse dialogue and plenty of bare-knuckle action. (Malachi and Tack prefer to take action with their fists for the most part; Ilene, on the other hand, doesn't mind using a gun.)

Malachi has always been a violent character and "dearly loves a fight," Tack tells us. Staying in the thick of crime suits Malachi.

But as the series progresses, Tack notes that Malachi's adventurous streak may be ebbing, which is something of a surprise for a pulp series:

> Since the war, we had been barging about Florida, looking for excitement and finding enough to keep us busy. Now that the restlessness engendered by action under fire was wearing off, he had shown signs of getting ready to settle down. ...
>
> He had millions, but these are not times to let money stagnate. Pretty soon no money, I figured. It was time to go into business and be busy and progressive. Florida, the land of opportunity! Ilene and I both wanted Malachi to get into something which would keep him occupied.
>
> Failing that, Ilene wanted to go to New York and start something up there. "The Big Time," she said, "is the place for Malachi. Besides, I know a bar where they make the best Daiquiris in the world. A girl can always amuse herself in New York."
>
> But Malachi was a Floridian and he had been investigating fruit concentrates, cattle, oil, the fishing industry. He had even considered politics, since his deepest interest lay in cleaning up government in its relation to crime. But he lacked the pomposity so necessary to running for office in the South. ("Death Wins an Oscar," June 1946)

It's a running theme that Ilene would rather live it up in New York on Malachi's dime than hang out in Bay City. Like Tack, she's destitute without Malachi.

Her uncle, who was murdered in the first story, squandered her inheritance on his failed political career. She is left with only $7,000.

But it's more than money that keeps her involved with Malachi:

> Did I say Ilene is red-haired and gorgeous?
>
> She has known Malachi since childhood, undoubtedly far too well, and that is probably the reason they do not marry. But there is a fascination between them which precludes either wedding someone else. This is too bad, since I, for one, would gladly marry Ilene tomorrow — today! ("Slay-Belle," October 1945)

Tack admires Malachi too much to pursue Ilene, and by the final story in the series, Tack begins considering other women. And Ilene, meanwhile, makes no mention of wanting to go to New York.

Had the series moved to New York, Cox most likely would have been able to write knowledgeably about it since he was born in Peapack, N.J., and reared in Newark. But Florida was where the series remained for all nine stories. It was also a place Cox was familiar with.

Cox moved to the Sunshine State soon after he started selling his fiction to the pulps, living first on Anna Maria Island, a barrier island at the mouth of Tampa Bay, near warm-weather residences of several pulp fictioneers, such as Wyatt Blassingame, MacKinley Kantor, and Talbot Mundy. But by mid-1948, he was divorced and headed to California to break into the television industry.

"Popular Publications was my home," Cox says in *The Armchair Detective* interview. *"Dime Mystery, Dime Detective,* and *Detective Tales* were my markets, plus the sports and westerns which filled out the scheme of things. I averaged 50,000 words per month, played tennis every day, took trips, enjoyed life, drove a Lincoln Zephyr, owned a fine house in Florida."

By 1940, he and his wife at the time, Lee, were living in a bungalow on Davis Islands in Tampa Bay, just over a bridge from downtown Tampa.

Davis Islands makes an appearance in the series' final two stories as "Mavis Isles":

> Malachi and I ... went to the little house we had managed to build out on Mavis Isles, a suburb of Bay City situated over a bridge in the bay, but adjacent to town. We used this house for headquarters and had an old housekeeper of ebony hue named Hattie who ran it. ("Death Wins an Oscar," June 1946)

Other Florida locales — actual and fictional — play prominent roles in the stories. Cox was clearly familiar with Florida's west coast and its culture, its blend of resorts and rural areas, and anchors the stories in authentic settings.

Cox takes us from the metropolis of Bay City (which may play the fictional role of Tampa in the series) to the west coast resort town of Gulf Town (Clearwater or Sarasota, maybe?). From the Gulf Lodge — "quite a place, strung out along the beach in two-storied, modern buildings erected just prior to the war" — to Dugan's Bar-B-Q — "just a Florida joint — a bare, barn-like structure with a bar at the side, a nickel-grabbing jukebox which played the worst records of the day, some tables with scarred tops and uncomfortable wire chairs." From swank tennis courts to tropical swamps.

Arguably, MacDonald's Travis McGee, and other Florida private eyes such as the late Tim Dorsey's Serge Storms and, more recently, Carl Hiaasen's Andrew Yancy, owe a debt to William R. Cox and Malachi Manatee.

MALACHI COMES HOME

HE IS A BAD CHARACTER, THIS MALACHI MANATEE. HE IS TOUGH AND JUST PLAIN DON'T GIVE A DAMN, BUT HE IS GOOD IN A PINCH. AND THIS IS A PINCH, BELIEVE ME, WITH BAY CITY'S POLITICOS AT EACH OTHER'S THROATS, TWO OF THE OPPOSITION ALREADY NEATLY DISPOSED OF—AND ME AND MALACHI HOLDING THE BAG.

MALACHI MANATEE said: "This is my home town. There is an election going on. That man over there with the white hair is running for office. He wants to clean out the crooks who have been infesting Bay City for twelve years."

We were in a small night club near Bay City, Florida. The white-haired man was handsome, florid, prosperous looking. Accompanying him was a girl with reddish hair in which she had tied a checkered ribbon that made her seem much younger than she was. She was exceedingly beautiful. Her eyes were very bright and slanted a little, giving her an appearance of alertness.

I said: "Who is interested in a political race in your home town? Let us go some place and do something. I tell you I cannot stand this inaction."

Malachi stretched his bad leg. He is six feet four, tops me by one inch, and although at that time he had not regained his normal poundage, he was a noticeable figure every place we went. He has blond, satanic good looks and a certain magnetism which springs from his brooding slant on life and from an unorthodox and speedy mind. He said: "Tack, you've got to simmer down. You are no longer in the Marines. You are a crock. I am a crock. You are out of the war. Look at all these people. They are not fighting a

3

war. They buy a bond, support the Red Cross—and go on with their jobs."

I said: "I have not got a job. I cannot play football with this bum lung. I do not want to be a wrestler. I cannot pass an examination for the cops. Who wants to hire me?"

"Look!" said Malachi. "There is the gambler who runs Bay City's rackets. His name is Tom Gruber. The two ugly men with him are Ike and Mike, no one knows which is which. They are his bodyguards."

Gruber was a fat man who had once been tough. You could tell by his upper chin, which still looked hard. The other chins bobbled beneath it as he stared at the white-haired man with the pretty girl. Ike and Mike looked amazingly alike considering that one was four inches shorter than the other. They wore sports clothes, for it was springtime in Florida, and no hats on their sleek, round heads. They followed Gruber to a reserved table and sat flanking him. I wondered where they packed their guns under their light clothing.

Malachi said: "The reform candidate is George Carver. The girl is Ilene Carver, his ward and niece."

ALONGSIDE US a skimpy little man in a dirty white apron said: "Here's your drinks…" His voice dropped to a whisper. "You innarested in Carver and Gruber? I got somethin'…."

Malachi said: "What's your name?"

"Mickey," said the waiter. "I useta work for Gruber, dealin'. For a C-note…"

Malachi said: "Skip it. I'm just a tourist." The little man sneered. "You're Malachi Manatee, the kid with the millions. I seen you play football…"

Malachi handed him a bill and said: "Skip it." The waiter hesitated, stared at me, then shut his weak mouth tight and went away.

Another party came in. There was a hulking, bald man with a scar and the fair skin of a Scandinavian, a lean vulture of a man and two heavy-shouldered individuals with "cop" written all over them. They had assorted females with them, none beautiful. The two policemen went in the back of the place and seemed to be interrogating the proprietor, a Latin chap.

Weevil tried to kick Malachi, but got a sudden reverse jolt as Malachi's right elbow split his cheek open and dropped him.

Malachi said: "This assumes dramatic proportions. There is Ivar Dolsan, the incumbent mayor, whom Carver opposes. The skinny buzzard is Chief of Police Jake Weevil, a cracker boy come to power. All the elements of the bitter election are here in the Star Club."

"Please, Malachi," I said. "Will you tell me why you brought me to Bay City and what sort of an idea is in your screwy head? You are not fighting Japanese on Tarawa now. You are home, with a bum gam, discharged from service. All right, you have got a million bucks. I am Tack Hinton, remember? I am a poor guy."

Malachi turned his full attention upon me. He said: "I know who you are." He has eyes which can be very tender and good when he wants. He is a bad character in lots of ways, this Malachi Manatee. He is tough and he just plain don't give a damn when he gets started on something. But he is a good one in a pinch, believe me. He said: "This is hard to get out. We've been together for two years. Lots of people didn't like us. You suit me and I want you to stay with me."

He had never let go of me since we were discharged. We made the rounds of private hospitals, clinics, good docs, trying to get his leg and my scar tissue fixed. Lots of times I thought I was doing it on my own, because I paid my bills as long as the cash held out. But now I realized that he had tooled me along with that persuasive manner of his.

He said: "You know how I am, Tack. Erratic. Neither of us feels very good about—things. I want to offer you a job as my secretary… hell, to take the raps in the jaw I collect— like you know about."

I said: "Now wait a minute, pal. You know better than that—"

He said quickly: "Not as a paid companion. Don't get me wrong. I'll find things for us to do."

"Nix, chum," I told him. "I'll make out I've been broke in hard times. The shipyards—"

"A week," he said. His brows contracted and he was, I realized suddenly, pleading with me. "Stay with me a week. If things don't develop, you can go. If I haven't legitimate need of you, I'll say so myself. One week."

"This is screwy," I said.

Malachi said in a very low voice: "We're not sentimental. But when Jojo and Johnny Jump and the others died out there and we lived, something went out of our lives. It left a feeling that is not good. We understand that. Other people can't possibly."

"It's all past," I said roughly. "Forget it."

"You can't forget," he said. "But in action you can lose it for a little while. Let's get some action."

I sat frowning, looking about the room. It was just a small, roadside joint, with some pretensions as to decoration, with fair food and a small, sad band. People danced and they lowered the lights. I was thinking thoughts which were not good, and when the lights went up it was by chance that I noticed anything wrong with the layout.

The girl was sitting at the table alone. George Carver had disappeared. Gruber, the gambler chief, and his two bodyguards were going out the rear door. The mayor was sitting, staring at the back of Ike or Mike, whichever was the last one out, and his face was stony with some emotion I could not read. The chief of police leaned towards Dolsan and said something and the mayor shrugged and got enough control to grin feebly.

AT THAT moment the girl got up and came directly to our table. She stopped and looked at Malachi and said: "Hello, character. Where's the uniform and the medals?"

We struggled to our feet. She had a husky, pleasing voice but her manner was almost insolent. Malachi said: "Sit down, Ilene—and don't crack wise all the time. It's unbecoming."

She said to me: "You are Tack Hinton. I saw you play tackle for the Giants once. You're a better fullback."

"Sure," I said. I liked her, somehow. She was nervous and talking tough to cover up. "But Owens needed flesh in the line that year. Did you see those Bears kill us?"

"It was Washington and they murdered you," she said and then she grinned and I liked her even more. We all sat down. Mickey came, his eyes sliding nervously around the room and absently took our order. Ilene wanted a double bourbon, but she did not look like a whiskey drinker.

Malachi said: "How is the political campaign?"

"I wouldn't know," she said. "Are you settling down here?"

"No," said Malachi. "Has George a chance?"

"He thinks so," she said. "Are you as brutal as ever?"

"More so," said Malachi. "Are you still meaner than hell?"

She glanced at the rear door. The Star Club is on the beach and when the noise stopped at times you could hear the Gulf of Mexico lapping at the white sand. There was a breeze and the stiff palm fronds rattled like skeletons. She said: "Let's not fight. Will you dance with me?"

Malachi said: "I keep my dancing in Tack's name."

I dance like any football player, but I knew he wanted me to take her out there. The band started to play and I did, and Malachi got up and limped towards the back of the place. She stopped and her body became rigid as a post, watching him. She said: "I didn't know he was hurt that badly."

"You think the Marines would let him go otherwise?" I said. "He was one hell of a soldier."

We muddled about on the crowded floor. I happened to glance at the table where the mayor's party sat and Ivar Dolsan's flinty face was directed at us, following us. Jake Weevil looked morose, but he, too, was watching Ilene, I thought.

She said: "I was in love with him once. He's cruel."

"You are nuts," I said politely. "He is a right guy."

"Listen, bub," she said, "I know that character. He stood me up, but good, one time. We even had the license, but he just never showed up."

"Maybe he had a good reason," I said.

"He was joining the Marines—if that is a good reason." She frowned a little. "Maybe it was, at that. I'm a lot older than I was then. Maybe he was right. I'm sort of mean myself."

She had one of those large handbags that women carry. It got in the way, but she clung tightly to it. We edged on the outer fringe of the mob and came to our table and by mutual agreement we stopped and sat down. She drained her big drink.

I said: "Tell me more about you."

"Just a moment," she said. "I'd better powder my nose. Malachi hates shiny noses. Maybe I'm going to like him again."

She wandered off toward the rear of the place. I sat and played with my drink. Malachi had never mentioned this girl. She was a strange one, all right, without artifices. The powder business was such an obvious stall I could ignore it. She was, like Malachi, one of those people who don't give a damn. I wondered if they would have been happy....

Malachi came back in and sat down. He said: "Where is that female Commando?"

"She's fine," I said. "I like her."

Malachi took a big drink. Then he said: "You're a damn smart guy, Tack."

"No, I'm not. I'm dumb. But I know what I like."

"She's too tight, inside," he scowled. "I never saw her like that... I wonder what's keeping George Carver outside so long? Gruber and his two hoods went out after him. George has been raising hell about Gruber and his mob and the mayor and the chief of police and everything connected with Bay City's governmental setup."

"Stop manufacturing excitement," I said. "Carver's probably making a nice little deal with Gruber to sew up the election. You know politics."

He grinned, because what I had said was cynical and he liked being tough. Ilene came strolling back, her nose powdered, but pinched at the nostrils. She sat down and said casually: "I'm a little worried about George. I wonder if Tack would go out and take a look around back? I couldn't see him out there."

I figured she wanted to be alone with Malachi, so I got up and drifted away. The rear door opened right onto the beach and there was a boardwalk for a ways. The palms made fantastic shadows against a bluish night sky over which a moon presided faintly, and the water was ink in motion.

THERE WAS a warmth beneath the cool breeze and I lit a cigarette and strolled. Between the club and the water was a stretch where scrub palmetto spread darkly, then came the shining sand, chopped into shadows by footmarks of meandering lovers and brave early bathers. I threw away my match at the extreme edge of the scrub and it flared for an instant.

My eye caught the heel of the shoe. I went over in two jumps and bent to stare. The foot was oddly twisted and the leg of the prone man did not seem natural in its awkward position.

I lit another match, cupping it in my hands. The white hair of George Carver was clotted with something dark and sticky. I lit another match and saw that he was not breathing. The back of his skull was mashed.

I stood there, finishing the cigarette. I'd seen a lot of dead men lately, but this was different. I was a little sick, and then I was mad. People shouldn't go around killing other people unless it is in a war. No matter how many battles you've been in, murder never seems right. It is a foul thing and within everyone is a loathing for a killer who slays for profit.

I looked around, but my detective experience was limited to six months as a private operator, a lousy job of getting divorce evidence. There were many footprints in the sand, none of which meant anything. I saw that Carver's pockets had been emptied, but that was to be expected. I noted the way he had fallen, crumpled, on his side and decided someone had handled him, probably after he was dead, because that one leg was stuck out all wrong.

I resisted an impulse to straighten out the corpse and went indoors. When I sat down at the table, Malachi said: "What's wrong, Tack?"

"You'd better get ready," I said to Ilene. "It's not good."

She gripped the table and said: "It's George!"

I nodded. "Someone attacked him…"

She tightened her jaw muscles and said: "He's—dead?"

"The chief of police is over there," I said. "We'd better tell him about it. There were two cops around..."

Ilene said: "Take me to him. I've got to know."

Malachi had her by the arm. The big bag was still clutched in her hand and she was as white as paper. He said: "Steady, Ilene. I'll take you out there... Tack, you speak to Weevil."

I got up and went over to the table where the mayor and the chief were sitting. I said: "Excuse me, but could I see you gentlemen privately for a moment?"

The women looked haughtily at me, but Weevil got up and walked a few feet away from the table. He said impatiently: "O.K., bub, let's have it. And none of Manatee's funny jokes."

"This is a fine joke," I said. The cops appeared from somewhere and came close behind me. I did not like that, so I moved where I could keep an eye on them. I said: "Your opposition just got knocked off. Carver's lying out there with his skull caved in. Does that make you happy?"

Weevil snarled: "Don't get funny, I told you. Mose, take a look... Where are those two going?" He pointed at Malachi and Ilene with his chin. He had a narrow, thrusting chin.

I said: "How do I know? You're pretty tough, eh, Chief?"

The other big detective came closer. Weevil looked at me and said: "I know Malachi Manatee. And I'm tough enough."

"Well, I don't like tough cops," I said. "You want to make something out of that?"

Ivar Dolsan, scowling, stepped to my side. He said: "Er—can I be of assistance, perhaps?"

Weevil said: "One of Manatee's playmates don't like me."

Dolsan said: "None of that, Chief. What's the complaint?"

Weevil said: "He says Carver's been conked."

In the doorway, the cop called Mose was beckoning strenuously. Dolsan said: "Carver? Why—he was here a moment ago."

"So was Gruber—and his guns," said Weevil significantly. "They're all gone, now."

He and the second cop, whose name was Pete Gann, started out of the place. Dolsan stared at me and whispered: "Is Carver dead?"

I said: "He ain't kicking."

Dolsan never answered me. He looked quite ill. He went back to the table and sat there, not answering the questions of the women. After a moment he herded them all out and a car drove away and then he came back and went through to the rear.

When I got out there, Weevil was barking orders about the coroner and telephoning and warning Malachi to get back and out of the way. Ilene was weeping quietly. Malachi took her over and put her in his car. The Latin proprietor was wringing his hands. Mose and Pete, the cops, were blocking the body from casual view. George Carver was just lying there, not caring.

Weevil said: "You—big guy. You found him? Stick around."

"Sure," I said. "I love watching the police work."

Weevil growled something to his two cops and they glowered at me. I waited while the coroner came and pronounced Carver dead, while the morgue basket was trundled out and the dead body placed in it. There were a couple of flashlight pictures taken and the crowd inside became unruly and uniformed policemen quieted them. Weevil was right in the middle of it, and he certainly was a decisive character.

He said: "I want Gruber and his gunsels picked up at once."

Pete and Mose moved off. The crowd was thinning. Weevil had taken my deposition and I was walking back to where we had parked our car. A voice whispered: "Pssst!"

Malachi's convertible was gone. There was a big, beat-up Buick standing nearby. Mickey the waiter, was crouching beside it. He croaked: "Take me inta town. I got somethin', I tell ya."

He saw Weevil, just behind me, then. He broke and ran like a scared rabbit. Weevil didn't seem to see him, so I let it go. The parking attendant said: "Mr. Manatee said you should take this Buick in."

Weevil said: "No, you don't! That's Carver's car. I got to look that over."

I said: "Well, look at it. He wasn't killed in the car, was he?"

"How do I know?" said Weevil. He turned on a flashlight and examined the interior of the sedan. I saw the stain as soon as he did. It was on the back of the front seat, as though Carver had been sitting in conference with someone who had simply reached out and beat in his skull. I saw the picture at once. Weevil said to me: "Well, wise guy?"

I said: "You scored one there." I walked back and there was a party leaving, somewhat flustered. I bummed a ride from them and had to hold a skinny blonde on my lap all the way to Bay City. It wasn't a pleasure.

IT WAS three days later. We were in Weevil's big, gloomy office in the antiquated Bay City Headquarters. Mose and Pete formed a background for Weevil's sharp exposition. Mayor Dolsan fidgeted on a chair and seemed unhappy. Ilene, Malachi and I sat in a row, like school children and listened.

Weevil said: "George drew seven thousand dollars from the bank that day. He went out to the Star Club, a place he never frequented, and Gruber came in there with his bodyguards. They all went out back. When we found George the seven grand was gone. That looks open and shut. Gruber pretended to make a deal of some kind with him, sat in the car to talk it over, then had George killed and took his money."

"Except it didn't happen that way," said Malachi. He was sitting quietly, his bad leg crossed over the other, his blue eyes mild. He seemed perfectly at ease and without guile, but he was coiled like a cat about to spring.

Weevil said: "Do you want to tell us about it?" He hated Malachi with a passion. It stuck out all over him.

Malachi said: "Gruber has two alibis. One, the waiter, Mickey, who saw him drive away while George Carver was still alive. Two, a filling station attendant who recognized the car and Gruber at the exact time which coincides with Mickey's story."

Weevil snarled: "Show me a crook as big as Gruber without an alibi ready."

"Maybe I could, at that," said Malachi. He let that drop among them and was silent.

Weevil said: "George was our opposition, but we don't like this killing at all. It looks damned bad for us. If we can't solve it, we get a black eye. If Miss Carver knows something, or if she heard anything about a deal between her uncle and Gruber, I want to know it."

Malachi said softly: "If Gruber and Carver made a deal, you boys would be out on your ears. Gruber controls a lot of the votes that put you in here."

Dolsan fidgeted and said: "That is neither here nor there. We are trying to solve a foul murder. George Carver was one of our most respected citizens."

Ilene said clearly: "If I knew of any deal between Uncle George and Tom Gruber, I wouldn't tell you characters." She was wearing a beige dress, with no mourning. She had completely recovered her magnificent aplomb. She did not like these city officials and was not averse to showing it.

Weevil said: "You'll be subpoenaed before this is over. You'll be put under oath…"

Malachi uncoiled. He stood, watching Weevil's angry face. The chief stared back at him. Malachi said: "We came down here voluntarily. We're leaving. And be careful of threats, Weevil. I don't like threats."

"You can't bluff me, playboy," said Weevil tightly. "I knew you when. Your old man's dough spoiled you years ago. Bay City doesn't need you or your smart boy friend."

I looked at Malachi, then at the two big cops. Scar tissue on your lung doesn't really slow you down except in the long run. For a few minutes you are as good as ever. This seemed like a good time for action to me. But Malachi just grinned like a satanic cat. He said: "I hear you talking, Chief. So long."

We walked out. We got into Malachi's car and started driving out of Bay City. It was early in the evening and quite warm. We were on the road leading to the Star Club.

Ilene said: "Let's get out of town. I've got a cousin in New York."

Malachi said: "I'm amazed that George didn't leave anything for you, Ilene. It worries me."

"He was never a businessman," she said. "He put a lot of money into this campaign."

"That seven thousand," said Malachi. "That was a lot for him to take out of the bank. Even to make a deal which would insure him of the election."

"George was a politician," she sighed. Then she said: "I really think I'll go to New York. I'll make a reservation tomorrow."

Malachi drove along slowly. He said: "I could lend you some money, Ilene." That seemed like a hell of a thing to say to a girl he had once been engaged to, and I looked sharply at him. His face was without expression.

Ilene said: "Thank you, Malachi. I have enough to get started. I can model—or something."

NOTHING MORE was said. We stopped at a place set back from the road where a dim light showed. It was Tom Gruber's place, known as The Dive. We got out and went up the path and the door opened and a big Negro looked us over. I gave him a slight shove and we went past.

The gaming room was empty. You could see where the tables had stood, but they were gone. Gruber had closed up until the heat was off, which was very smart. We went across the room and found an office. The door was open and Gruber was walking up and down, a fat man worried to death. Ike and Mike leaned against the wall and glowered at us.

Gruber began talking right away. "I'm glad to talk to you folks. I've got nothing to hide. City Hall is trying to frame me. There's cops all over this place."

Ilene sat down. Malachi said deliberately: "You're a damned liar, Gruber. All crooks have something to hide."

Gruber's one tough chin got hard. The others bobbled. Ike and Mike came away from the wall. Gruber said: "You can't talk to me like that, Manatee. I'll—"

I stepped in and took him by the belly, getting a firm handful of flesh. I started him back toward the gunmen and pushed. He split them and I got a hand on each. I cracked them together, quite roughly, and dumped them on top of him. They made a conglomerate heap on the floor. I kicked a couple of small automatics loose from them and said: "We might as well get set straight in the beginning. We want something close to the truth."

Gruber struggled to his feet. He said wildly: "I didn't kill Carver. I wouldn't kill him. I tried to make a deal with him, but he wanted to shut me up. I couldn't stand being shut up. It'd break me. Damn it, Manatee, can't you see I wouldn't knock him off? I didn't have to. I could support Dolsan and get by."

Malachi said: "You sat in the Buick and talked to him? You got out and left him sitting in there?"

"Ask Mike and Ike!" said Gruber. "They saw it all."

Malachi looked at the two gunsels and without a smile said: "Is that right?"

They nodded furiously. They wanted a crack at me. I said to them: "Just take it easy. I didn't hurt you. I might have, but we are not sure about you yet."

Gruber said: "You don't have to strong-arm me. I know you two have been overseas and are tough enough. I'm a gambler, so all right, I'm halfway honest. Legally I got alibis. They never found a print on that car George was killed in. They got nothing on me except that I was in the Star that night."

He was stubborn about it. He had taken the mauling I handed him and was not sore. I watched the three of them and wondered. They were sullen, but somehow they were not scared.

Malachi said: "I'm going to see Mickey. The cops have not yet got around to working him over. Maybe we are tougher than the cops, even Mose and Pete. Maybe I will see you later, Gruber."

The gambler said: "I know you guys—I know what you'll do. I'm not dumb, and I know you're making a try for the gal. But any time I steal seven grand, it won't be off a corpse. See Mickey… I wish you could protect him. I'm a little scared, Manatee, I admit it. There are people who would like to take over the stuff I control. You know there always will be gambling in Bay City. George couldn't have stopped it. He knew that, too. George was a politician."

Ilene got up abruptly and Malachi said: "O.K., Gruber. I heard you."

We went out and drove to the Star Club. Mickey was not in sight. Malachi called the proprietor and said: "Where is Mickey?"

The Latin spread his hands. "He came… he went— Who knows? This trouble is not good, hey?"

Malachi said: "When did he disappear?"

"He did not disappear. He walk out, maybe fifteen minutes."

I got up and went out the back door again. I had a terrible feeling of repeating the action of another time. I even lit a cigarette and threw the match into the scrub palmetto.

This time it was a hand, and it moved. I got down on my knees alongside the frail figure of Mickey and lifted his head. It was pretty bad, but not as bad as George Carver's had been. Mickey said in his hoarse voice: "Toldja I had somethin'… Kept clammed… Tried t' git to ya—George Carver was—"

I said: "He was making a deal with Gruber."

"Yeah…" the voice began again. "Gruber… dive… They got me—"

THAT WAS all. Mickey was dead, in almost the same spot where Carver had lain. I took another look around the spot, then went back indoors. There was some blood on me. I went into the men's room and washed it off.

I dried my hands thoughtfully and went out. The ladies' room was smack next door. I went into the main hall and there were Weevil, Pete and Mose. The two cops had their guns out and were watching me.

Malachi said: "Now you are acting like a double damn fool, Jake."

Ilene looked like a red cat, her eyes shooting green fire. Weevil said: "We saw him, this time. He dropped Mickey and walked away cool as ice. He's broke and jobless. He could use that seven thousand George had on him. Why should Gruber kill George? He didn't have to. Hinton killed him, Mickey saw it, and he just killed Mickey. Look at him! He's strong enough to smash a man's head with anything he picks up. He could toss the weapon into the Gulf—"

"You're talking too much, Jake," said Malachi. He was lounging at the table, but his face was careful and alert. "You're trying to make up a case as you go along."

I did not say anything, because I was having a brainstorm. I just looked at Ilene and at Malachi. The two cops held their guns waist high, pointing at my middle. Weevil said: "I know what I'm talking about. I'm taking Hinton to jail."

The people in the place were all huddled down at the far end, staring at us out of parchment faces. The Latin proprietor was hopping about, distracted, at his wits' end. The door opened and Mayor Dolsan bustled in. Behind him were Gruber and the two hoods with the rhyming names.

Malachi said: "Everybody got here all of a sudden, didn't they? Are you sure you don't want to arrest me as an accessory before or after?"

"It may come to that," said Weevil, his eyes hot. "You think you're a big shot because your old man once ran this burg. You throw your dough around and show off—"

Ilene blurted: "Stop his mouth, Malachi!"

Malachi said: "So you want to put Tack in jail? That is very quaint. Tack could take you apart, right now, guns and all."

"You killers come back and assault private citizens as you were taught in the war—"

Malachi said: "Talk, all talk. Where is your evidence against Tack?"

"I'm arresting him on suspicion of murder," said Weevil.

There was a kind of embarrassed silence. It seemed as though Weevil wanted me to make a plea of innocence, or make a break, or do something. I stood pat, waiting.

Malachi said: "It all seems to hinge on that seven thousand dollars. But Miss Carver has that, right here, in that big bag she totes everywhere. Show them, Ilene."

She hesitated, and I could see it was a complete surprise to her. But she slowly opened the bag and bills tumbled on the table. Malachi said: "George was too smart to take all that money out among crooks."

Mayor Dolsan, Gruber and Ike and Mike were part of the circle around us, now, staring. Without anyone noticing it I changed my position to get them all where I could watch them.

Malachi said: "Now where is Tack's motive?"

Weevil was more amazed at sight of the money than anyone. He said quickly: "How do we know that's the same dough?"

"Don't you remember?" asked Malachi gently. "The bank has the number of the bills. George Carver insisted on that. He meant for that money to be traced… Or are you going to pretend you don't know that?"

Weevil said: "Now see here, Manatee—"

Malachi said: "You and the mayor sat in here while George was killed just outside. Now you want to hang the murder on anyone at all, so long as it is solved quickly. You even try to pitch the killing of a waiter in with it. How do you know Mickey's girl, or an enemy or some itinerant tramp didn't kill him? You see Tack walking away from him and right away you want to arrest him."

Weevil said: "I'm getting awful sick of you, Manatee."

Malachi said: "You were sitting right here when it all happened, you and the mayor and your party. You made the remark that George Carver never frequented this place… I happen to know you and your party were never here before, either. But the night George is making a deal with Tom Gruber, you all come trooping in. And your cops get very nosey, asking the owner questions about the layout and who went where. That sounds phony."

Weevil said: "I'm going to haul you all in as material witnesses to both crimes. Take him, boys."

MALACHI HAD already given me the signal. I picked out Pete, who was nearest, and gave him the Commando rush, which bounced him into Mose and allowed me a second's time. I hit Mose with the edge of my hand across the bridge of his nose and stuck two fingers into Pete's eyes. They floundered about and I cracked each of them with a left hook, short and inside. They went down and Malachi heaved over the table at which he had been sitting.

The table took Dolsan off his feet and then Malachi had Weevil in his hands and was removing a gun from the chief's holster. Weevil tried to kick Malachi, but got a reverse jolt as Malachi's elbow split his cheek wide open and dropped him.

Tom Gruber had not moved. Ike and Mike had their eyes wide open in admiration. Gruber said: "I'm ready to tell it all on the witness stand, Manatee."

"That's good," said Malachi. "I have an idea the town'll be a lot better off."

"Mose and Pete must have killed George," said Gruber. "We had made the deal. I was scared to say so because George was dead and I had to get along with these gougers."

Malachi said: "They were taking you for plenty, weren't they?"

"Too damned much," said Gruber grimly.

"You saw them in the back?" prompted Malachi.

"Yeah," said Gruber. "I saw Mose and Pete and scrammed away, telling George to pay me off at The Dive."

I said: "That's what Mickey was trying to tell me. He heard the whole thing. He knew George was to pay off at The Dive and that someone didn't want him to get there. If George and Gruber got together, Weevil, Dolsan and the boys were through."

"They couldn't stand an audit of the books," nodded Malachi. "Someone had better phone the sheriff. We seem to have used up the local constabulary."

Gruber said: "You guys are awful tough. I'm glad it came out this way. I hated to run off the other night…"

"You're a crook," said Malachi dispassionately. "I don't expect anything of crooks—in any walk of life."

Gruber flushed and Malachi scooped up the bills which had fallen on the floor and put them in Ilene's bag. The prone bodies were stirring. A siren sounded outside and a man with a star pinned to his vest came striding in. Malachi said: "I'll take Ilene outside, Tack. You handle it."

I did and in a little while they were all bundled into the sheriff's car and the morgue wagon was coming for poor Mickey.

Then I joined Ilene and Malachi. He drove towards town in silence for a ways. Then he said: "It's a weak case, with Gruber and those gunsels testifying for the State."

More silence. Then I said: "Did you see George lying out there when you were in the men's room?"

"No," said Malachi. "I saw him get into his car with Gruber."

Then Ilene said very quietly: "All right. You both know it."

Malachi said: "Certainly we know it. But not all of it. You had to see his body, because you went out there at the right time. You took the seven thousand off him. You had to move him to do it."

She said: "Please, Malachi! It wasn't pleasant."

He said: "You thought you wouldn't get the money, that someone might steal it, or that it might be held in escrow. You knew George was broke, and that this was your money—the money he held in trust for you."

She said bitterly: "You're guessing, but you're right. George cleaned me, long ago. I was penniless, except for this money. George was a politician and I was against this deal with Gruber. You know he was going to let Gruber operate and take his cut like all the others before him. You heard Gruber admit the deal was made. I'll testify, Malachi—"

Malachi said: "That's how I figured it out. They were all crooks. They got playing that political game for keeps and it bred murder. I wonder how often that happens?"

Malachi had an idea. I saw it beating its wings inside his head. I said: "O.K., boy, I'm sold. I take the job."

"I gave you action, didn't I?" he said with satisfaction. "I'm liable to dig up some more, around and about. I think I like this sort of unofficial butting into people's business."

We drove into Bay City and pulled up before a bar. Ilene said: "What about me?"

"Come in and have a drink," said Malachi, "You're not so bad in a crowd, at that."

We went in and had a drink.

MALACHI BUTTS IN

MALACHI IS SIX-FOOT-FOUR AND I'M NO SHRIMP MYSELF. WE'VE BEEN THROUGH TARAWA AND WE DON'T SCARE EASY, BUT WHEN IT COMES TO UNDERHANDEDNESS AND BACK-STABBING, GULF TOWN'S POLITICOS COULD TEACH THE NIPS A FEW THINGS.

W E **WENT** into the bar and sat down at a table and had a drink. Malachi Manatee said: "That is Tom Sack sitting with the Chief of Police. What did you learn in Jax?"

Tom Sack was a burly man with big-city copper written all over him. His flat gaze was fixed on the table where Ilene Carver smiled upon a bald, rubicund man and a dark, handsome woman. This was Gulf Town, a nice resort on West Coast Florida where Malachi had spent many vacations in his youth. This was a nice drinking place called Queen's Taste, with a small but noisy band and many soldiers from the nearby air base.

I said: "Tom Sack has operatives in each big Florida city. People come here to get divorces. Tom Sack watches them. If they step out of line, he gets in touch with the spouse up north and tries to create a little trouble. He sometimes makes plenty."

Malachi moved the bad knee he had picked up on Tarawa. He is six feet-four and can see over the heads of folks, which is a great help to him as he is very curious about things.

He said: "The dark woman with Ilene is Rose Frascatti, once connected with Chicago interests. Billy Dill, the bald man, has the slot machines. Over yonder is Charlie Dill, the chief of police, with Tom Sack. Sack, Billy and Charlie all are after Rose Frascatti. And this is supposed to be a clean, quiet town." He lifted his blond eyebrows into a V and grinned. He was very happy because I had confirmed his suspicions about Sack's private detective agency. He was looking for trouble again.

Always he was butting into things and looking for trouble. Since we had come back and were discharged as unfit for military service, Malachi had been seeking out adventure. Corruption in public office was his particular interest and the carelessness of the American public in this respect was his despair.

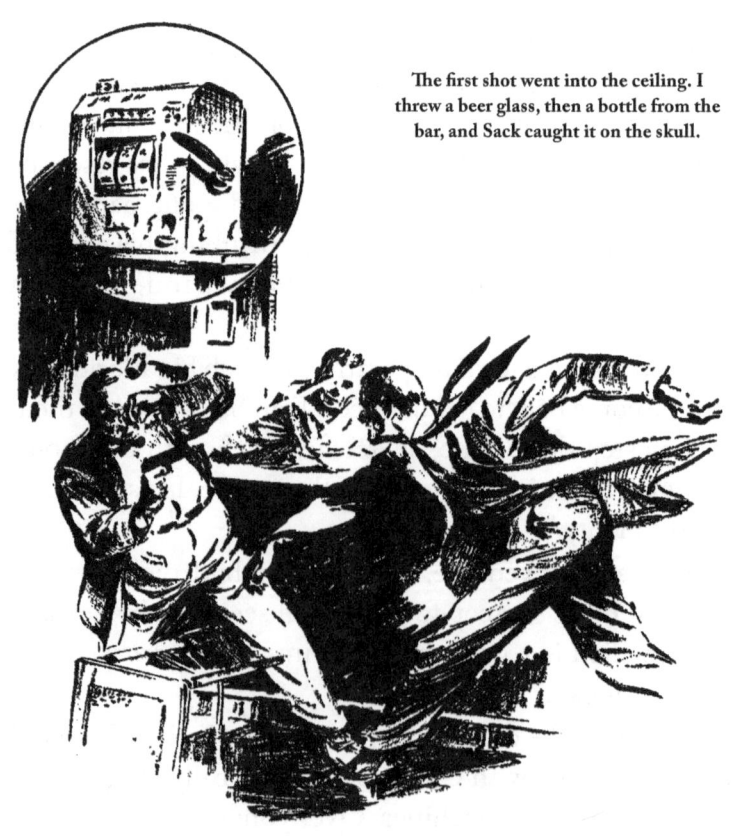

The first shot went into the ceiling. I threw a beer glass, then a bottle from the bar, and Sack caught it on the skull.

Ilene did not choose to recognize us. The reckless redhead was having a fine time, lapping up Scotch at Billy Dill's expense, giggling with Rose Frascatti. Rose was a full-bosomed, black-eyed, ball-of-fire sort of gal. Billy Dill had laugh wrinkles and no eyebrows, a fine paunch and wore silk and sharkskin, very expensive. In the rear of the Queen's Taste the one-armed bandits rattled, spun and paid off but seldom.

Malachi said: "They are taking the buzz boys. The airplane pilots fall for Rose, who leads them to the machines, or has them buy her drinks. Charlie and Billy Dill are silent partners in this place with Rose. Tom Sack is trying to muscle in. The mayor, Freddy Rutan, was a schoolmate of mine. A young squirt—4F. As much spine as a garden snake."

I said: "Sack is a jerk on wheels. But he has a license to operate and his victims can't testify. The divorce situation here is a ticklish thing."

A couple of cadets paused at Rose's table. Billy Dill ordered a round of drinks, took his in a pudgy paw and wandered over to the table where his brother sat with Sack. Immediately, Sack began to snarl about something.

I looked at Charlie Dill, the chief of police. He was a smaller edition of his brother, with the same pale, lidless eyes, the same curving mouth. He said nothing, watching Billy and Sack. I heard Sack say: "You'll deal me in or else, Billy…"

THE BAND played too noisily and the two girls got up to dance with the soldiers. Ilene Carver was as beautiful and unpredictable as ever. She was working her way into the gang, I knew, at Malachi's request. She could be as tough as any of them, if she wanted. Tougher. She was hell on wheels. She was an orphan and had no money and did not give a damn. She had known Malachi Manatee all her life and why they did not get married was more than I could figure. They would make a fine pair of hellions.

The Dill brothers were dead-panned. Sack talked. The dance music stopped, Billy Dill went back to his table and the cadets faded to the slots. Tom Sack, his face red, stalked out of the place.

Charlie Dill came over to our table and said to Malachi: "Manatee, you've put it over. The mayor left town tonight—on a vacation." The pale eyes registered faint contempt. "He left orders to clean out the machines. And to clean up the town."

"Are you going to do it?" Malachi asked him.

"Fred appointed me. He done me favors," said Charlie Dill. His pallid eyes surveyed me, then went back to Malachi. "I ain't denying we made something. People didn't seem to care. Everybody gambles. It'll be tough on Billy to stop, but he'll do it. I can make him do it. I can make Rose act nice."

"Yeah?" drawled Malachi.

"But I can't handle Tom Sack," said the chief flatly. "He's wired in at Tallahassee somehow. He's too big for me. I'm not scared, Manatee, not of him—nor of you. I'm taking orders from Fred and that part's O.K. But Sack's dangerous."

Malachi said: "I hear you talking, Charlie. You close Billy up and take care of Rose. I'll be around a while."

Charlie got up and said: "I don't know how you do it, or why. But you sure are looking for trouble."

He went outside onto the main street of Gulf Town. In a moment we followed him. The city was neat and orderly, without a beach of its own, but adjacent to the keys of white sand and bright shell which adorn the West Coast. Wealthy people lived here and the air base annoyed them so that they kept their daughters under lock and key. I watched two drunken enlisted men wrestle a third and drunker companion toward the air base bus and could not blame the residents too much, even if it did mean playing into the hands of Rose Frascatti and her crowd.

This was a problem we could not solve, this unhappiness of youths far from home, adjacent to small, decent towns, longing for companionship, but deterred from enjoyment thereof by actions of their comrades who would not behave in nice company. Malachi and I had seen all sides of that. We still did not know the answers. All we could do was mess around, hunting for trouble.

It was about eleven and I was tired from the trip, so we went to the Hibiscus House and up to our room, which was big and had a ceiling fan and fine inner-spring mattresses. Manatee rubbed his wounded knee and said: "Ilene is over at the Jacaranda Hotel, where Rose and Billy and Sack stay. Sack has two gorillas named Lib and Eck who are bodyguards and nuisances. There should be some fun."

I said: "If Billy Dill is pulling in his horns, why should Sack demand to be dealt in on something? On what?"

Malachi said: "You heard him too, huh? You're getting to be a regular detective, Tack."

I said: "What other racket have they got?"

"I don't know," said Malachi. "But they're all at each other's throat about Rose and I'm willing to let them start the trouble. Ilene has been helping by telling tales, in order to arouse jealousy among them. That Frascatti gal has some figure, huh?"

"You better not let Ilene hear you say it," I told him.

"Ilene is a firecracker which never quite goes off," said Malachi. "She is a tease and she annoys me."

I went to sleep on that. Ilene was in Malachi's blood like the malaria which had put me down and out and the pneumonia which had left spots on my lung. However, I had no intention of telling him so. Minding my own business has always been a virtue with me. It was Malachi who butted into things. I just went along because I was out of the war and could not play pro football any more and a fellow had to have some action.

I was not particularly interested in Malachi's campaign to save servicemen from getting trimmed by slot machines because it was my firm opinion that they would rather have it that way than be bored. Their dough was bound to be spent by payday and who eventually got it made little difference to me. Furthermore, Malachi did not give a damn. He just wanted a peg to hang a crusade upon and one was as good as another so long as he got excitement. We were, actually, a pair of slaphappy cynics, looking for an argument. It was not pretty, but it kept us alive.

I AWOKE to find Malachi standing over me, dressed in slacks and a tight T shirt, with his muscles bulging. He had that gleeful, devilish glint about him and he said: "Get up, Tack. The parade has started and they are waiting for us in the reviewing stand."

I said: "What the hell time is it? I'm sleepy."

"It's one o'clock and someone murdered Charlie Dill," he said.

I put on some clothing and said: "Where? How?"

But Manatee just led me out of the hotel and down the street and around the corner to a square, yellow brick building with green lamps beside the door. A young man with trembling hands and a tanned, thin face met us.

Malachi said: "This is Fred J. Rutan, the mayor. He came back and found Charlie dead. It upset him and he called me."

"For God's sake, Malachi," said Rutan. "This is awful. You've got me in awful trouble."

He was all shot, but he led us into the office marked chief of police. Charlie was still there, down behind his desk, with a swivel chair pushed awry. There was a small hole in his chest, over his heart. The coroner was there, a local undertaker, a dignified doctor who looked supercilious, and two cops, one a sergeant.

The sergeant said: "I'm Jeter. This heah is bad, Mr. Manatee."

Rutan said: "Charlie had visitors—Miss Frascatti, with a red-haired girl, then Billy, then Tom Sack. Sack left about midnight. We found poor Charlie at 12:45."

"Which one of them could have done it?" asked Malachi of the doctor.

"Any one," said the medico curtly. "He may have been dead an hour, or a half hour, or any time between eleven and twelve-thirty."

The undertaker-coroner gave orders to two sleepy helpers with a basket. They lifted Charlie Dill and took him away. His face was white and still and there was something in it which I had liked and which stayed with him in death, a certain integrity which was deep within him.

There were footsteps outside and Tom Sack came wheeling in, followed by two hulking characters. He said in his throaty voice: "Howdy, Mayor. I'll take charge here if you like. You got no detectives in town."

He ignored us. He bustled about. I had already seen the hole in the screen. It was a small, evenly cut hole, and it was the right height. Sack pointed to it, bent and sighted needlessly on the swivel chair. He said: "A rifle—.22, no doubt. Charlie heard something, turned, and got it in the heart. Might even have recognized who did it. That alley ain't so wide."

I looked out of the window. As near as I could make out, the alley led both ways behind Headquarters to streets which ran north and south. Across the way was a low warehouse without windows. A loading platform conveniently made a perfect place for a man with a .22 rifle and long cartridges.

Eck and Lib, the characters with the bumps and muscles, stared admiringly at their chief. Rutan sighed helplessly. Sack said: "I'll have my men help search the town. Why, I saw Charlie an hour or so ago and talked with him. This is terrible." He did not sound as though he thought it was terrible. He sounded pleased.

Billy Dill came in the door and looked at Sack. He just stood there, his round face white and pinched and wrinkled. The private operator said: "Billy, I'm soft as hell…"

Billy Dill drew a short-barreled revolver. He almost got it trained on Sack, too, only the gorillas snapped into it. One hit him low, the other high. The gun fell away.

Sack's face got hard and he stepped forward, swinging a kick at the prone fat man. Rutan groaned: "No!"

Malachi was already in action. He jerked Sack around, hit the big man a terrible blow with the heel of his hand, landing on the nape of the neck. He stepped on Sack's toe with his full weight and lifted his shoulder under the other's chin, then stepped away to let him fall.

Eck and Lib were trying to get to Malachi. I split them, grabbed them and knocked their heads together like coconuts. Then I slapped them a couple below the belts and let them fall on Sack.

Billy Dill got up and made no effort to retrieve his gun. He said numbly: "Sack did it. He hated us. Charlie told him off tonight and Sack threatened him. Rose…" His voice trailed off.

Malachi said in the gentle voice he can assume so easily: "Go home, Billy. Take a sleeping pill and we'll talk tomorrow. Go home!"

The sergeant named Jeter said: "Gees! I never seen nothin' like it! Gees!"

Rutan wrung his long, thin hands, "What will we do, Malachi? Sack is very powerful politically. He will make trouble…"

Malachi said: "Let us leave Mr. Sack and friends to recover. Let us talk some."

We went out of Headquarters and walked around behind the building to the loading platform of the warehouse. I climbed up and could see Jeter still staring at Sack and his troglodytic pals. I got down and went along with Malachi and the quavering mayor.

ILENE AND Rose Frascatti were waiting in the lobby of our hotel. We all went up to our ample room and I kept looking at Ilene's red hair and her red lips and her ankles and hips and thinking what a damned fool Malachi was.

The Frascatti bosom was heaving and her black eyes were fearful. Malachi asked them a lot of questions about when they had been with Charlie and what had been said.

Ilene, still pretending not to know us, said: "Mayor Rutan came home and called us. He asked us to come over. We just made a social visit with the chief, at eleven—"

Rose cried: "No use, Ilene. It was about the machines. Charlie said they had to go. He lectured me. Jeter heard it all. He was in the next room. Poor Charlie…"

Ilene addressed Malachi: "Jeter left the room and went out. I saw him bring back hamburgers, as we were leaving. He and the other cop on duty couldn't have known what happened, or when."

"Where was Tom Sack?" demanded Rose. "Was he where he could have shot Charlie? Where is Billy? There should be a guard over Billy. None of us is safe. Tom Sack was trying to take over everything in this town. Even the mayor is afraid of him."

Rutan's hands simply would not be still, but he said without a tremor: "I am not afraid of Sack. If he is guilty, I will arrest him myself."

Malachi said: "You saw Charlie tonight?"

"Yes," said Rutan. "At ten-fifteen. When I came in."

"Everybody saw him," said Malachi. "But nobody killed him. Sack's got his men to alibi him. How are the rest of you fixed?"

Ilene said: "I was with Rose. Except when she talked to the mayor, at eleven-thirty."

"Where did this take place?" asked Malachi.

"At the hotel," said Rutan. His hands were damp with sweat. "Nobody saw us. I had been warning Rose to clean up the Queen's Taste. I came back because I knew I had to see Charlie and Billy and Rose, Malachi. I couldn't leave it to you. It wasn't right to leave. I had to come back."

Malachi said: "That's fine, Fred. Does you credit, old boy." He was as insincere as a Jap diplomat. He talked to them some more. He was not listening to their answers and neither was I. Both of us had the feeling that we were waiting for something to happen. Tom Sack and his boys would not remain idle. But after an hour, with the clock pointing to two-thirty, Malachi called it off.

Ilene went with Rutan and Rose Frascatti without blinking an eye at us. We went to bed again, but did not turn out the light. In five minutes the phone rang. Malachi took it and I could hear Ilene's unexcited voice say: "Rose could have done it easily. She left me, but did not meet Rutan for fifteen minutes. We are almost next door to Headquarters."

Malachi said: "What do you think, darling?"

"I think you are a dumb jerk to let this happen to Charlie, who was a good guy," she said calmly. "I think Sack or Rose would kill anyone for a buck or two. That gal is tough."

Manatee said: "And built, too!"

"You should know," said Ilene. "You and your goggle eyes. Are you going to clean up this mess or let them find out about me and kill me, too? I want to go to New York."

"You stick with Rose," said Malachi. "She may be tough, but my money is on you. And don't let her get away again. If she shot Charlie, it's your fault."

Ilene cursed him fluently, but he hung up, grinning. "Some character," he said. "You know what? I can't see Rose sashaying around with a .22 rifle in her mitts. It had to be a rifle, didn't it, Tack? And why didn't someone hear the shot."

I said: "Could be a Woodsman Colt. A silencer would take care of the noise, you dope."

Malachi said: "Any one of them could have done it. Charlie had passed the word that the rackets were busted. Rutan was back to enforce his rulings. Sack was mad at all of them. Rose stood to lose much of her income. Even Billy must have been enraged."

I said: "Once I was a private detective. I was very broke and played Peeping Tom with married folks on the loose. It was nauseating and the Giants signed me and I quit. I never could stomach detective business since. I am going to sleep."

Malachi sprawled slantwise on the bed, which was too short for him, and supported his bad leg. He would lie there and use his peculiarly unorthodox brain for hours, with the light on. Neither of us minded sleeping with the light in our faces. We liked lots of light, ever since Tarawa....

IN THE morning, we went down for breakfast and Jeter, the cop sergeant, was waiting for us. He had a lantern jaw and the weathered red neck of a Cracker lad, but he was not a dumb cop. He said over coffee: "Manatee, you-all better watch out. Tom Sack and his two boys are pretty mad. They will get you whenever they can. I can arrest them afterwards, but the harm will be done."

Malachi said: "Thanks, Jeter. Who murdered Charlie?"

The sergeant sipped his coffee. He took his time about answering. Then he said: "You better see that snooty doc. I ast him a couple questions about the wound and all... I'm workin' on this thing my way, Mr. Manatee. I had the FBI course once."

He was proud in a modest fashion. We talked with him about the fishing down at Boca Grande and he left.

Fred J. Rutan came in shortly after, dark hollows beneath his eyes.

Malachi said: "I'd make Jeter the new chief, Freddy."

Rutan said: "Tom Sack wants the job."

Malachi grinned and said: "Sure he does. He wants to operate the slot machines, too. I wouldn't be surprised if he wanted to clothe his rotten divorce business in official-dom… He wants Rose Frascatti, too."

Rutan flushed. "That woman! I—I don't know how to handle her, Malachi."

Even Manatee's old friends called him by his full name, I noted. There was something about him that precluded nicknames, even in the Marines.

Malachi looked at Rutan and said: "She's dynamite. Ilene respects her. You know Ilene."

Fred said: "Ilene is in danger, too. I don't like all this, Malachi. Maybe you had better withdraw. I'll appoint Jeter, who is honest, and let him work it out… Billy Dill is around this morning, sad and sick. All the fight has gone out of him. Sack is breathing fire and threatening you. The town is in an uproar."

Malachi said: "Let 'em roar. It's time they woke up. If Sack wants to get tough, that's fine with us. Tack loves tough people. He could eat one right now, for breakfast."

Rutan looked desolated. He moaned: "I've got to see the city councilmen. They will be awful. Couldn't you—"

"No," said Malachi. "I couldn't even speak to them. Run along, Freddy and spiel them. You're the charmer."

Rutan went out, shoving his hands in his pockets so that people would not see them flutter. He had the worst case of jitters I had ever seen.

I said: "Your pal is not rugged."

"Always the bright boy," said Malachi. "Always the campus cut-up, in a Boy Scoutish way. And women—they loved him. Just the lad for a small-town mayor."

Malachi has a strong ironic strain. We went out without speaking. Tom Sack boiled us. We went over to the Jacaranda and hung around the lobby for a while. Eck and Lib came from the elevators and glared, but went out without speaking. Tom Sack boiled in a few moments later and went upstairs, ignoring us.

Malachi said: "He didn't choose us on sight after all."

Ilene came at last. She sat in a chair near us and spoke politely, as though we were comparative strangers, recently met. "Sack is after Rose. Something about rackets and how they should be run. Also something personal. He admires curves."

Malachi said: "He should see you in a bathing suit. Why didn't you stick around and learn more?"

She said: "He caught me listening. Malachi, Rose liked Charlie best."

Malachi batted his slanting eyes. He said: "Catch the next train or bus for Tampa and we'll meet you there. We're going to clean up this thing. Can you pack as soon as Sack leaves?"

She said: "You go to hell!" She got up and walked out into the street.

Malachi groaned. I said: "She won't leave until the payoff. You should know that. Sack is confident of being chief, huh? Working over Rose already…"

Malachi went out and I followed him. He was worried, I could see. There was no sign of Ilene. Billy Dill wandered down the street, pale and pinched and broken. He came up to us and said: "Sack did it. I should shoot him, but I haven't got the nerve."

Malachi said: "You're sure it was Sack, Billy? Why?"

"Charlie told us to close up," said Billy Dill. "Sack had a fit. He said he would never do it. He's tough, Manatee. And he wants Rose—bad. Rose was Charlie's girl."

Malachi said: "You'd better go down and talk to Jeter. Stick with him. Jeter's on the level."

"Yeah," said Billy. "I'll do that." He seemed dazed. He started for Headquarters, but I watched him. He hesitated before the Jacaranda, plunged in.

Fred Rutan came along and stopped us. I was uneasy and did not care about the councilmen and what he had said to them. I had a strong hunch and wanted to get away. I finally mumbled an excuse and hurried back to the Jacaranda.

I went in and walked upstairs, quickly. It made me breathe too hard, but I did not want to be seen coming from the elevator. I went down to Room 450 and rapped on the door.

There was no answer. I went in, tearing the latch loose with my shoulder. I called: "Ilene!"

The room was empty. I looked it over thoroughly. Ilene's and Rose's things were undisturbed, neatly hung up. The maid had made the beds. I was puzzled. I went back out, sorry now that I had wrecked the door. I went down in the street but did not find Malachi. I walked back to the hotel and as he did not show up, I killed the afternoon reading a murder mystery in our room.

AT SIX the phone rang. Malachi said over the wire: "All hell has broken loose, They found Billy Dill a suicide in the Jacaranda. He shot himself in Room 452, next to Rose and Ilene. With a pistol, a .22 carrying long cartridges. Rutan appointed Sack as chief and politely asked us out of town."

I said: "Wait, Malachi. This ain't right. Billy never shot his brother. Himself, maybe. He was low down. But not Charlie."

Malachi said: "Grab something to eat and meet me at the Queen's Taste for a drink about eight. I'm looking into something right now… You're right, of course. Billy didn't do it."

I found Jeter in the Queen's Taste. He said soberly: "Billy was in that hotel room with all the windows locked, the doors locked, and the gun beside him. It sure looks like suicide."

I said: "Between 450 and 452 there are two doors, right?"

"Each has got one knob and can only be opened from the far room," he nodded. "If someone in Rose's room wanted to get in 452, he would have to get the occupant of 452 to open his door. There ain't even a latch. Jest the knob, on the inner side."

I said: "Who's got alibis?"

"Everybody," said Jeter darkly. "They alibi each other. Rose and Sack—Eck and Lib. Not that they need 'em. Coroner said suicide. Sack said suicide. Tom's the chief now."

"Everything is ducky in Gulf Town," I said. I saw Eck and Lib come in and line against the bar. Rose entered by the back way. Ilene wandered in behind Rose, looking wonderful and somehow pleased with herself. Eck and Lib drank fast whiskeys and kept looking my way. It made like trouble.

It was too early for the soldiers. The bar was deserted except for Eck and Lib and Rose and Ilene and a couple of bartenders who would be no good to me. The door opened and Tom Sack barged in. It became so still the air-conditioning machine sounded like a B17 buzzing on a damp morning.

I do not like things to get away from me like that. I saw Eck and Lib going toward Ilene, heard Sack say: "Arrest that girl!"

Sack had caught her eavesdropping and as chief he could accuse her of loitering, soliciting or any other trumped-up matter.

I got to my feet and started into action. Rose Frascatti shrank against the wall, her olive face expressionless. She made no move to save Ilene, her supposed friend.

Eck and Lib were waiting for me, of course. They had Ilene blocked off from the back way, with Sack between her and the door, and they wanted me. Each had a badge, I saw now, and a blackjack. They had guns, too. They were newly appointed cops!

I stopped. They waited, grinning like gargoyles.

Tom Sack said: "Why don't you start something, Hinton? Go ahead, cut yourself a piece of local law."

They had their blackjacks dangling, playing happily with the new, shiny little toys. I let my shoulder slump and said: "If that's the way you're going to play…"

Then I hit them. With a spot on your lung you do not have much time. You give out quicker than of old. So you move very fast and do not use genteel tactics. I put Eck into Lib, or vice versa, as I never did get them separated in my mind, and then I stabbed them with pronged fingers in the eyes and kicked them severely in the groin. One kick each was enough.

I yelled: "The back way, Ilene, and quick!" She went and Rose followed.

Sack had a gun. He stood there and there was a red light in his eyes. He had those straight-browed eyes and an undershot jaw. He looked like murder, all right. I pitched a chair at him.

The first shot went into the ceiling. I threw a beer glass, then a bottle from the bar. Whiskey spattered around. A bartender had a club or something and I backhanded him and got a soda bottle. I threw it, too, and Sack caught it on the skull. He shot twice more, but bullets do not affect me unless they clunk into me.

I took his gun and beat him over the nose with it. I never encourage people to attack me, so I broke it three times, carefully. He was screaming, but I was sore. I slugged him behind the ear.

Malachi came in and said: "Holy hat! What the hell are you doing, Tack?"

"It's a game," I said. "Break-up-the-joint. I made it up."

I looked and Ilene was gone. Rose was gone, too.

I said: "They were going to pinch Ilene. Rose was not helping us any."

Malachi said: "Jeter will be along to clean up this mess. Then we will go down to Headquarters and see what is what."

"Where the hell have you been?" I demanded. "These characters like to kill me!"

"Yeah," he said, "You didn't even bust a knuckle. Drink your drink and come on."

Sure enough, my bourbon was still unspilled on the table. The remaining bartender ogled me darkly as I drank it down. I threw the shot glass at him but he ducked. It broke a mirror.

WE WENT out and down the street. As we approached Headquarters, I saw Rose and Ilene tumble out of a parked car. Ilene got a hammerlock on Rose and shagged her up the steps to Headquarters. Somehow I was not too surprised.

Fred Rutan and Jeter were waiting. Jeter went out after Malachi told him what had happened. We all went into the office marked chief and there was Rose, her bosom showing off in great heaves, her black eyes snapping. Ilene was saying to her: "You play any more tricks on me and I'll mow you down."

Malachi said: "Don't be so rough, baby. Rose will be good. Rose loves everybody, don't you Rose?"

The woman said something in Italian. Malachi laughed and said: "Naughty, naughty!"

We waited and Jeter came back with a couple of his local constables and Sack and his two boys were rolled in. They were in sad shape, especially Sack. He said to me: "I'm going to kill you if I burn for it, Hinton. Remember that."

"Listen, pal," I said to him, "I've got one lung and a bad disposition and I smoke and drink too much. Are you trying to scare me?"

He lapsed into silence, watching Malachi. Rutan sat gingerly in Charlie Dill's swivel chair and presided, sort of, very prim.

The mayor said: "Have you facts for us, Malachi? Really, I can't approve this brawling, you know. Hinton takes too much for granted."

I bawled at him: "Your stinking chief was about to arrest Ilene Carver in a gin mill, you sissified jerk! I got a notion—"

Malachi said: "Whoa! Wait a minute!"

I subsided, but I kept an eye on them all. They were a crummy crowd, all of them, to me. I did not see any saving grace among them. Malachi lounged on the edge of the desk, resting his bum gam, talking easily. He said: "The last shall be first—take the killing of Billy Dill."

"Suicide," corrected Rutan.

"Killing!" said Malachi pleasantly. "Billy went up to Room 450 of the Jacaranda to see Rose. He loved Rose. Everybody loves Rose around here"—he cocked an eye at the fiery dark woman—"except me. I do not love her. She and Tom Sack, one or both, killed Billy."

"They couldn't have!" said Rutan. The key to 452 was on the inside of the door. It's impossible!"

Malachi said: "Billy came in. Ilene saw him. Rose and Tom were in there. Billy never came out."

"But—but…" Rutan's eyes bugged out.

Malachi said: "They shot Billy. He knew too much. He knew who had killed his brother. They shot him and then Sack went downstairs and swiped the key to 452. He opened it, went in, then opened the connecting door from the 452 side. They lugged Billy into 452. They slammed the door by pulling hard and stepping out of the way. The latch caught. They left the key inside the other door of 452, then closed the connecting door on their side. Simple, wasn't it?"

"Can you prove that?" demanded Rutan. "Jeter, arrest Sack and Rose!"

Neither Sack nor Rose said anything, except that they wanted a lawyer. They were smart people. They had been in jams before and wanted to see some proof.

Ilene opened her handbag and took out a black cylinder. She said: "I found this silencer."

Malachi said: "Where, darling?"

Ilene said: "It couldn't have been used on the pistol, you know. The barrel is too short."

Malachi did not repeat his question. He said to Rutan: "Now about poor Charlie. He was sitting right the way you are now when he got his."

Rutan frowned and said: "No, he had his face to the window."

"Impossible," said Malachi calmly. "Right, Jeter?"

The sergeant said: "According to the doc, the bullet sloped downward into his heart. If he was shot from that loading platform over yonder, the bullet would have ranged upwards!"

"Exactly," said Malachi. "Charlie sat facing the door. Someone came in with a rifle, silenced by this gadget, fired a shot into him, then one through the screen. Anyone with a magnifying glass can see that the tiny prongs of the screening bend outward!"

"If we had the gun," Jeter said eagerly, "we could prove that. I found the other bullet, mashed against the wall out there."

"The gun?" asked Malachi innocently. "Why don't you look in the rack right in the next room? There are several .22 rifles in there. Guess you boys hunt with them, at the city's expense."

JETER PLUNGED into the next room. Tom Sack bared his teeth and said: "I suppose you're going to say I killed Charlie?"

"You'd love to have me say so," nodded Malachi. "Because if that were disproven, you'd beat the rap on Billy. And I've got you placed on the scene in Billy's murder, and a witness who will stand up. Miss Carver. Then you tried to arrest her, which also makes it look bad for you, although you didn't know for sure she would burn you when you tried that. You're not so smart, Sack! In fact, you're pretty stupid.

You fell for Rose, like all the rest of them and it warped your judgment and made you a killer. Billy had too much on Rose to allow him to live."

Rutan said: "Well, I guess that settles it. We'll never find who killed Charlie, I'm afraid. If it was one of our guns and Sack did not do it… or if he did, one murder is enough to burn him."

Malachi said: "Fred, what time did you see Charlie last night?"

"Before eleven," said Rutan. "Remember? I came in—"

"I wasn't here," said Malachi gravely. "Now Jeter was here. He went out for hamburgers and when he came back he gave you one. That was after eleven-thirty."

"Oh, I was here," said Rutan, smiling. "I was hanging around, gabbing with the cops."

"Yeah," said Malachi. "Making sure of your alibi. You couldn't possibly have been across the street, shooting through the window at Charlie. But you could easily have gone back and grabbed a gun and shot him through the door."

Rutan said: "Are you crazy, Malachi? Why should I shoot my own chief of police?"

"Tell him, Rose," said Malachi.

Rose had come up off her chair. She was chalky white. She choked: "You—you did it! You knew I—you knew…"

"Rose really loved Charlie best of all," said Malachi in his calm, easy voice, "You see, Freddy? Things catch up with you. In college it was always the same. *Cherchez la femme* and find Freddy! Off the deep end for Rose, and Rose loved solid old Charlie, who represented everything in the world which was not like Chicago and the rackets and tough guys like Tom Sack. You were tied into things around here too deeply, and after you came back and rescinded the order to clean up the town and Charlie asked you how you were going to get around Tack and me and the council-men, you argued with him and got hot. Then you brought Rose into it, and he got you told off, plenty. You went out, brooded while the others came and went. You saw Rose go in, slipped into the gun room and spied on him. You heard Rose say she loved him. You lost that temper of yours and shot him."

Rose was sobbing, collapsed, the fire momentarily gone from her. Sack looked sick. Lib and Eck hadn't any more fight in them. Jeter came back with a rifle and said: "I think this is the one."

Ilene said drily: "I burgled Rutan's home after you tipped me off, Malachi. I found the silencer there. It was under a picture of Rose, torn in two. Down in the trash barrel, as you suggested. Sometimes, Malachi, I think you are a pretty smart fellow."

Jeter called for someone and a cop came with keys jangling. They had nice clean cells in that building. Rutan looked awful. Jeter handcuffed Sack and his two heroes and then he put a pair on Rutan. The mayor stared down at his wrists, emitted a terrible sob, and fainted.

Rose Frascatti said: "And he thought I'd go for him! If I had known the punk killed Charlie I'd have fixed him myself!"

Ilene said: "Look, Rose. You're not such a bad guy, at that. If you turn State's evidence—"

Rose almost spat at her. "You dirty spy! Before I'd stool I'd fry ten times! What the hell do you think I am?"

Ilene said calmly: "I'm beginning to think you're a killer. Sack is pretty tough, but I am awakening to the fact that you are tougher."

"If I was loose I'd show you how tough," raged the Chicago girl.

Ilene grinned at her. "If you ever swung on me I'd bust your pretty nose," she promised. "With your padding you couldn't free wheel a good punch to save your life!"

Jeter and his cops took them all out. They had to carry Rutan.

Malachi looked after him and said: "You see? That's what's the matter with us. We elect clunks like that to office. Then we can't understand when they go wrong. The councilmen who sent for me couldn't understand anything except that things were all fouled up in Gulf Town."

"Sent for you!" scoffed Ilene. "Nobody ever sent for you, you big busybody! You just butt in."

"They sent for me after I had investigated here for a week and mailed an anonymous report," Malachi said with dignity.

"Recommending Malachi Manatee!" snapped Ilene. "I want to go to New York. A certain colonel at the air base is going on furlough tomorrow and has offered to take me, all expenses paid. If you insist upon cleaning up every town in Florida, I'm going!"

"You're an immoral red-headed witch," said Malachi. "And I can talk plainer than that. Let us repair to the Queen's Taste and have a drink."

"Of what? Blood?" demanded Ilene hotly. "Are you going to take me out of this murderer's roost?"

"O.K.," said Malachi. "We'll go up to Tampa. Maybe we can go on to New York from there."

I said: "You go ahead."

"Why?" demanded Malachi. "What's eating you?"

"That other bartender in the Queen's Taste," I said. "He meant to tag me, but it didn't work out for him. I got to go back down there and Christianize him."

"Oh, nuts!" said Ilene. "Let's go. I'll drink blood!"

The barkeep had already left town, so we just had a couple of Scotches. Ilene was certainly beautiful. I kept thinking how she had tied this case together for Malachi and how she had handled Rose. I kept thinking she was so wonderful I would like to sock somebody just for her.

After a while she and Malachi got to arguing. That's always the way it was. But what the hell, I couldn't sock *him*. It would be like beating myself on the jaw. It's a hell of a life sometimes.

MALACHI ATTENDS A PARTY

A GAL LIKE ROSE LEE WAS BOUND TO DIE YOUNG—AND NOT FROM NATURAL CAUSES EITHER. HER PRESENT HUSBAND CALLED HER A GORGEOUS, GOLD-DIGGING BORE AND A SCORE OF EX-SWAINS AGREED WITH HIM— BUT IT WASN'T BOREDOM THAT CAUSED SOMEONE TO BURY A BUTCHER'S KNIFE IN ROSE LEE'S LOVELY RIBS.

THIS GULF Lodge to which Malachi Manatee had brought Ilene Carver and me was quite a place, strung out along the beach in two-storied, modern buildings erected just prior to the war, all fine glass and masonry, cool in the Florida sun. We lay on the beach among the rich people and if Malachi did not remember another beach, on a Pacific Island, with dead Marines all around and him going down with a bayonet in his knee and me trying to get to him—well, that was better not to remember.

All this luxury was Malachi's natural prerogative. He had seven million dollars tucked away here and there. Ilene Carver, although penniless, had been reared in a like atmosphere. Me, I am a lug, but I can get used to things. Gulf Lodge was all right with me. It kept Malachi from messing into other people'; business for a while. It gave me a rest between battles with crooked politicians and honest criminals....

Ilene is the world's most beautiful red-headed woman. She said: "Rose Lee was always no account. Even if you did give her a whirl—as who didn't in Bay City? But a party is a party and I'll go if you say so."

Malachi rubbed his head. His hair was short and the sun had bleached it almost white. He is six-feet-four, and not thin. If you did not notice his scar, you would think him a rich, 4-F lounger. My scar, being on my lung, does not show at all.

Malachi said: "Ray and Max and Ned will be there. It's a corny old gag to show off her old flames to her new husband. But Ray and Max and Ned are dynamite in their own way. It's a trouble brew and I want to see it."

"You keep your cotton-picking hands off that woman," said Ilene. "I remember when you drove her all over Bay City in that red roadster of yours."

"Rose Lee was always agreeable," said Malachi. "It will be interesting to see how Broadway has spoiled her."

Ilene and Malachi were bending over a body on the beach. It was Rose Lee with a knife buried in her lovely ribs.

I said: "I caught her on the radio. She is extremely mediocre. Jay Conger put her in a hit show and married her. Jay hasn't got any sense about women."

"You know Jay Conger?" asked Malachi.

"A right guy and a good producer," I replied.

Malachi said: "Max Standish is Bay City's success story and an important banker on the West Coast. Ned Royall is a political power in spite of congenital drunkenness. Ray Arrango is the leading gambler in this part of the woods... Rose Lee must have had something even in her salad days."

Ilene said: "You know what she had, you nasty thing!"

A small girl with a deep tan, violet eyes and slim limbs came along the beach almost timidly. She waved at Ilene, and dropped to the sand in a small heap. She said: "Going to the party, darling? I hope so. It'll be awful, won't it?"

Ilene said: "Mrs. Betty Royall, Tack Hinton. You know the great Malachi, of course."

Mrs. Royall had a nice smile. "I grew up with Malachi, Wasn't he the bad one?... How are you, Mr. Hinton?"

I said: "Malachi keeps me well, thank you."

They talked about this and that. I lost interest and lay silently on the beach wondering why quiet little girls like Betty Royall married loud drunks, and what perverse thing kept Malachi from marrying Ilene Carver.

Betty Royall's voice became unexpectedly sharp. "Rose Lee is a trouble-maker and you know this party is arranged to make me seem foolish. I'm tired of being pushed around, Ilene..."

I sat up. A party was approaching. There was a tall, luscious-bodied girl wearing a scanty two-piece bathing suit and a flimsy cape fastened only at the neck. That was Rose Lee. There was Jay Conger, a step behind, thin, dark, sardonic-looking. There was Ray Arrango, short, Latin, black-eyed, quick. There was Ned Royall, obese, but powerfully built, his face red-veined beneath the fashionable tan.

There were three large, quiet men in the background. They stopped short of our spot on the sand and were not introduced. But I knew them. They were the Baerlie brothers and where Ray Arrango went, they were not far behind. I wondered if he would bring them to Rose Lee's party. Arrango was a big operator, all right.

A third man came hurrying, a serious, compact fellow with a firm mouth. That was Max Standish, the banking figure of Bay City.

Rose Lee was in her element. She posed and gave with the bended knee to make her legs look Hollywoodish. She was not a bad looking girl, but she was not that good, either.

She said: "We're having French 75s, my dears. It will be vurry noice, I think…" She talked like that all the time, but she never missed giving the boys the glad eye.

Ilene said: "A gun you don't need, my dear. You've done very well without bullets."

"Oh, you darling! Same old Ilene!" cooed Rose Lee. "French 75s are a drink. Wonderful, rahlly…."

The conversation sickened and finally died. I went into the warm waters of the Gulf and wished my lung was all right so that I could swim out a mile and float like in the old days.

THE WAY you make a French 75, you take a half barspoonful of sugar and some bitters and muddle them in the bottom of a large sherbet glass, add a lump of ice, pour champagne and lash with brandy. So by midnight it was a hell of a party.

Maybe thirty people came and went, but finally it narrowed down to the crowd from the beach that afternoon. Arrango's three bodyguards were not in evidence. There were just Rose Lee's husband, her ex-lovers, Ilene, Mrs. Royall and me. Rose Lee was making with Malachi like mad, to annoy Ilene, and kept insisting that Malachi had discovered her. She even went to the piano and played and sang *Lover* because she had sung it to Malachi some years before and he had told her she ought to go on the stage.

Ilene said: "Just like the lecherous harpy. But she won't tell you that Ray Arrango put up the money to get her to New York."

Betty said in a tight little voice: "He did? She's very clever. She got a couple of thousand from Ned, too!"

Ilene said quickly: "Wives shouldn't know those things, darling, and if they do they should forget them."

Betty said: "I hate her! She's flamboyant—"

"Sex machine," nodded Ilene. "Ned is getting very stewed, baby. Why don't you take him home?"

"That has been tried," said Betty. She was nervous, but underneath it she was wiry-tough, I thought.

I said: "Standish seems out of place here. Did he kick in for the big career, too?"

"He gave her a ring," said Betty. "She hocked it. They were engaged, I think they called it."

"That gal certainly got around," I said.

There were half-empty glasses and soggy canapes and soiled paper napkins all over the place. It was a fine apartment with a luxurious setting, but filled with people who were getting cantankerous—especially Ned Royall.

He wandered over to where Jay Conger was mixing a fresh Scotch for me because I do not like champagne drinks and said: "Holdin' out the good stuff, huh? A hell of a host you are! Gimme a Scotch."

Jay looked him in the eye and said coolly: "You've had enough, old fellow."

Royall put down his empty glass. His face got purple. He said: "Listen, you Broadway sharpie, don't come down here among southern people and show off…"

It was Ray Arrango who stepped in. He said calmly: "Downstairs, Ned. You'll get us all into trouble. Downstairs, outdoors."

Royall wheeled and said: "You keep out of this, you dirty little Cuban racketeer!"

Ray Arrango's face did not change expression. He reached out, grabbed the big man and threw him out the door. I held it open and shoved Royall down the stairs.

Those things happen so quickly it's almost impossible to retrace the sequence of events. The next thing I knew, everyone was running down a flagged walk, with light showing from a lamppost and some windows behind which rudely awakened folks were snapping switches. Instead of Jay Conger, it was Ray Arrango who had chosen to tackle Ned Royall….

That happens often, too, among drunks. Two characters will get into a scramble, another will check into it, and first thing you know it is Johnny-change-partners, and usually a Donnybrook on top of that with everybody having a word to say or a punch to throw. In this fiasco, Jay Conger seemed to get sidetracked completely, because I lost sight of him and of several others, but that was because the Baerlie brothers suddenly appeared.

They must have been hanging around, waiting for Ray Arrango. They moved in on the two contestants, who had squared off in the full light. Rose Lee made a brief appearance, screaming: "Please, boys! Think of the publicity!" Then the three big men blocked her skillfully out of the circle of light and that was all I saw of her. Arrango was feinting Royall out of position, and I had to get a load of that, because Arrango did it almost too well. He had an educated left, and he wound it around Royall's neck, drew him in close and deliberately punched his nose.

The thing was, he could have punched Royall on the button and kayo'd him then and there. But he took short chops, expert and neat, tearing the big man's nose, breaking the bones, bloodying him something fierce. Betty squirmed away from me, without a sound, and started into the crowd. She bumped into a Baerlie and turned, her hand to her mouth, looking like sudden death. Then ran off toward the beach.

Malachi, however, was right there by this time. He came in closer and said: "That's enough, you guys."

The Baerlie brothers moved respectfully but firmly upon Malachi. Their man was winning by a mile. I edged in. Then there was a great turmoil, and never afterwards could anyone swear to what happened, exactly.

One of the Baerlies touched Malachi's arm, which is like setting fire to a hunk of T.N.T. I got behind him—he was the biggest one—and stuck out a leg. Malachi pushed him and he fell over my leg. I hit him.

Then Malachi hit the second one, very quick, with a rabbit punch. He fell down, too. I got the third with a semi-block and elbow jab to the throat. That made quite a pile of Baerlies on the ground. Malachi and I gently plucked Arrango off Royall, who was beginning to resemble an overripe tomato which has been thrown at someone and had not missed.

Royall mumbled thickly: "The dirty little crook... I'll take him yet! Gimme a chance! I'll outlast him and all the rest of that damned outfit..."

Malachi said: "Not tonight you won't. You need a doctor for that proboscis, my friend."

Royall put a hand up to his face. It seemed to me that everyone had been outside the circle of lights, but now came back in, standing around nervously. Other guests had arrived. The manager had finally come running, querulous, slightly afraid of his lustrous though disorderly patrons. A man said he was a medico and busied himself with Royall's nose.

Max Standish said to me: "Where is Rose Lee? The poor kid must have got scared and run."

Jay Conger, quite sober now, said: "She went toward the beach with the bout. I think Betty Royall is with her."

Arrango seemed a bit dazed. He said to me: "What makes with you, pal? I didn't think you'd take chips for a heel like Royall."

"Your playful chums chose to pick on Malachi," I explained.

He looked at the Baerlies, who were slowly getting up, said: "So that's the Manatee-Hinton treatment?"

"Not the full treatment," I told him. "We did not wish to harm your pals."

"Where is Malachi now?" he asked.

"Me, I'm just a bystander," I said. "I just look on— He and Ilene seem to have a date on the beach or somewhere."

Malachi's voice came suddenly, in that tone I know so well: "Tack! Bring the doctor!" I took the medical man away from Royall and started toward Malachi's voice.

ILENE AND Malachi were bending over a body on the beach. It was Rose Lee. She was lying on her side, one knee hunched up. She was still very warm, and a little blood oozed around the knife buried between her ribs on the left side. Malachi was staring at her, his cigarette lighter flaming in his hand.

The doctor said: "Someone call the sheriff. I don't think any of you should leave…"

Max Standish, Royall and Arrango were all there by now. Betty Royall stood close to her husband, a handkerchief against her mouth. The Baerlie brothers, still dazed but throwing vengeful glances at me and Malachi, grouped behind them like the Three Fates. No one spoke for a full moment, then they all broke into excited speech at once.

Jay Conger stood nearest me. He muttered: "Now why should someone kill her? God knows she was a bore, but why that?"

I said: "Why did you marry her, Jay?"

He looked at me from some far place and said: "Did you ever hear of sex appeal? She had it! It gets me every time. She was the third and I'm not yet forty."

"You had better soft pedal that talk and act the grieving husband," I said. "These Crackers are not like metropolitan cops. They're sort of simple."

All in all, it was a frightened crew who gathered in the overdone, but luxurious Conger apartment. The Baerlie brothers seemed strangely out of place, standing against the wall, their wide-cheekboned faces blank, their eyes narrowed. Arrango walked up and down, but said nothing. Ned Royall administered to the weeping Betty. Max Standish looked out the window where the hotel attendants were keeping the space about the body cleared. Jay Conger poured a straight drink and swallowed it.

Malachi took Ilene's arm and led her into the bedroom, giving me the nod to follow.

He closed the door and said: "These people swing a lot of weight down here. The Sheriff will be mighty careful how he moves. What do you think of it, Tack?"

I said, trying to clear it in my mind: "Nobody liked Rose Lee very much… Royall and Arrango had staked her, each thinking she was his girl. She hocked Standish's engagement ring—then came back to twist the knife in the wounds, with a husband who was bored by her. Arrango and Royall, however, were busy attempting mayhem on each other when she was killed. It looks as if it must have been either Standish or Conger—"

"Or Betty Royall," said Ilene.

"Not that kid," I said.

Malachi said: "Could have been. The knife looked like a heavy-handled butcher's blade, worn thin by honing. My guess is it came from the hotel kitchen, which is two hundred yards from here. That makes it premeditated murder, huh?"

I said: "Those Baerlies were right in on the fight. Arrango is the type, but he couldn't have done it, and anyway, he seems a pretty decent sort of guy. Boy, he sure can hit!"

"He was a boxer as a kid," said Malachi. "Did you hear what Royall said when we stopped it?"

"Something about outlasting the rest of the damned gang," I said. "If he thought he could handle the Baerlies, he's nuts."

Malachi said: "The set-up is like this: Max Standish heads up a reform element which is trying to get Arrango's gambling interests eradicated. They're using Royall's political machine to further their schemes. Royall's bunch is out, right now, having been defeated in the last primary, but with Standish behind him, Ned figures to get in again…"

Ilene said: "Now wait, Malachi. What has this to do with the killing of a Broadway soubrette from Bay City?"

"I dunno," said Malachi. "But that's the story. It's all behind the scenes, as usual in politics. The people think Max, a Sunday school superintendent, is sacrificing much in entering politics as a running mate to Royall. What they don't know is that Ray Arrango's Latin Bank is giving Max's interests hell. Ray is a shrewd business fellow. Max is simply playing the game to maintain supremacy in his field."

"All these sidelights are interesting, if true," I said. "But who is going to take the rap for slipping a shiv into the girl-friend of six other guys?"

Malachi said: "You'd better be prepared to have the finger of suspicion pointed at your pal, Conger. He's the only outsider."

Ilene said: "He didn't do it. I can alibi him."

"You were with me," said Malachi.

"I can lie, can't I?" said Ilene serenely. "I think I hear the voice of the Law. Let us go and tell our stories."

We went back in and Sheriff Battle gave us a glare. He was a lanky man, all politician. He was very polite to Royall and Standish and scared of Arrango and his men. He asked routine questions, corroborated the fact that the knife had been taken from the hotel kitchen, then left.

Malachi said to the assemblage, now quite ready to go to bits: "The coroner's verdict will be what you all want it,

never fear. 'At the hands of person or persons unknown'…
Battle is up for re-election too, you know."

Most of them looked relieved. But Jay Conger said into
a thin silence: "She was married to me, remember? I'd like
to know who killed her. It was one of you—"

"One of *us*," said Max Standish meaningfully.

Ilene, who had evidently adopted Jay, said: "Oh, I think
we'll find out who did it. Malachi is very smart that way,
didn't you know? He and Tack have worked out a few killings between them. Tack used to be a private detective in
New York City."

They all looked at me. Since my detective experience was
limited to six months as a divorce snooper, it was an effort
to look nonchalant, but Ilene always had a motive behind
her remarks, so I tried.

Malachi said: "This thing will have to be cleared up, or
you'll all have a tough time at elections. The sheriff will
let it ride, but he'll run independently and leave it in your
laps."

Max Standish said: "We'll risk that, Malachi."

"This is our business, Malachi," added Royall.

"We can settle it," Arrango said significantly.

Jay Conger said, drawling nastily: "They all get together
quick, don't they? Manatee, if you can solve this, I'll do
anything for you. One of these people, including Mrs.
Royall, by the way—she hated Rose Lee—killed my
wife—"

We had to stop another fight, then. Ned Royall came
charging like a bull at Conger. Malachi went for the Baerlies, confronting them, bluffing them with a sharp word.
I grabbed Royall and slung him. He was heavy, but too
angry to be any good.

AT THAT moment the door opened and the sheriff came in. He posed dramatically, then unwrapped a handkerchief and laid on an end table a knife still bloody. He said: "You people better look at this."

It was one of those heavy-bladed, heavy-handled butcher's knives. The unusual thing about it was that the point had been sharpened, so that it came to a tri-cornered sharp point....

Everyone looked at it. The sheriff had an unexpected sense of theatrics. He re-wrapped it and, without a word, left the apartment.

The Royalls were the first to gather themselves and go. Betty leaned on her husband's arm, but I noticed her legs were not shaky. Arrango swaggered out among his bodyguards. Standish was last, and seemed anxious to say something to Manatee, but afraid to do it among witnesses. Finally he said: "I've a suite under yours in the main hotel building. Come in and see me before you go to bed."

That left just Jay Conger, who busied himself with another drink. He said: "The slobs! Rose wasn't bad—she was just avid—of life and success. She was stupid, but not bad..."

He gulped down his drink, added: "If you solve it, Manatee—I know I can't pay you, but I'll do something for you—somehow..."

We got away from him, headed for Malachi's suite on the second floor of the hotel, and sat down to a bottle of Scotch.

It was close to three A.M. Malachi drank slowly, his V-shaped eyebrows going up and down like a nervous window-shade. Ilene was amazingly silent.

All the time I was trying to piece together the few things I knew....

More and more it pointed to Arrango, the spurned Latin. Yet he had been punching Royall's nose in plain sight of everyone. The Baerlies had been right in there getting theirs from Malachi and me. Someone had killed Rose Lee while the action covered the crime. It could not be any other way.

I said as much, finally, when the silence among us got on my nerves. Ilene just looked at me, as though she did not hear, then said: "Betty slipped away while Ned was fighting. She has always hated and feared Rose Lee. Once, when Betty was young, she had a nervous breakdown, they called it, and they had to put her away for a while… I like Betty, Malachi…"

"Somebody ground that knife," I objected. "Could Mrs. Royall have done that? Can you see her doing it?"

"If she was jealous enough and hated enough."

Malachi said, his voice low and clear: "Someone else is going to get killed tonight unless we can figure this out."

"You keep tying it up with politics," I said. "You got crime linked with politics in your brain."

Malachi said: "You didn't catch the significance of that knife. Why was it sharpened in that manner?"

"So it would slip into a person easily," I said. "You remember Jake? He used to do that to his jungle knife. Said he could skewer a Jap and take it out in one motion."

Malachi said: "I'm going to take a walk. If something occurs to you, look for me on the beach."

Ilene smoked two cigarettes in silence, then suddenly blurted:

"Tack! Malachi said someone else was going to get it. We'd better go after him."

But at that moment a bright light dawned in my thick skull. I said: "Ilene, tell me all you know about Royall, Standish and Arrango. About their past, what they did. Everything!"

She said: "Come on, I'll try to remember while we walk."

We went down on the beach. There was no sight of Malachi's tall frame.

Ilene talked. She was a good, straightforward reporter when she took the time and trouble. I got a good picture of all the people about whom I was curious. Betty, trying to marry Ned Royall, getting sick, going away—and that was how, in the end, she got him, for he had a contradictory streak of tenderness, which I had already suspected... Max Standish, trying to get ahead in the bank, ruthless in business, unfriendly to people unless they could help him, falling only once, for Rose Lee... Ned Royall, born to the purple, drinking, fighting, but making friends in politics with a shrewdness which matched Max's... Arrango, the boy from the Spanish quarter, a flashy kid, a good boxer but too smart to take the bumps in the ring, handsome enough to go on the stage, a lad who had tried everything, including circus performing until he got started in the *bolita* racket, where he grew like a weed to top rank....

I said: "Ilene, Standish asked us to stop in. Malachi isn't on the beach. Hurry!"

I HAD it then. We dashed for the hotel where Max had his suite on the ground floor. We could see light in his window.

We slid silently into the hall and listened outside the room. A voice was telling somebody something. Ilene raised her skirt and took a small revolver from a holster strapped to her thigh.

I hit the door. They don't make hotel doors to withstand a good fullback's best plunge. It opened.

Standish was on the floor, bleeding. There was a knife in him, but he was alive, because he flicked us a grateful look.

Malachi was against the wall. When Ilene came in behind me she fired one shot, and then Malachi came away from the wall.

I began slugging with all the dirty tricks I learned in the Marines. I hit one of them with my pronged fingers, smack in the eyes, then I kicked him where it hurt the most. I got another by the wrist and broke his arm before I smashed his jaw to bits. The third was stone dead, because Ilene can shoot like a sniper.

Malachi had Arrango in his hands and that was not so good for the gambler. Malachi was taking him apart, limb from limb, when I stopped him by touching his arm, just gently and saying: "He's out like a light, pal. Let him be."

Malachi dropped Arrango and said: "Max had it figured out. He got Max, but the light was out and his aim went bad…"

Standish was on his feet. His shoulder bled, but his hands were cool, ripping the shirt away. Ilene was calling the doctor on the house phone. The place was lousy with Baerlies. They were all down and not liable to get up without help.

Malachi said: "Those knives were balanced for throwing. But I had forgotten about Arrango's circus career—he never meant to kill Rose Lee at all."

"I was sure of that," said Max Standish gravely. People were coming in, Jay Conger, the Royalls, others. Standish said in his precise voice: "He meant to get me. I thought I heard something whizz by me. Rose Lee was getting away from the fight—she was humiliated, you see. Ray threw the knife then got into the fight to provide an alibi. It was very clever. I wasn't sure, Malachi, I wanted to talk to you about it."

Malachi said: "I walked right into it. They were inside the room, with the lights out, and Ray had thrown the knife. Max was bending over, getting ready for bed, and caught it in the shoulder. They were in a hell of a spot, so they stuck me up. They had to kill me, too, and make it look as though Max and I had fought it out."

Ilene said: "You big dummy! Going out without your bodyguards! You might have got hurt!"

Malachi said with dignity: "It was a political deal, as I suspected. Ray wanted Max out. He could handle Ned's crowd, had done it before, but Max's money was too much for him. Now there'll be an open scrap—and I hope you lose, Max, I hope you lose."

The sheriff came, gathered up the Baerlies and their boss, all unconscious, and took them away. Malachi and Ilene and I went upstairs. Conger came with us. We had a drink and Conger said: "It seems worse, in a way, killed by accident. Not even a reason for her death…"

We didn't say anything. After all, you can't tell a guy that his wife had traveled in bad company and through them had met her end.

Ilene said, after a while: "Have another drink. Who are we to pry into the imponderables? All I know is Malachi was a dope to walk into it the way he did."

"I was just about to take the gun away from that Baerlie and make him eat it when you dropped in," Malachi said loftily.

That precipitated an argument which brought the manager again. It was a hell of a night for the Gulf Lodge, all right. It had had the full Manatee-Hinton treatment.

SHAME ON MALACHI!

IT'S THE STANDING AROUND,
NOT SURE OF WHAT IT'S ALL
ABOUT, KNOWING THERE'S
A KILLER LOOSE THAT GETS
YOU. I'M OF THE HIT-FIRST-
AND-THINK-ABOUT-IT-LATER
SCHOOL. BUT MALACHI
HAD SOME REGRETS ABOUT
THE FINAL FIST-FEST. "I'M
ASHAMED, TACK," HE TOLD ME
LATER. "I SHOULD HAVE BEEN
ABLE TO HANDLE AN OLD
WOMAN WITHOUT SLUGGING
HER."

MALACHI MANATEE and I were living in one suite, Ilene Carver was living in another, all very kosher, and on the ground floor lived Mrs. John Sudan and her bachelor son, John Jr. It was a fine apartment house, called the Poinsettia Arms, owned by Mrs. Sudan, who owned a good deal of Bay City, a town on the West Coast of Florida. Malachi's father had known Mrs. Sudan many years before and she must have been one hell of a girl in her heyday....

Malachi is quite a character, of course, being so tall and blond and arrogant and kindly and tough and ruthless all at one time. Ilene is the best looking redhead in America. Before the Japs put scar tissue on my lung I was a tough sort of fellow, I suppose.

But Mrs. John Sudan was something else again.

We were in her place, drinking bourbon, the kind you can't get any more. Mrs. Sudan had cottony white hair, very neatly arranged atop her head, the remnants of some beauty, and black, snapping, young eyes behind steel-rimmed spectacles. She wore dark clothing, obviously expensive, yet somehow ancient in style. She was not quite *Godey's Lady's Book,* but she was not up to date either. She drank from a tumbler and took plenty of drinks.

She said: "A man named Doney Beedle controls the vice in this town. He's a vicious, depraved character. He poses as a citrus grower and has ingratiated himself with Dolf Cartier and the leading men of this community, who have no social responsibility. He even got himself into our poker game!"

Malachi said: "You still play with the men, Mrs. John?"

"Cartier, Solvey, Marshal, Carey Flowers and I have played poker for twenty-five years," she said. "Now they let Beedle play. He cheats."

John Sudan, Jr. said: "Now Ma! That's not true!" John Jr. had no hair at all and his eyes were too close to his big nose. He looked like a tired old billiard ball. He didn't work at anything in particular except jumping horses, of which he owned several, yet he did not look like a horseman. He was not jaunty.

I got away from the table and blocked off any possible interference. Malachi took him by the nose, twisted it and said: "That's just a beginning."

Mrs. John said: "I lost seven thousand dollars to Beedle last night."

John Jr. didn't bat an eye. "That's not surprising. You always play two pair too strong before the draw."

"You fool!" snapped his mother. "You play them too strong *after* the draw!"

John Jr. said stubbornly: "Doney Beedle is not a cheater. He was a bootlegger, yes. He came up the hard way. But he's a legitimate business man and Dolph deals with him and so do all the others. They trust him."

"They're all fools!" declared Mrs. John. Her black eyes gave off fire. "I've been rooked by a damned Cracker crook who has crooked cops like Sam Heppner and his partner, Lodi, do all his dirty work and I won't stand for it."

Ilene sat in a deep chair with her legs slung over the arm, drinking a highball. She said: "Hear! Hear! You tell 'em, Mrs. John. Malachi can fix it for you. He loves fixing things."

Malachi said: "I knew Doney Beedle when he was legging the boot. I was only a kid, but Father always said Doney was square."

John Jr. said: "That's right. Ma's just sore because she dropped some money."

"Seven thousand dollars!" stormed Mrs. John. "Is that hay?"

"The way you talk!" John said admonishingly. "Like a Yankee tough!"

Malachi said: "Dolph Cartier is no fool. The others have played a lot of poker. How could Beedle cheat them?"

"Me!" shouted Mrs. John. "He just cheated me!"

"Why?" asked Malachi.

"To get my money, you dolt!" Mrs. John spat at him.

It was a comfortable room, with old furniture and a fireplace with real andirons and things. It was spring in Florida, very nice and warm. I looked at Ilene's wonderful legs and wished she was in love with me, instead of with Malachi and wondered for the millionth time why they didn't get married between squabbles some day. Old Mrs. John was beginning to bore me with her big squeal.

Malachi had been looking into things in Bay City, as he usually does these days. There was a tie-up between the cops, under Chief Asa Larabee, a porcine moron, and the gambling and vice interests. Things like that excite Malachi. He's against them. He's a crusader. He hires me to crusade with him, and although I was raised on Tammany, it's nice to go along with Malachi and be supported by him and occasionally get some excitement. Malachi and I had had a lot of excitement before the Japs winged his leg and my chest and put us out of it. Now we need some action once in a while.

Malachi was saying: "O.K., Mrs. John. I'll see Doney."

Ilene said: "A lot of good that'll do. Sam Heppner and Lodi and Chief Larabee will see you and raise you."

Malachi said: "I'll see Dolph, too. And Ilene can check with the women."

"What women?" demanded Ilene suspiciously.

"Dolph's wife and the wives of the others," said Malachi. "I want to know what they think about Doney Beedle playing in the game with their husbands. And if they think he cheats…"

"Those bags!" Ilene screamed. "You mean I've got to sit with them and listen to their arteries harden and hear about their operations?"

Malachi said: "You want to help Mrs. John. You got me into it. Do your part or shut up."

Mrs. John said: "I don't blame the child. Those women…"

WE GOT out of there while they were still arguing. John Jr. followed us to the street and said anxiously: "You won't be hard on Doney Beedle, will you Malachi? Fella like that, he's sensitive. Came up from nothin', you know."

"Friend of yours?" asked Malachi.

"It's not that," said John Jr. rather too quickly. "I just hate to see Ma indulge her grudges. She's too tough on folks."

Malachi said. "Beedle and Larabee are cutting things up, aren't they?"

"I wouldn't know," said John gloomily. When he frowned he looked even more pathetic than usual. He was a likable enough fellow, with an honest way of looking straight at you when he talked. "I don't go around town much—I'm busy at the stables. But I know Doney isn't such a bad egg."

"Why doesn't Mrs. John like him?" asked Malachi.

"I don't know that, either," sighed John Jr. "I'm dumb. But I'm for the underdog, Cartier and the rest have been nice to Doney. Why can't Ma?"

Malachi said: "It's true that Sam Heppner and Lodi have been shaking down the little gamblers and everyone else who will hold still for a touch. If Beedle's in with them, you needn't feel sorry for him."

John Jr. put his hands down in the pockets of his riding pants and said, half-defiantly: "That's none of my business, what people do downtown. Everyone knows there is graft. We don't pay our public employees enough to keep them clean."

Malachi said: "Same old story… Well, let's not go into that now. People like you, John, don't help matters."

We got into the car. Malachi was burned up and John Jr. knew it. He seemed unhappy, staring after us, the wrinkles flowing up and down his baldness like little waves.

Malachi said: "He's too moronic to lecture to." He drove down Aiken Street to the Flamingo Hotel. We got out and went into a dimly lit grill. In a corner a man sat alone. We went over and sat down at his table.

Doney Beedle was carefully barbered, but he had the weather-beaten red neck of a man who had spent his youth outdoors at arduous labor. He had narrow shoulders and clever, watery eyes. He said to Malachi: "Am I glad to see you!"

He stared hard at me and Malachi said: "This is Tack Hinton. He works with me. He doesn't bite."

"He could," said Beedle. His voice was flat and toneless. "With both his teeth, I betcha."

Malachi said: "You want somebody bitten?"

"No," said Beedle. "I just wanta give you some dough."

He took a wallet from his pocket. He counted green money on the table. When he reached seven thousand dollars, he said: "For your old pal, Mrs. John. She claims I cheated her at cards."

"Why, Doney!" said Malachi innocently. "You wouldn't cheat in a card game!"

"I couldn't," said Beedle in his expressionless voice. "I ain't that smart... What's she got against me, Malachi?"

"How would I know?"

Beedle said: "She led into me. She waited until she knew I had her beat, then threw seven grand at me. Then she beefed all over town that I was a cheater."

Malachi said: "Sounds batty."

"Not Mrs. John," said Beedle. "She never was batty, not one little bit. She owns half the burg. She's richer'n Dolf Cartier and he owns the 'lectric company. She's got it in for me, all right."

Malachi lit a cigarette. He said: "Could it have anything to do with the vice take, Doney?"

There was silence. A waitress came and we ordered a drink. She brought it and still no one had spoken. We drank half our portions. Two beefy men drifted past the table, batting their eyes at Doney Beedle. They were Sam Heppner and Lodi, his partner—a couple of crooked gees wearing detective shields. They went out the door and Doney Beedle said: "Some things ain't nobody's business…"

Malachi put the money in his pocket. He took an envelope from his wallet, wrote a receipt on the back of it and gave it to Doney Beedle. Then he said: "I've been away. I've been busy with guys who are still busy doing what I couldn't finish. Those guys are taking it because they believe they have a good home to come back to. They think places like Bay City are the best places in the world."

"My brother's on Iwo Jima," said Doney defensively. "I buy a war bond every week for him."

Malachi said: "With the graft? I hear you're quite a politician nowadays. I remember when I bought a shine from you, and now you're telling me to mind my own business in my own home town."

Doney Beedle said: "Now don't go off half-cocked, Malachi…"

I got away from the table and blocked off any possible interference. Malachi leaned over and said in Beedle's face: "You'll clean it up, pal. You'll clean it up inside a week. Or else!"

Beedle said: "You can't talk to me like that…"

Malachi took him by the nose and twisted it hard. Beedle tried to reach inside his coat, but Malachi's other hand snapped him against the wall and held him there. After a moment, Beedle screeched with pain and defeat. Malachi dropped him and said: "That's just a beginning. Every time I see you it'll get worse. Unless you clean house."

We walked out of the hotel. It was late afternoon and Malachi was burning. We stormed into police head-quarters. Chief Larabee, his thick neck sweating, sat and listened for a moment or two and then tried to interrupt. "We closed all the houses, didn't we?" he whined. "You cain't butt in on us, Malachi. If I di'n't know yore pappy…"

Malachi said: "One week! Then I'm coming at you with everything I own and can hire."

We went out and Malachi felt better. Sam Heppner and Lodi passed us going into the Chief's office. We got into the car and drove to the other side of town.

PEOPLE DIDN'T seem to want to let us into the office of the president of the power company, but Malachi brushed them aside. Dolph Cartier barely had time to get the blond secretary off his knee. He was a big, white-haired man, handsome in a pink-and-white way. He started to storm, then recognized Malachi. He said stiffly: "Really, my boy, this is no way to enter a man's private office…"

Malachi said: "Sit down and cool off, Dolf. What about Doney Beedle and how come you associate with him?"

Cartier said: "You're very abrupt. What do you mean?"

"Doney was a common bootlegger, then a grove owner. Now he's a political boss," said Malachi. "You and Ed Solvey and the rest play poker with him—and allow him to cheat Mrs. John."

"Ridiculous!" said Cartier angrily. "Mrs. J. made a fool of herself, tilting at Doney. She threw money at him, a large amount."

"What hold has Doney on you?" Malachi insisted. "John Jr. defends him. You defend him. Yet he's tied in with Larabee and taking vice money hand over fist."

Cartier said: "Malachi, you were always headstrong. But this time you've gone too far. If you're insinuating that I and my friends are intimidated by any man…"

"Stuffed shirts!" Malachi said, sneering. "My father's friends! Scared silly, all of you, except Mrs. John. Bah!"

We went out, got into the car and Malachi drove toward home. He said: "Doney Beedle's pretty tough, eh? He's running the old town. All the old families are taking him up. All the old idiots are scared of him and all the young guys who could eat him are off to war. A hell of a thing!"

I said: "I don't get the part where Mrs. John throws dough at him. Did she think she could run him out by accusing him of cheating? Hell, even a dope like Cartier didn't go for that."

Malachi said: "Mrs. John isn't scared of him. The others are. Her own son…" He quieted suddenly, fell into thought. He almost ran down a lady who was walking against the green light at an intersection. A police car swung around and nearly ran into us and I saw the two hulking figures of Heppner and Lodi in the front seat. I figured those two would be watching us now, and it made my hands itch. I hate fat, crooked cops.

We got to the apartment and rang Mrs. John's bell. There was no answer. It was late in the afternoon and the Florida sun was pushing long shadows behind it. We went upstairs and found no trace of Ilene. We came back down again. Both of us were uneasy. I listened at Mrs. John's door. It didn't seem right that she wasn't at home, since she never went out for dinner and it was after six o'clock.

Malachi said: "I'll try the back door." I waited in the hall. After a while I heard movement within. Then Malachi opened the front door, nodded to me and I went in.

John Sudan, Jr. lay in the middle of the living room floor. Sun came through the slats of a partially open Venetian blind and shone upon his balding head, making a nimbus of dripping scarlet. The rug was stained with it.

Malachi said: "John is not with us any more."

"Dead as hell, ain't he?" I said.

"Mrs. John always would keep the fire-set out all summer," said Malachi. "Said it looked cozy."

The old-fashioned, heavy poker lay alongside John Jr.'s body. There was blood and hair on it, but no fingerprints, I decided, leaning close for a look without touching it. There was no sign of a struggle, which seemed funny, as John Jr. kept in fair physical condition.

Malachi said: "Either someone distracted his attention, or he was conked from the side. Could have been either way."

"He's still warm," I said. "It wasn't long ago."

"Could have been while we were upstairs," said Malachi. "Could have been before we got home. He's still bleeding a bit."

"He sure is dead," I said. "Where is Mrs. John?"

"In the bedroom," said Malachi. "She's alive."

We went into the bedroom. There was a bruise on the old lady's temple, on the right side. She lay across the bed on her left side, her skirts disarranged, one shoe off. Malachi put her head on a pillow and got some whiskey.

She strangled a bit, then came up fighting. She felt for her hair first thing and her fingers flew, fixing it into place. She said hoarsely: "Who did it? Who hit me? I'll break every bone in his damned body, the son—"

Malachi said: "Just how did it happen?"

"I was giving John Jr. hell, the fool!" she said. "I came in here to get—something—and someone hit me."

Malachi said: "Someone hit John Jr., too."

"Not hard enough, I'll bet," she snapped. "The dolt!"

"Too hard," Malachi said gravely.

Her hands dropped from her hair. She stared at Malachi. She said: "You mean… someone killed him?"

Malachi said: "With your poker."

She slid from the bed, wavered, but managed to remain on her feet. She said: "He was my son… He was an awful fool, but why should they kill him?"

"Why?" echoed Malachi.

For one instant she was a weary, frightened old woman. She held onto the bedpost, looking into space and there were a thousand lines in her face. Then she stiffened, got her chin up and began walking toward the parlor.

We were in the hall when the door banged open and feet marched heavily into the place. A harsh voice said: "Look! Another damn corpus!"

Sam Heppner heaved into view. He held a gun in his hand and he held it right, low and steady. He said: "You two git away from Miz John. Yore under arrest!"

Mrs. John said: "Don't be dumber than usual, Sam. These men are my friends. They didn't kill John."

"Mebbe not," leered Sam Heppner. "But they shore as hell kilt Doney Beedle!"

Lodi was waiting, with another gun, as we all marched into the room where the body still lay before the hearth. Malachi said sharply: "Put away that gun, Heppner. You know damned well we didn't kill anyone."

"No?" said Heppner. "You gave Beedle a receipt for seven grand. Think that'll git you anythin'? If you got seven grand on yore person it's his'n an' yore it, brother."

Malachi said: "Ten people saw us leave him in the Flamingo Grill."

"Ten people seen him foller you out," said Heppner, "inta the alley alongside the hotel, where you gave it to him, you and yore buddy."

Lodi also knew how to handle a gun. I was very careful not to make a bad move. If Mrs. John hadn't been there, I might have tried....

The door to the hall leading outdoors was open. If I could have made a play on the two of them, the way was clear to our car. We needed time, right now. I remembered that Malachi had made himself obnoxious to Chief Larabee and to other people that day. I could see the rubber hose coming at me, down at Headquarters. Heppner was getting out his handcuffs....

Mrs. John was staring at her son's body. She didn't approach it, just stood, looking at it. Heppner suddenly remembered that John Jr. was her son, I guess. He backed up a step to let her get by, not relaxing his vigilance, however. This placed him right in the doorway.

I NEVER saw or heard Ilene. But all of a sudden Sam Heppner buckled at the knees. As he did, Malachi dove head foremost at Lodi. I went in as fast as I could behind Malachi. As Lodi's gun came down, aimed at Malachi's head, I grabbed it and took it away from him and smacked him on the jaw with it.

I was in time to kick Heppner on the skull. Ilene held a limp blackjack in her hand and said: "I heard the tail end of the hippodrome…. My God, is that John Jr.?"

Malachi said: "You take it from here, Mrs. John. We'll be back and give you John Jr.'s murderer."

As we went out the door, I heard her say: "Never saw such quick shenanigans in my life! Lawdy me!" She was a tough old girl, all right, say what you will. She never tried to stop us from lamming out of there.

The police sirens were coming closer, like banshees in the dusk. The three of us got into the car and Malachi drove slowly out the street, turned a corner, then stepped on it until we had put a few miles between us and the Poinsettia Arms. There was a small saloon he knew, in the poorer section of town and the man let us have the back room all to ourselves.

Ilene drank a quick bourbon and exhaled hard. She said: "Those clowns! They could never have made it stick. People know you in this town, Malachi. Seven thousand dollars wouldn't tempt you to murder. What goes with our comic cops?"

Malachi said: "They only wanted to get us downtown and beat hell out of us, or maybe just detain us… Now why would they want to detain us?"

I said: "Beedle killed—John killed. They were pals…"

"Mrs. John quarreling with her son," said Malachi. "Hating Beedle, for some reason we don't know."

Ilene said: "I saw all those women. They were having a meeting of their silly Garden Club. Mrs. Cartier with her asthma and her bangs from 1925. The Solvey with her thick, drippy southern accent. The Marshal with her relatives in Chicago, rich like mad. Mrs. Carey Flowers, all nose and big mouth. Ugh!"

Malachi said: "What did you learn?"

"They hate Mrs. John. She's always played poker with their husbands for high stakes and usually wins. The night Beedle won made them the happiest old hags in Florida. Most of them hate their husbands, too—especially the Cartier. She thinks he cheats. At his age!"

I remembered the blonde sliding from Cartier's lap as we barged in on him at his office. These pink-cheeked old guys who resemble Esky on the mag cover always have hand trouble… Things began to piece together just a little bit.

Malachi said sharply: "There's a clean-up going on. Beedle was eliminated as part of it. But it's not a clean-up of the city vice. It's a civil war among the grifters."

"Those two coppers," I said, "could have done it. They could have been coming from Mrs. John's when we saw them driving down Aiken Street. They could have bumped Beedle, then rushed back and closed in on us."

Ilene said: "Then there will be a next. Those women, hating their husbands, hating everyone, those old, tired women and their Garden Club, which is a gossip soirée…."

I said: "We can't hide out here forever. I got some sports clothes I'd hate to lose back at Poinsettia Arms." I had Sam Heppner's gun in my pocket, too. It was loaded and felt very good. Going against cops or robbers without guns is all right sometimes, but the steel felt cold and fine to my touch.

Malachi said: "That is a point well taken, Tack. I think we can return, by devious ways, to our rooms."

Ilene said: "They'll have a guard."

Malachi was onto something. I could tell by the slow way he spoke, the angle at which he cocked his head. He said: "There are a few things I'd like to check, just for the hell of it. Such as why did Mrs. John hate Beedle so? And what about the seven thousand dollars? Also some things I heard today which didn't make sense at the time. Let's return to the scene of the crime. Let's kill a few birds with a couple of stones."

"When he talks like that," said Ilene bitterly, "I always have need of my trusty blackjack. And usually I get my clothing torn. Let's have another drink."

We had another drink. Then Malachi borrowed the car belonging to the saloonkeeper, an old battered Chevvy. We all scrooched down, as we are very tall people, even Ilene, and easily recognizable. Malachi drove carefully around town. There were squad cars all over. We made a detour through the select residential district near the golf course. Malachi paused a moment before a large house set well back from the road.

A big sedan came out and rolled swiftly toward town. Malachi followed it. The car didn't pause until it was near the Poinsettia Arms, then the driver hesitated, pulled to the curb and stopped. A man got out and walked along the shadows.

Malachi parked behind the sedan, which gave us cover to crawl out and follow. The man turned into the Poinsettia and disappeared immediately from our view.

Malachi said: "Two and two make four and carry six."

"I don't like this pussy-footing," muttered Ilene. "It gives me the lurgy wampus."

Malachi said: "I'll take the back way. Tack will do in front. You bring up the rear guard, Ilene. You always make such a fine rear…"

"If you say 'end' I'll hit you with the blackjack," Ilene warned. "You get too damned cute when you think you know something and refuse to tell us. What's this all about?"

"It's a charade," I grumbled. "Malachi's playing games."

"Don't kill anyone until I give the word," said Malachi. "Mostly just spy around and wait for me."

"Those are damned poor orders-of-the-day," I complained.

"He's a damned poor actor," said Ilene. "He thinks he's Dick Tracy—in technicolor."

Malachi had already gone through the alley of the house next door to the apartment. His hurrying tall form disappeared from sight. Ilene sighed and said: "Why do I love that big extrovert? Why don't I marry some safe, nice guy and raise babies?"

"How could a safe, nice guy stand you?" I asked. "Why don't you marry Malachi and go ahead and raise babies? It would make one of you settle down."

"That would be me," she said darkly. "He'd never stay still. He'd always prowl nights, looking for trouble. And you with him, you big trambo! Hadn't you better go ahead and keep him from getting killed?"

I went up to the front of the Poinsettia Arms the quickest and quietest way, jungle style. I slid up to the front door which was open. There were no cops. This seemed odd. There should have been someone around to guard Mrs. John and watch the premises from which a murdered man had recently been removed.

I got into the hall without trouble. There was a light shining beneath the door of Mrs. John's apartment. There were low voices, which I couldn't hear. I thought I recognized the man's voice, but wasn't sure. Mrs. John was sounding off, as usual. She was certainly a rugged old gal.

WAITING IN a dark place is bad, no matter what experience you've had in warfare. It never gets any better, the standing around, not sure of what it's all about, knowing there's a killer loose—or killers—which is worse. They can come at you from two sides. The way John Jr. got it, while one distracted his attention....

But if there were two in on it when John Jr. got his, how did they manage to keep him from battling them? If Heppner and Lodi closed in, it was ten-to-one even John Jr. would have suspected trouble and attempted to ward it off....

The whole thing was giddy. It had happened so suddenly, with so many people involved, that I got dizzy trying to follow my own train of thought. Malachi knew these people, which made it easier for him. It's better if you know what to expect from certain parties....

I wondered where Malachi was, and if there were cops prowling the neighborhood and if Ilene was in any danger. Bay City is a pretty good-sized town, but if anyone hurt Ilene we would take it apart and throw it into the bay.

I was getting a complete set of nerves when I heard Malachi's voice. He was inside the apartment. He had, of course, come through Mrs. John's back door. I heard him say: "No you don't, not this time!"

So I hit the door. It was a tough door and I had to hit it twice. Down the stairs men came tumbling, shouting orders. There were Sam Heppner and Lodi, at last! The door gave and we all seemed to pile into Mrs. John's apartment at once.

Heppner tried me high and Lodi tried me low. I caught one glimpse of Malachi, all tangled up with someone. I took another quick look, my mouth hanging open and Heppner seized the opportunity to slug me with something hard alongside the jaw. Lodi was trying to throw me to the floor.

I had to turn a little to get Heppner within range. I forgot all about the gun in my pocket when he socked me with the mace. Lodi had not been trained on the football field and could not get my legs together to throw me. I got an arm free and rapped my knuckles into the spot behind Heppner's ear. He stumbled just a moment, which was all I wanted.

Ilene came charging in. She stopped dead in the doorway and cried: "Malachi! Shame on you!"

I stabbed two stiff fingers into Heppner's eyes. He reeled into Ilene and without pausing to think, she hit him with her blackjack on top of the head, collapsing him into a heap on the floor. I leaned down and got Lodi.

He was a chunky guy, full of fight. He busted me one in the groin, but I turned my hip and kneed him a little. Then I got him on his feet and hauled off to belt him out. But Ilene again absent-mindedly swung the blackjack and Lodi went limp in my hands. I deposited him atop of Heppner and turned to see what in hell Malachi was doing.

Malachi was picking Dolf Cartier off the floor. He was placing Cartier on the couch in the corner of Mrs. John's comfortable living room. Outside someone blew a whistle and Chief Larabee came wheezing into the apartment. I held Heppner's gun on the fat man and the cops behind him. Ilene started to slug him from habit, then refrained as Malachi said: "Hold it, everybody. This is all cleared up."

I kept looking at Mrs. John. She was groggy. She was holding her jaw with both hands. She sat on the floor near the hearth and was shaking her head slowly back and forth.

Ilene said: "Malachi, are you completely insane? I saw you slug Mrs. John!"

Larabee said: "You're under arrest, all three of you!"

The cops didn't say anything. They looked from the gun in my mitt to Ilene's swinging blackjack and were quite still. On the couch, Dolf Cartier moved and whispered: "She—she would have—done it..."

Malachi said: "You should have known it, you dope. She owns half the property in the old vice district."

Mrs. John sat on the floor. She stopped feeling her jaw and began fixing her white hair. She said in a muffled voice: "They thought they could move in on me. I showed 'em..."

Malachi said: "You certainly did! You tried to bribe Doney Beedle by tossing him seven thousand dollars in a poker game. Cartier couldn't understand that, and almost got killed for questioning you about it just now."

She said: "You're too smart. I thought you'd clean 'em up. I thought you'd be on my side."

"You had the vice racket going your way for years," said Malachi. "You owned the property and you had connections."

Larabee said hastily: "That's enough doubletalk. You're all under arrest."

"Talks like a parrot, doesn't he?" grinned Malachi. "All he knows is to arrest people. If they oppose him, arrest them. Consider yourself finished, Larabee. You and Mrs. John ran things long enough. You had it all your way until Doney Beedle moved in. Then he took most of the vice graft away from you, building his political machine. John Jr., who was ashamed of your racket, threw in with Doney Beedle. He didn't know that his income depended mainly on the take. When he found out, he turned on you and you picked up the poker and let him have it, didn't you, Mrs. John?"

Her face changed. It broke into little pieces, right before us. She whined in a voice I had never heard: "I'm an old lady. You're persecuting me... I want a lawyer—Dolf, get me a good lawyer..."

Cartier got off the couch. I saw the poker, then, under the chair. He had a bruise on his face. He said in a low voice: "She's lost her mind, hasn't she, Malachi?"

"You can call it that," said Malachi. "All I know is that she and Larabee have been shaking down gamblers and petty crooks for years. She got her gambling money that way, she increased her holdings that way. I don't care whether she goes up for murder. I just want Bay City cleaned up—for guys like Doney Beedle's brother and your own son and others who are taking it the hard way and hope to come home to a decent living here some day."

Cartier said: "Mrs. John, the killer of her own son—"

"And of Doney Beedle," said Malachi grimly. "Heppner and Lodi are grafters and crooks and thugs, but they were on Doney's side in this deadly warfare. It was Larabee and Mrs. John against the newcomers. She slid downtown, parleyed with Doney in the alley outside the Flamingo Grill where he always was available and killed him. Then she came home, slugged herself and pretended she had been attacked. Heppner and Lodi were dumb enough to think we might have been in on Doney's killing because Doney and I had a little argument about cleaning up the town."

Mrs. John said in her trembling accents: "Malachi Manatee, you should be ashamed of yourself, hitting an old woman!"

"An old murderess," Cartier said sternly.

Malachi said: "Larabee might be called an accessory, I imagine..."

Lodi got up first, then Heppner. They looked at Larabee and grinned through their bruises. Larabee immediately fell to squawking. He directed his talk at Cartier. He squawked loud and long. He laid it all on Mrs. John. He protested he had had nothing to do with any murders. He said the old gal went berserk when John Jr. jumped her and tried to warn her off the vice take. She had hit John Jr. without meaning to kill him, and then had gone after Beedle, blaming him for what had happened. It was a very bad beef and Larabee looked bad delivering it, but it was mostly the truth.

They all got out, after a while. Cartier kept saying: "I can't believe it. I've known her all my life…"

Malachi looked him in the eye. "And always knew she was an old rip, grafter, and the owner of fire-trap property. Think it over, Dolf—it nearly got you killed. Think it over the next time you get that blonde on your lap. Your wife is hating you, too! Maybe you'll get a dish of poison from her some day. You stand for anything while it's under cover, you and your kind. Then when it's brought into the open, you holler in dismay. I hope your son is safe in Germany. I hope he comes back and you can face him—I hope!"

We went upstairs. Ilene poured a quick drink, then another. We finished a bottle. Ilene said: "Let's take a trip. Let's do something. I didn't like this affair."

Malachi said slowly: "I never thought I'd hit an old woman. You know what? I'm ashamed. I should have been able to handle her without slugging her…"

SLAY-BELLE

THE WIDOW MORGAN
SHOULD HAVE STUCK TO
HOUSEWORK AND RAISING
BABIES INSTEAD OF RAISING
CAIN WITH THE LOCAL
POLITICOS IN GRANADA.
SHE JUST DIDN'T HAVE ANY
LUCK WITH MENFOLKS—
THEIR MORTALITY RATE
WAS TOO HIGH. EVEN HER
LATEST ROMANCE HAD
BEEN "INTERRUPTED" BY A
WELL-AIMED FRUIT KNIFE.

FLORIDIANS, LIKE Yankees, go to the beaches in the summertime. The tourists return north and the natives take over the resorts which are cooler than Florida cities. Malachi Manatee, being a West Coast boy, took us to Granada that July after VE Day to bathe in the invigorating blue waters of the Gulf.

Granada's beach is on Granada Key, a strip of sand and hummock containing innumerable cottages and Casa Granada, which combines the features of hotel and drinking club. Floridians go in for Spanish nomenclature, probably because De Soto landed at the mouth of the Manatee River and went all the way to the Mississippi before he finally kicked off.

Malachi says his family took their name from the river at a time when their own name would have proved embarrassing. Ilene suggests that now would be a good time to change it back, since Malachi is becoming somewhat notorious, but Ilene is red-headed, impetuous and beautiful, and resented attending the murder trial. Furthermore, Ilene always wants to go to New York and play—on Malachi's money, of course.

Anyway, we were not on the cooling beach, but in a sweltering courtroom, listening to John "The Mouth" Metzger defend one Leb Anchor, charged with murder. Metzger is a wiry little lawyer and Anchor is a giant Cracker, even bigger than Malachi's six-foot-four.

Malachi was acquainted with Metzger, with Judge Selvey, who had rehearsed the case for us and invited us to attend the finish of the trial. Malachi has an awful yen for justice—his own brand, of course—and six or seven million dollars to back him up.

Metzger was pouring it on the jury. He had a loose mouth and a glib orator's tongue. He wrung out the flag, mothers of mankind, the Constitution and what not in equal parts, none of which made sense to me.

Leb Anchor sat slouched in a chair which creaked under his weight, cleaning his nails with a long, sharp fruit knife, a spring-bladed affair which many Crackers carry with nonchalance, but the mere possession of which would get a New Yorker a jail sentence. It seemed a hell of a weapon for an accused murderer to be handling. Anchor's heavy, unintelligent features were blank and he seemed totally disinterested in the fact that he was on trial for murdering Daniel Morgan, a respected citizen of Granada.

Metzger rose to screaming heights. "If there is a man among you worthy jurors—and I doubt it men, I doubt if there is a man among you who would brook insult over a trifling debt of twenty miserable dollars—if there is a man among you who would suffer the fascistic gibes of a man of money, a man noted for his penury, a man avid of mere monetary gain, if there is a man among you who would not defend himself when violently attacked…"

The jury was eating it up, swaying under a sort of hypnotic spell. I decided it was not what he said, but the way he said it. It was ridiculous and disgusting, but Metzger was making it work.

Judge Selvey sat on the bench and glowered. He was a stout, muscular ex-football player, a budding politician. Malachi had known both Selvey and Metzger at school and Selvey had warned us: "John is the best trial lawyer in Florida. He drinks constantly or he would be practicing in Miami or Tampa and richer than Croesus. He chases every skirt in town, mainly to get information which will help his cases, the rat. He's a terrible crook—but smart, Malachi, smarter than me, I'll admit."

"Mouthy Metzger," Malachi mused. "I never liked him…"

The jury filed out. Malachi turned his attention upon the prisoner. Anchor closed the jackknife and handed it to Metzger, who put it carelessly in his pocket, sat down and began conversing with his client. Anchor just stared

Leb came at me with the chair, then Ilene said an unladylike word and tried to belt Mary Jo on the chin.

at his hands, which were exceptionally long and clean for a character of his sort, I thought.

I looked at Mary Jo Morgan, widow of the deceased, inheritor of the hardware business. She was pretty in a sketchy, febrile way, a wisp of a girl with helpless, narrow shoulders. She wore unbecoming black and stared straight ahead, as expressionless as Anchor.

Malachi stirred himself and said: "Let's catch one while they're out."

Ilene muttered: "Why do I stay and listen to this? If I don't take the next plane for New York…"

DID I say Ilene is red-haired and gorgeous? She has known Malachi since childhood, undoubtedly far too well, and that is probably the reason they do not marry. But there is a fascination between them which precludes either wedding someone else. This is too bad, since I, for one, would gladly marry Ilene tomorrow—today!

Ilene went on: "That crook, Metzger, could free Judas Iscariot. Especially against that pitiful prosecutor. It's degrading!"

Malachi led the way into a bar next to the courthouse. He said: "As long as we elect prosecutors to small-paying jobs, we will not be able to hire star lawyers. Metzger is an accidental character in that he remains here because he drinks too much, but it happens often that under our judicial system clever criminal lawyers free crooks… Let's have a drink."

"Mary Jo Morgan could have afforded a special prosecutor," Ilene said. "The little fool sits there stony-faced letting her husband's murderer go free."

"Metzger probably has her on his side," replied Malachi, shrugging. "And why should she have to buy justice, anyway?" But he ordered a champagne collins, and I knew he was more perturbed than he cared to reveal.

In the rear of the bar a hand beckoned, and there was Judge Selvey in a private booth, glooming over a highball. He had a round, smooth face, a slightly balding head, and he looked very unhappy. He growled: "Nothin' to it… Metzger oughta be hung."

Malachi said: "The Mouth stays inside your laws."

"That's no excuse," said Selvey. "He's all rat. I wish you'd pry into his business a little, Malachi."

"Anchor is a moronic killer if ever I saw one," Malachi mused. "I can't do anything about Metzger, of course. But Anchor must be wrong in many things."

"He runs a still," said the judge. "He's a brute. But they're all afraid of him except Sheriff Blake, who is powerless."

Malachi said: "We came here to enjoy your beach. Your murders are none of my business, I'm afraid."

"Yeah," sighed Selvey. "I guess you're right… Stop at City Hall and get a cabana, Malachi, on me. You can dress on the beach without walking from the hotel in a bathing suit. We built some new ones, the city did. I'll mebbe see you over there tomorrow."

He went back to his court and after we had finished our drinks we returned also. The jury had returned already, too quickly, I knew, for justice to prevail. The foreman said defiantly: "Not guilty!"

There was a slight flurry, and Mary Jo Morgan came up the aisle and went past us, her face buried in a large man's handkerchief with an initial in the corner. Malachi stumbled on his bum gam and almost knocked her over. He apologized, holding her elbows in his hands. She tore away and ran out of the courthouse.

Judge Selvey was lacing into the jury. He called them some very fancy names, meaning that they were a dumb lot of prejudiced clucks. He spoke of charlatans of the law, without naming Metzger, dismissed the jurymen without thanks.

Metzger, however, grinning from ear to ear, went among them with outstretched hands. He ignored Selvey as though the burly judge did not exist. He came back to where we stood and said with cynical laughter: "How'd you like it, Malachi? Pretty smart, huh?"

"Very clever, Mouthy," said Malachi disdainfully.

Metzger sneered and said: "Don't look down your nose at me, Malachi. You never heard a smarter lawyer."

"Peace, Mouthy," said Malachi, "you're wonderful."

It was the way Malachi could say things, of course. He could take a man's hide off with his tongue, his blue eyes boring into him. Metzger got angry all in one instant. I saw it coming and also saw Leb Anchor, his heavy face puzzled, looming near Metzger.

The lawyer snarled: "You big stiff, I always hated you. Just because you inherited a lot of filthy money from your thief of a father…"

Malachi said easily: "Oh, go to hell, Mouthy." He put his hand on Metzger's shoulder, twisted him and chucked him into the hall, where he bounced off the wall and went flat on his face.

Anchor roared and started forward. I took him from the side, on a sort of lateral block, the way I used to in my old days with the football Giants, and that put him on the benches.

I could have left him there, but he was, I thought, a murderer and his man had started it, so I gave him the treatment the Marines had taught me before I got mine on Tarawa. It left him cooled off among the splinters of the bench. Then I picked him up and threw him after Metzger, and the two of them sprawled on the concrete floor.

Sheriff Blake, a nice young guy, walked over and said: "Tsk, tsk, you may have hurt them, Malachi!" He winked.

Malachi said: "Put away the gun, Ilene." She had a .22 automatic in her hand, the safety clicked back. Blake blinked, and Malachi said: "She has a license for it. Tack and I don't carry them, but Ilene likes the feel of a gun."

Metzger glared up from under Anchor without trying to arise and sputtered: "I'll get you for this Manatee! You and that slob Selvey and your tough boy-friend... I'll get you all!"

Malachi said: "That'll be the day, Mouthy..."

We went out and got into Malachi's car. Before we drove away I saw Selvey leaning out of the upper window, waving at us. He was chortling with glee and giving us the prize-fighter's mitt.

We stopped at City Hall, and the clerk gave Malachi a key to the cabana, but he insisted on having three and paying for the other two. Then we drove over the causeway to Granada Beach, had a few drinks and tried to relax. The thing about coming back from the war is that you crave action—then when you get it you stay keyed up, and it's hard to relax. But we tried....

WE WERE staying at this hotel, a stucco building of no great pretensions, a few blocks from the beach. Ilene was in her room, napping or something. Malachi and I played gin rummy, and he beat me as usual. He never works at cards, and with his luck he doesn't have to. He just lays them down. He says they help him think—about other things.

He said suddenly, as I was trying to decide what to do with an unwanted ace I had drawn: "Anchor undoubtedly killed Dan Morgan over a twenty-dollar debt. Metzger got him off. That's bad, huh?"

"I'll go down with seven," I said, holding the ace.

"I seem to have only six," said Malachi. "That makes me out in all three games. You owe me eight dollars."

I paid him. He won a lot of money from me that way, but what the hell, he paid me too much in the first place. It was the best job a guy ever had, stooging around with Malachi. Boxing and football were not for me, with scar tissue on my lung, and Malachi seemed to need me, ever since Tarawa, if only as sounding board for his conversation.

He said: "And I don't like the Mary Jo Morgan angle, either. Metzger has a way of fouling up everything in skirts."

I said: "This is a vacation. How about a swim?"

We went down to the beach. I had cabana Fifteen, Malachi had Sixteen, Ilene Seventeen. I went in and undressed. The cabanas were nothing more than lockers, set in a semi-circle under one roof, all connecting but with no doors in between. They were each about six feet square, with high walls, no windows, electric lights and a useful little fan in each. They were built of concrete block, with cement floors, insect-proof and really efficient.

We went out and had a really good swim in a Gulf calm as a lake, and then we stretched on the sand in the afternoon sun. Ilene came down, went into her cabana and reappeared in a swim suit which did not cover too much of her fine body. She sat cross-legged between us and said: "This is a hell of a place. Metzger's here some place, stinking drunk. Leb Anchor drove him down. Mrs. Morgan is at her husband's cottage and Judge Selvey lives down there in that big house."

Malachi said: "All the actors in a little drama… Come on, I'll race you for the drinks."

He meant in the water, as the Japs had made sure he wouldn't race on foot again. He could really swim, but so could Ilene. They got up and Ilene put a rubber cap over her red hair. She said: "It's disgusting, these clowns literally getting away with murder, then celebrating where I can see them. And there'll probably be a fight. You know Metzger and Mary Jo were like that—before the trial. Now I hear Anchor and Mary Jo were cheating on Dan Morgan and that's what led to the murder."

Malachi blinked once and was quite still. I said: "If there's going to be trouble, I choose Anchor, He's my man. I'll fight him every day and twice on Sundays—for nothing."

"He shoots people," Ilene said. "Come on, Malachi, I'll swim you to the pavilion."

Malachi said: "I'd like you to fight Anchor, Tack, for keeps. Metzger, too, and some others."

"You want a war for your money?" Ilene said. "I think we ought to go to New York."

"Yes, I want a war. Against thugs like Anchor and crooks like Metzger…"

"And dumb widows like Mary Jo Morgan," added Ilene. "Were you just gabbing about that race, Malachi?"

They went down to the water to begin their race northward, about a quarter mile. I took off south, leaving them alone, which I did as often as possible, on the off chance they would break down and begin pitching woo. The drift was my way and I took it easy. Porpoise blew not fifteen feet from me. I was startled, but a man swimming nearby said: "Don't let them bother you, Hinton."

It was Judge Selvey, and I realized I had floated down opposite his house, which was right on the beach. He said: "Porpoise will never bother you. They patrol just like cops, up and down. They're friendly to man, you know."

"I'm never too friendly with a fish that size," I said.

We floated side by side. Selvey was stout but powerful, and I could see he was a hell of a swimmer. He said: You took care of that big Anchor all right. Water is just not your element."

"Right," I said. "Anchor is a pushover, really. Muscle-bound, and unpracticed in using his hands for defense. That's why he shot Morgan—he's a weapon-user, not a rough-and-tumbler."

"Say, that's right smart," said Selvey. "Come on up and have a drink and we'll talk a little."

We walked out of the water and up to the house. There was a colored servant who could mix hell out of a julep, and the judge had good bourbon. We sipped in perfect contentment and he said: "That case bothers me. I liked Dan Morgan."

I said: "What about his wife?"

"Weak," said Selvey promptly. "Not bad… ignorant. Metzger hypnotized her and she gave mighty poor evidence."

I said idly: "There's a rumor she and Anchor were palsy."

Selvey's big hands clenched. He said slowly: "Now that would be a hell of a thing. I never heard that. Morgan was a man's man. Kind of tough, I reckon, but hell, he was my friend and he had to do business with these Crackers and you know… But he was tough, all right. Older than me… I liked Dan."

I said: "You must feel lousy, believing Anchor killed him."

"It's one of those things," Selvey said. "A judge gets accustomed to seeing juries go wrong. Prejudice is so strong in the south… the duel is not a lost art to us."

I said: "I know what you mean."

We talked some more. He was pretty smart and very nice to me, and he obviously admired Malachi, so I liked him. He said his wife preferred Carolina in summertime, but that he stayed here and I guessed his own domestic life was none too smooth. He seemed lonely and I asked him up to have a drink with us at the hotel later.

I swam back, for the hell of it, and to strengthen my lung, and found Malachi and Ilene side by side, not quarreling for once in their lives.

Malachi said: "Hey! Let's dress and have one."

The judge's julep had started me and I was willing. I followed them up to the nearby cabanas. They were sure a fine-looking couple, long-limbed, tanned, clean looking like thoroughbred horses. Malachi's limp suited him—he was so tall and handsome he needed a touch of humility to bring him to earth.

WE WENT up to the hotel, and Malachi was preoccupied again, and I knew he was thinking about the murder case. We went into the bar and had martinis and I felt mine, on top of the julep. The door banged and Anchor came in. He looked big and tough and drunk. I got down off my bar stool.

Anchor did not see us at first. He bellowed at the bartender: "Where the hell is Johnny?"

"Drunk, no doubt," said that worthy harshly, unafraid.

"Gahdammit," said Anchor, "I got to see him. Gahdammit, he cain't do me like this."

The bartender had his hand on a blue revolver. He said: "Metzger didn't ask for you when he left. Get out of here."

Anchor's eye rolled, came to me. He said: "Gahdammit, you ain't all that tough, y'know. Yo' was lucky."

I started for him. Malachi grabbed my arm and said: "Let him go this time, Tack." Anchor's hand was at his hip. I wrenched away from Malachi and dived for him, getting him by the wrist before he could draw the gun. I hit him hard with the edge of my hand, on the nape of the neck. He stumbled forward and fell to hands and knees. Malachi got to me before I could kick out his brains.

Malachi said: "No, Tack… Not now!"

The bartender said coolly: "Don't stop him on my account."

"I'd rather the law got him," said Malachi. "He's a murderer. They'll get him sooner or later."

Anchor had started crawling. He went out that way, on hands and knees, without trying to get up. Ilene said: "What do you mean 'they' Malachi? He can't be tried again for Morgan's murder. You expect him to do another one?"

"I meant, the Fates, I guess," said Malachi. "Something. I meant, I don't believe he can get away with it, but I didn't want Tack, slightly inebriated, to kill him."

"Sure," I said. "You're right. Let's eat. I'm sorry, Malachi, the guy gets me."

"Sure he gets you," said Malachi. "He's a beast. But let's forget him now."

We had melon, mullet with a fine salad, hot biscuits and some white wine. It was fine. Mary Jo Morgan slipped in and sat in a corner, ordering only melon. She seemed to be waiting for someone and left before we were finished. There was no sign of Metzger.

We went back to the bar and had a brandy, and played some three-handed hearts. Ilene ran into a streak of luck and won seventeen dollars. I lost all of it, Malachi breaking even.

I was sleepy after all the drinks and at eleven we went upstairs and to bed. We had a suite and Ilene a double room. It was a nice, cool layout, and the beds were comfortable. Ilene and Malachi played gin, but I slept heartily, with the cicadas singing through my dreams....

It was about eleven when we went to the beach. Looking down at the judge's house, I remembered that he had not shown up for a drink the previous evening and wondered why. We went into the cabanas and put on our suits. Ilene and I came out first and Malachi came a few moments later. We took a dip, then sat on the sand. The sun was really hot.

Mary Jo Morgan drove down and went to the cabanas. In a moment or two she came out, went into the water, and splashed timidly. She was quite tanned and sturdier than I had thought, and she certainly was better looking undressed than in the flouncy garments she affected.

Malachi said: "That woman lives in fear."

"She's a dope," said Ilene.

"A scared one," said Malachi. "I wonder how much she knows."

"She knows everything, but can't put it together with her mental equipment." Ilene said forcefully. "Women like her should be kept barefooted and busy raising babies."

Judge Selvey had come out of his house and was strolling down the beach toward us.

Malachi squinted at him approaching and said: "Well, this will make him happy, and I might as well tell you two—Metzger's dead."

"Now how do you know that?" demanded Ilene.

"I just found him," said Malachi, "in my cabana. Had a hell of a time dressing around him without getting blood all over me. Someone cut his throat. He was beat up and cut to hell."

Ilene said: "You found him? And you kept quiet about it, dressed and came down here. Are you crazy, Malachi?"

He shrugged. "We did more than that around Jap corpses—and don't raise your voice. Someone meant Metzger to be found in my cabana, of course. Let's be quiet about it for a while and see what happens."

I said: "You'll be blamed. You and he tangled before witnesses. And furthermore, how the hell did he get in your cabana? Those are good, new spring locks. Who had your key?"

Malachi said: "I'll answer those questions before the day is over. Meantime, let's not tell the judge."

Selvey came up, smiling. He had a towel and wrapped in it a thermos jug. He flourished it and said: "Gin and grapefruit juice. Best beach drink in the world. Icy cold."

Malachi said: "You're a pal. We looked for you last night"

We drank, but my mind was going around like a carousel. I was trying to imagine who had killed Metzger. There were many people capable of it, there were many, no doubt, who had cause. But, of course, I could not think of any outside the circle connected with yesterday's trial.

THERE WAS Leb Anchor. He would do swell. He was my favorite. He had been squawking in the bar last night before I worked him over. There was the long knife

Metzger had loaned Leb in the courtroom, then had taken back and shoved in his pocket.

There was Mary Jo Morgan. If Metzger had spurned her, once his purpose of freeing Leb had been accomplished, she would do for a suspect. Metzger had a record of being tough on his women.

Then there was Malachi, and there was me. We would undoubtedly be suspected. We had rowed with the mouthy lawyer and he had threatened us. No one would expect us to stand under threats from him.

Furthermore, we were the ones who had the key to the cabana. How could Leb Anchor, the moron, figure that stunt? How could Mary Jo get Metzger into the locker?

Judge Selvey was saying: "Well, I got to get back. Metzger wants to see me. I'd like to cut his damned throat!"

Ilene jumped about a foot, but Malachi said: "Have you seen him since the trial? I hear he was plastered down here yesterday."

Selvey said: "Nope. He phoned me. He has several cases on my calendar and wants a postponement or something. It's hard to play square with the little rat. Wish I could mess him up on some of his skulduggery."

Malachi said: "He'll get his come-uppance some day... See you later, Sam."

Selvey took his empty bottle and saluted with it. He walked back down the beach and Ilene said: "Good Lord! Throat cutting all over the place, real and imaginary!"

Malachi was watching Mary Jo Morgan. She had stopped wetting her knees, which were plenty good-looking, and was hovering nearby. She caught Malachi's eye, flushed and came over. She said in a low voice: "I heard Judge Selvey mention John Metzger. Did he happen to say where he is now?"

"No," said Malachi. He introduced himself, Ilene and me. "I was sorry to hear about Dan, Mrs. Morgan. I knew him slightly."

She said vaguely: "Yes… Wasn't it awful? Leb never should have done it."

Ilene said: "Aren't you red hot angry at Leb and Metzger?"

"Oh, no," Mary Jo said. "It was sort of a fight, you see. Dan was mad and so was Leb. John—Metzger was hired to do a job. No use being sore at them. It—just happened that way."

Ilene shrugged, but Malachi said gently: "Still, shooting an unarmed man in cold blood is bad business."

"Dan was mad," she repeated. "He cussed Leb awful. Did the judge say when John— Metzger was going to see him?"

She must have been listening pretty closely. Malachi hesitated, then said: "In about two hours, I think."

Mrs. Morgan said: "Well, thanks. Guess I'll be going, now. Uh… er… Thanks, all of you."

She walked off, her gait like a farm girl's, her hips swaying. Men looked after her with a faraway glint in their eyes.

Malachi said: "Tack, you'd better take a look at the corpse. We'll get dressed and start snooping around."

"See that you don't start snooping around that damned stupid woman," said Ilene sharply.

"That's your baby," said Malachi. "Keep an eye on her. If she starts out in the car, you take mine and follow."

Ilene said: "I should follow that witch? I'll have to get in line among the procession of two-legged male canines!"

Malachi said: "A man has been killed, darling. Mary Jo expects to meet him in two hours, but he's dead. It's necessary to keep Mary Jo in sight."

"It's necessary to call the sheriff," said Ilene. "You're beginning to get that police dog look about you, Malachi, and it's quite unbecoming."

"Go and—soak your head," said Malachi. "And follow that woman wherever she goes until I check with you!"

Ilene said: "Go and—play with your corpse, you necrophile!"

But she would follow Mary Jo, because I knew she was as interested as Malachi in who had done in the lawyer. She went into her cabana and Malachi opened Number Sixteen.

METZGER WAS huddled in a corner. There was too much blood on the floor, but a declevity in the cement held a strainer which allowed seepage from the wet bathing suits and the overflow from the little shower cabinet ran down a pipe. There was enough clean floor in which to maneuver and examine things. Metzger didn't look any better or any worse than a Jap who had slit his own throat and I took a good gander.

There were bruises on him. His throat was cut from left to right, so I figured someone had done it from behind, assuming the killer was right-handed. There was no sign of the weapon. Metzger's pockets contained some bills and his wristwatch was in place.

Malachi said: "Funny thing, there were no footprints leading to the cabana from north or south. It had been high tide just before we came down this morning and the beach is smooth in each direction. So whoever put him there brought him from the beach, before high tide. That puts the time of the crime around daylight, or before, say between midnight and five."

"Yeah," I said. "No rear entrance here. But he may have been killed someplace else and dragged here."

"Too much blood," said Malachi. "He may have been stunned elsewhere and cut here—" He stopped abruptly, his eyes wide. He muttered: "Well, I'll be damned!"

I said: "I never saw you so amazed since that Jap prisoner came out with the hidden grenade."

Malachi said: "Check, pal… Let's go up to the hotel and catch a drink."

"I thought we were going to investigate Leb Anchor," I said. "This looks like his work. Bruises on the victim—but a weapon to finish it. Leb's no good with his dukes, but Metzger was a little guy. Anchor could maul him and cut him with ease."

Malachi said: "I need a drink."

I went back into my cabana and dressed. It was evident that Malachi had a good idea who was guilty. When I went out, he was holding a handkerchief. He said: "This could be the one Mary Jo had when she was going out of the courtroom after the verdict. It has the same initial. And here's a laundry stain…"

I said: "So that's why you bumped into her."

"A man's handkerchief," he said. "I was curious, sure… Let's get that drink." He didn't show me the initial. We went up to the hotel and ordered straight bourbon.

The barkeep said: "Anchor was in again. I chased him out quick. He seemed scared and worried and kept asking for Metzger."

"He would," I muttered. "It would give him a good alibi, to his way of thinking."

The bartender said: "You sure handled him, Mr. Hinton. He has a lotta people around here scared."

Malachi said: "Is he a strong swimmer?"

"Yeah, he's tough all the way," said our informant. "He runs a still and some politicians are behind him."

"As usual," Malachi nodded. "I see Mrs. Morgan going out to her car down the road. Is she a good swimmer, too?"

"Why, sure," said the barkeeper, perplexed. "Most natives are, Mr. Manatee. So much water around Florida, y'know."

Malachi knew, all right. He was a West Coaster himself. But I was beginning to see why he had asked. I remembered Mary Jo Morgan piddling around in the shallows as though she were afraid of the water.

Malachi said: "Well, well, whaddya know, Tack—Miss Carver's going for a ride, too!"

Ilene was taking off fifty yards behind the Widow Morgan. She saw us with our drinks and made a terrible face. But she went on. Malachi drained his glass and led me out through the back entrance of the hotel.

There, amid palm trees and oleanders, where insects droned about our ears, we waited ten minutes. Malachi said nothing and neither did I, but we were both thinking a lot. I was wondering why we didn't wait indoors where it was cooler and more comfortable. Malachi was wondering how to trap a killer.

Then there was a noise, and a man appeared at the edge of the tangled growth about the patio. It was Leb Anchor, half drunk, his revolver bulging on his hip. I started after him, but Malachi was hauling me in the other direction. Anchor got into a big, fast coupé and raced the motor.

Malachi shoved me behind the wheel of the hotel station wagon which was on the other side of the hotel. In a moment, Anchor went tearing by. I followed him without question.

He headed straight for Judge Selvey's house. The distance was very short and I knew he would see me, so I drove off the sand road behind some trees a distance of a hundred yards from the rear of the house. Malachi jumped down, balanced on his good leg. He said quickly: "I'll cover for now. You look for signs of a man afoot taking this road in—a small man in a hurry."

He limped through the brush, which tore at his clothing and tangled his bad leg, and I wondered why he didn't take the road. I did, walking slowly, looking for signs of a man walking. I thought I discerned some footprints on the sod as I came to Judge Selvey's back lawn, but by that time there was confusion in the house and I had to move fast.

THE BACK door was still quivering, so I imagined Malachi had gone through. I saw Mary Jo Morgan's car in a wide driveway. The big coupé was there, too. Malachi's car was not in sight.

I hit the door and went into a kitchen. The sounds were in the front of the house. Ilene's voice cried: "The big stiff! I'll kill him!"

I went through a dining room and fell over a chair. There was a living room across the front, a large, pleasant chamber which I had noted from the veranda the evening before. The colored man lay across the threshold, groaning, his arm bent at a wicked angle. I leaped across him and ran smack into Leb Anchor.

He had a chair in his hand. He gave it to me, all of it, right over the noggin. I went down, rolled over. I saw Ilene with her gun out, and Mary Jo tackling her. I saw Judge Selvey.

The judge was shaking his head. There was a cut in his bald scalp. I guessed that Leb had used the chair on the judge, too. Selvey was against the wall, but he was not down, just out.

I got my knees up. Leb was right after me, his pig eyes gleaming. He almost frothed at the mouth, cursing me. I unfolded my legs, trying for his guts with my heels.

He was a good man when he had a weapon. He side-stepped at the right instant and slammed the broken chair at me. I managed to squirm away from the full force, but all this clouting was not doing me much good. I'm no longer up to a long bout. My lung won't stand it.

I wondered what had happened to Malachi. Ilene was tussling with Mary Jo who was not saying a word but keeping Ilene from using the gun. Selvey was trying hard to snap out of it, but not doing very well. Then Leb came at me with the chair. It was like a slow motion picture, like a bad dream. He kept coming, and I kept evading him, but he wouldn't let me up off the floor or give me a chance to swipe his legs from under him with a scissors. He was tough.

Ilene said an unladylike word and slugged Mary Jo on the bosom. The widow bit her lips and hung onto Ilene's gun arm with a grip like iron. Ilene tried to belt her on the chin, but Mary Jo had been hit there before, by her rough menfolks, and knew how to protect herself in the clinches.

Anchor tore a leg off the rapidly collapsing chair and hefted it, dancing around me. He could finish me with that, all right. I made a last effort to flip myself erect. It would have been fine if a throw rug had not caught my heel and tossed me for a loss.

Leb's laugh was maniacal. He leaped in, the rung of the chair leg like the blade of a scythe, ready to pin me to the floor.

Then Malachi strolled in. He came the front way, across the veranda, slightly scratched from the scrub, but debonair enough to make me unhappy at my plight. He reached halfway across the room, seemingly without effort, and took the weapon away from Leb. Malachi never seems to hurry or sweat over a job.

Anchor turned with a roar and reached for his pocket, suddenly remembering his gun. Malachi took another step, got close to him. He took a wrist and elbow hold and pivoted like an adagio dancer, to slow music. Leb took off, heavily, but definitely, like a B-29. He soared through the air, lit against the wall, crumpled into a heap. I crawled over and took his gun away. He was unconscious, but groggy. I said to Malachi: "You do it easier than me, dammit. Where you been, anyway?"

Malachi separated Ilene from the widow. Mary Jo's blouse was torn, revealing some very special equipment.

Ilene said: "Yes, you big clown, where have you been while this wildcat almost tore me apart!"

Malachi said: "You're bigger than she is. Why, I was delayed. I was checking on things."

Selvey came away from the wall and took out a clean handkerchief and mopped at his cut head. He mumbled: "A hell of a thing… He comes raving in here looking for Metzger. I haven't got Metzger!"

"No," agreed Malachi. "You sure haven't!"

Anchor said thickly: "He knows where Johnny's hidin'!"

Mary Jo, her hands at her blouse, panted: "You said yourself John was comin' here!"

"He meant to," Malachi said. "He got interrupted."

"Gahdammit," Anchor said. "He better not git too interrupted."

"He did get too interrupted," Malachi said. "You know that fruit knife he packed?"

Nobody answered. Selvey, Leb and the woman became still as statues. Malachi said: "Yep! Cut his throat all to hell."

I WAS watching Mary Jo Morgan. She stood plucking at her torn blouse, her eyes like dark pools in the white of her face. She didn't weep, didn't even change expression. She just stood there.

"He's in my cabana, right now," said Malachi. "But he was not meant to be there. When I first went into my cabana I noticed it had been put to use. I was going to check and then it slipped my mind. It's Number Sixteen. You happen to know anyone who rented Number Sixteen of the row, Judge?"

Selvey said: "You mean the clerk didn't give you Number Five like I told him?"

"I asked him for three," said Malachi. "It confused him. He's not very bright. There must be duplicate keys and he gave me the duplicate of Sixteen, forgetting it was rented."

Selvey said: "Well, I'll be damned!"

Leb Anchor pulled himself erect. He said: "Now, you ain't gonna blame me fer this! I stood the other rap, but you ain't gonna slap this one on me!"

"No," said Malachi. "They're not."

Ilene said: "What are you talking about?"

Malachi turned to Mary Jo. He said: "You testified you saw Leb Anchor shoot your husband. Did you actually see it?"

She faltered: "Why... he never said he didn't.... They were arguin'—loud!—Cussin' each other."

"Uh-huh," said Malachi. He reached into his pocket and took out a jackknife wrapped in a handkerchief. He said: "I guess this is enough evidence, Judge. The knife was in the garage, wrapped in a wet pair of bathing trunks."

Selvey said: "I guess it is, all right."

Anchor said: "I never done it! He loaned me dough fer my still, sure. But we only squabbled when we was drunk. It wasn't no killin' matter!"

"Someone killed him. Someone hit him, knocked him out, then took him into the Gulf. They swam with him down opposite the cabanas. It was dark, and they dragged him up at high tide, or almost high tide, and put him in the cabana. Then they swam away, leaving no trail. The body could be towed out to sea and sunk later, at the murderer's convenience," said Malachi. "Only the error of an underpaid clerk in the City Hall who has charge of the municipal cabanas messed up the deal."

Selvey said: "A hell of a note!"

"Uh-huh," said Malachi. "Just so!"

Leb Anchor said: "I won't stand no trial without him for a lawyer. I won't do it!"

Malachi said: "Who asked you to stand trial?"

The widow of Dan Morgan stopped trying to hold in her torn blouse. She said: "He did it! He's been after me and after me, and I never was cheap. Dan was meaner than dog meat to me, and John was good to me, in his own way... Generous, anyway, and he spoke so good, and was so eddicated an' everything. Leb admitted he killed Dan over twenty dollars... He did it!"

"He did it, and Metzger knew it," said Malachi. "Right, Judge?"

Selvey said heavily: "Yes, Malachi. I did it!"

Mary Jo dropped her arm. It had been pointing at Selvey, now it fell listlessly to her side. She turned her face away and her shoulders sagged. The life went out of her and she looked frightened and pitiful again. "John's… dead," she whispered.

Selvey said: "It was Mary Jo… She wouldn't go for me. But she went for that rat, Metzger. Dan caught me with her one evening, right after he quarreled with Anchor. He tackled me and I shot him. Metzger guessed, through questioning Mary Jo, that I had done it. He got Leb off, then he was coming for me. Blackmail of course. He'd have ruined me."

Malachi said quietly: "I always liked you, Sam."

"I know, I know… my wife and I weren't happy," the judge said. He was calm, all the way. "I've always loved the water, Malachi. I'm a hell of a swimmer—that's how I got the idea of getting rid of him that way. But I slipped up on the knife. And of course, that dumb clerk… Well, Malachi, I'll take a swim, if you'll allow it."

"I haven't called the sheriff," said Malachi. "I don't think Leb or Mary Jo will stop you."

The judge was wearing a robe. He took it off and he had trunks beneath it. He nodded politely to us. The colored man on the floor moaned and Selvey said: "I think Leb fractured his skull. Look out for him, will you, Malachi? He's a good servant."

Then he walked down and into the Gulf. It took him quite a while to get into deep water. I watched him with a heavy heart. It *was* a hell of a thing! I could have watched Leb Anchor or Metzger or even the woman go to certain death without a qualm. But Sam Selvey had been a man, caught in the web of circumstance, murdering without hope of profit....

Ah, well, a murderer is a killer no matter how you look at it. He swam very strongly until we could see him no more. He was a right guy to the end....

Leb Anchor was up, trying to swagger. "You got nothin' on me. I'm goin'...."

Malachi hit him one on the chin, as pretty a punch as I ever saw. "Resist arrest, will you?" Malachi said. "You hit the Negro, didn't you? You'll do a stretch for assault if I have to spend a million."

"No use talking to him!" said Ilene. "He can't hear you!"

Leb lay at full length, his nose pressed to the floor. Mary Jo Morgan said lifelessly: "What you want of me, now?"

"Not a damned thing," said Ilene. "Just get out and keep your fool mouth shut. You'll have another man before autumn!"

Mary Jo stumbled out the back toward her car. Malachi looked out to sea. There was no sign of Judge Selvey. Malachi shook himself and said: "It had to be him. He always was the best swimmer in the state. The body had to come from this direction and by water. And that handkerchief..."

"You mean it wasn't Metzger's handkerchief she carried?"

"No. It was initialed *S*," said Malachi. "And I stopped and called the City Hall from next door. That's why I was late. That cabana Sixteen is in Mrs. Selvey's name. As you know, she's away. Evidently one was issued to her as a piece of petty graft. Since the Selvey house is so close, maybe she used it for friends. The judge did. He offered us his locker, which was Number Five. Just another example of political petty thievery, infinitesimal in this case, but costly."

"Yeah," said Ilene inelegantly. "It cost Granada one judge and one crooked lawyer—an even score, I'd say. Well, at least I learned something."

"Like what?" I asked gullibly.

"The Widow Morgan," said Ilene, "does not, as I first believed, wear gay deceivers!"

VACATION— WITH SLAY

THE CRAB CAY BUNCH HAD KNOWN MALACHI SINCE HIS SALAD DAYS, THEY WERE ALL WELL-TO-DO AND, DESPITE THEIR FRIENDLINESS, THERE WAS A POLITE CLANNISHNESS ABOUT THEM WHICH EXCLUDED GUYS LIKE ME. A TIGHT LITTLE UNIT, AND TO BE OSTRACIZED BY THIS SNOB-SET YOU HAD TO DO SOMETHING REALLY BAD— LIKE COMMITTING A MURDER, FOR INSTANCE.

MALACHI MANATEE led us down to the wharf and cautioned us for the last time. He wasn't really talking to me. I'm pretty quiet and, if let alone, very reasonable. He was worrying about Ilene Carver, who is the most beautiful redhead in the world, but of an unpredictable temper and with no guards on her sharp tongue when aroused.

Malachi said: "This is a vacation. We're going out to Crab Cay, an exclusive island owned cooperatively by Ed Beech, Porky Dunn, Bunny Drake and Robert Carson, the munitions magnate. We're going to swim and fish and loaf and dammit, Ilene, you're not to start a riot by flirting with any of my friends."

Ilene said: "You mean this Carson is richer than you are? H'mmmm. What am I hanging around you for?"

Malachi said: "Nuts! Carson is married. Anyway, we won't see much of him. Ed, Porky and Bunny are my friends. Carson just happens to be in on the co-op which owns the island."

"So he's married," mused Ilene. "All rich men are—except you. Well, if I can't get a single one, I'll take what I can get. I'm sick of stooging for a giant with a crooked brain…"

"Shut up!" said Malachi. He was really indignant and he looked like a tall, blond devil, with his inverted V eyebrows and his thin, ascetic features. We were almost at the boat, and I could see the three men lounging there spring to attention at sight of Ilene's curves and her shoulder-length bobbed locks.

Malachi said to them: "You know Miss Carver, I think... This is my guy, Tack Hinton. He was with me when I got my come-uppance. In fact, if he hadn't toted me away, I would have been rubbed out by those nasty little yellow fellows."

They shook hands with me, soft-spoken, tanned Florida men, all three recently discharged from the Service. Ed Beech was the leader, a powerful guy who had been a famed

I got him with a lateral block, nailed him to the wall. The gun sounded very loud in that pleasant room.

southern back, a clean-cut, ruggedly handsome fellow, with short black hair. Porky Dunn had been his block and he looked it—round skull, low brow, a big, good-natured grin for everyone. Bunny Drake was a little, sharp fellow with a nose like a fox and eyes half-concealed by heavy lids, which made him look older than the others. They had all known Malachi in his salad days, they were all well-to-do, and somehow I felt that, in spite of their friendliness, I was not going to enjoy this vacation Malachi had planned for Ilene and me.

There's something about these "scions of wealth," as the more sensational reporters limn them, something politely clannish which excludes guys like me, rough guys with no social background. As soon as we boarded the fifty-foot cruiser which Beech had loaned to the Coast Guard and had regained only that day, they gathered around the wheel where Beech stood and began reminiscing about old times.

I went aft, beneath a canvas shelter, and sulked with a Scotch bottle I found alongside a pail of ice and a pitcher of water. The boat picked up speed, and I could tell it was a hell of a good boat, even though I am a complete landlubber. Ilene came under the shelter and threw herself into a chair opposite me, her long legs stretched out alluringly. I mixed her a drink. She drained it, a bad sign, but I gave her another. Hell, I'd give her my right eye! I never will understand why Malachi doesn't marry that gorgeous woman.

I said: "Pull your skirts down, you're a big girl now."

She said moodily: "You're the only man on board who'll enjoy the view, so the hell with it! This is a damned clam bake for Malachi, but it's not going to be much fun or excitement for you and me, Tack."

She knew about the excitement and how, since the Pacific war days, Malachi and I, both somewhat crippled, needed stimulation to keep our minds from ourselves and our ills. Malachi limps in his left leg. I can't last very long at anything violent on account of my scar tissue. It irks us. Malachi was always a violent character. I was a professional football player and once something of a prize fighter.

I said: "Malachi pays the bills and he can call the turns for me any time."

"I know," she said. "Sergeant Hinton and Lieutenant Manatee."

"The hell with that!" I said. "We saw it through together."

She said: "Crab Cay. A hunk of sand covered with bungalows where the rich go native by wearing white pants for two days instead of one hour. Lousy with Scotch and soda—without ice. That's being rugged. I wish we were back hunting a nice, messy murder."

The little one, Bunny Drake, came up just then. His hooded eyes opened, then closed. He said: "Murder? Perish forbid! Wait until you meet Robert Carson, Ilene. You'll want to commit murder. His wife will be about your age—you'll like her. Only Carson won't let her play." He rattled on about Carson's great position in Washington, his political ambitions, his allegedly shady past. Bunny was a gossipy little guy, it seemed. He was one of those snobbish fellows, rich enough himself, but envious of the richer people who sat in the seats of the mighty of the land. I left him to Ilene, who drank another Scotch and made no effort to listen, I was sure.

I FOUND a sandwich in a hamper and ate it. Malachi came over and we leaned on the rail. He said: "Maybe we ought to have a boat. Maybe we could have more fun."

"I don't like boats," I said.

Malachi said: "Look, Tack, I'm sorry. This was a bad idea. Now they tell me nobody can get along with Carson. Ed says he's a complete jerk. I think we made a mistake."

I said: "I've never punched a multi-millionaire on the nose."

"He has a tough chauffeur, who carries a gun," said Malachi. "Ed just told me. Ed's a very good guy, one of the few college friends I have, Tack."

"Sure," I said. "He seems O.K."

Malachi said: "Ed says Mrs. Della Carson is a good egg, but that Carson beats her down whenever she wants to have some fun. He's twenty years older than she…"

I said: "Ed likes this Mrs. Carson?"

"Oh, Ed wouldn't—I mean he's not that kind," said Malachi. "It looks as though we were going into an unpleasant situation, though. The island is small and Carson's grounds adjoin his. If Ilene gets tight…"

I didn't say anything to this. Ed Beech called Malachi just then and I sneaked back to find Ilene sitting with her eyes closed, and Bunny Drake telling her she was a knockout. He stopped when he saw me, and I knew right away this was no pal of Malachi's. Ed Beech might be all right, but this was a little gadfly of a jerk. He lowered those eyelids when I came up, mumbled something and beat it.

Ilene opened one green eye and said: "Is it gone?"

"Like a wittle wabbit, he wunned away," I said.

"He's been trying to make the Carson woman," said Ilene. "He talks all around it—you can tell."

"So has the great Ed Beech," I told her. "Malachi gave it away. Malachi is worried."

Ilene sat up. She said: "Worried? In that case, I won't get too stiff. Maybe we won't be spending too much time on this damned island."

So we drank a little more slowly and only did away with the one bottle of Scotch. Then we sighted the island.

Crab Cay was small, but it had palm trees and bougainvillaea and hibiscus and a bit of mangrove and it looked quite attractive. Ed Beech brought the boat in smartly, made it fast, and we all piled ashore.

The bungalows were in sight of the dock, and of course there were no roads and no automobiles and the air was clean and bright. It was October and the bugs were gone. Florida is a swell place and the Keys are wonderful without mosquitoes. We walked up a shell path and there were three bungalows about fifty yards apart, painted brightly, well-kept.

Malachi and I shared one of them, Beech's, and the three alumni took the biggest which belonged to Bunny, the littlest guy, which is life all over for you. Ilene had the middle one all to herself. She plunked down a bag, looked around at the comfortable cane chairs of a square, well-aired living room and said: "I've been in worse traps." It was a concession, from Ilene.

Malachi and I unpacked. The general rule was for everyone to be on his own, with no community activity. Each one got his own meals, whenever he wished, except dinner, which was at seven and cooked and served by Mama, a solid character in glistening ebony. That part was fine. Malachi and I started on a bottle of bonded bourbon and, as the afternoon waned, this seemed pretty good after all.

It was almost dinnertime when the ruckus started. Malachi and I were in the water, floating on our backs. We hadn't seen any of the others for two hours. Ilene, we imagined, was sleeping. The loud voices came from the north, where Robert Carson's land began. There was a high hedge—a spite hedge—and you couldn't see anything of his place. But the voices coming from the other side of the hedge were easily distinguishable.

Thunderous bass accents rolled to us over the water. "I've warned you young wastrels to stay off my land time and again. None of you is worth a damn and killing you would be a pleasure and a virtue—"

Ed Beech drawled back: "Mighty harsh words, Carson. But neither you nor your tough friend is going to kill anyone."

A harsh voice said: "You hoid what d'boss said, joik!"

Malachi raised his head and eyed me. "Brooklyn?"

"Bronx, I think," I said.

Carson raved on: "Beech, you take your friends and get out. I've put up with you because Della knew you, but I won't be trespassed upon any longer. Now get out before I have you thrown out."

Malachi said: "This Bronx person must be very rugged."

"A gun," I said. "He shoots them off."

Ed Beech was saying coolly: "O.K., Carson. You're a terrible hog, aren't you? Sometimes I wonder why our national government tolerates a person like you."

They filed through a gate in the hedge, Bunny first, then Porky, and finally Ed Beech, who was grinning. Porky looked mad enough to hit somebody and Bunny's thin face was vicious with rage, but Ed Beech was shrugging it off. I had come in close to shore and was wading through the shallow water when I caught a glimpse through the hedge of the belligerent millionaire and his hired thug.

Carson looked spare and fit in a pair of wet trunks, with very little belly for a man of his years. He had iron gray hair and was not bad looking, although his eyes were mean. His bodyguard wore an ill-fitting sky-blue sports ensemble which did not match his bruised and very ugly face. His name was Katz and he was Bronx, all right—and poisonous. I knew what he was like in that brief second. A gunsel off the streets. It seemed funny that Carson should have a man like that around him, but then Carson was a very important character and a gun is a gun.

Beech came down to the water and said to Malachi: "Nice neighbor, huh?"

They all dove into the water. They swam out quite a way, saying nothing more about the incident. Malachi and I sat on the beach, where we could squint through the hedge, and Malachi said thoughtfully: "Now I wonder why our friends go over there when they're so obviously unwelcome?"

I said: "Look and you'll see."

A willowy blond woman was walking past the gap in the hedge. She was undulating along sinuously and you could tell she was angry. She had an oval, piquant face and her hair was loose and she was built like a shapely eel, all fluid and lean, but with plenty of what it takes.

"Mrs. Carson, no doubt," Malachi murmured.

Another figure came along, hurrying after the blonde. It was an extremely dark young man, with sideburns, a neat black mustache and a marcel wave. He was pretty, too, in a Latin sort of way, and he looked very perturbed.

Malachi said: "Carson's secretary, Ricardo Perez."

"All that and your friends, too? Mrs. Carson must be quite a gal!" I said.

"She's got trouble in every line," replied Malachi. "For the small number of people it contains, this Crab Cay is loaded."

"And might go off any moment," I added.

Five minutes later, there were footsteps again on the Carson side of the hedge. The bass voice was purring, now. It said: "My dear, it was a pleasure to show you around. It is not often we are so honored. Now, please, I do hope you and Mr. Manatee and Mr. Hinton will come over for a drink around nine."

Ilene Carver stepped through the hedge and purred: "We wouldn't miss it for the world. Malachi's friends are *so* boring with their chitter-chatter. Thank you, Mr. Carson!"

I DON'T know which was the funniest—Ricardo Perez trying to conceal the fact that he was wildly in love with Mrs. Della Carson, the spectacle of Katz serving drinks like a waiter in a beer joint, or the way Mrs. Carson kept looking askance as Ilene poured Scotch down her gullet during the bridge game.

Malachi and Carson were in a corner of the long, high-ceilinged room in a heavy political discussion and the other four of us played hearts. Ricardo was so anxious not to give the queen of spades to his love that they were both duck soup for Ilene and me. We were playing for a nickel and a half buck, peanuts to them, and I won eighty dollars. Thus the poor triumph over the rich—once in a blue moon.

Ilene, who also doesn't have a dime, although she was born with dough, won sixty dollars. By this time it was twelve o'clock and Katz was beginning to look at Ilene with adoration as he poured her a drink from the second bottle of ancient whiskey.

Malachi dragged his six feet-four erect and said: "This island life makes me sleepy early. What say, kids?"

Carson came forward, rubbing his hands. He seemed pathetically pleased with the evening. He said: "Oh, have another drink!"

The blond woman, whose conversation was, I had found, confined to brief statements of her wishes, said: "I'm going to bed." She gave Malachi a look, glanced briefly at me, patted Ilene's arm, kissed her husband on the cheek, ignored Perez, who groveled, and wafted her hips to the stairs.

The Carsons had a two-story, E-shaped hacienda which would have made a house and gardens magazine editor weep in his tea-with-lemon. There were six big bedrooms upstairs, each with a bath. They must have had the biggest cistern in the world.

Carson watched Perez bow out with many genuflections and rang the bell for Katz. The tray with ice came in and Katz said: "I gotta check d' power plant. See ya tomorra, sir."

Carson said kindly: "Good night, Katz. Thank you."

Katz said: "I didn't do nuttin', boss. Them collechiate joiks—" He batted his slant eyes at us, stopped and went out.

Carson said: "Er—I know Beech is a friend of yours, and he's not a bad fellow. But that big footballer and the little snide chap are terrible lechers, Manatee. I've had plenty of trouble. I used to have white maids, but couldn't keep them here with those men chasing them all hours around the island."

Malachi said: "I understand, Carson. You're entitled to your privacy."

Carson smiled and let it go. He was a cool customer, and no nonsense about him. We chatted, and you got the feeling he was really powerful—I mean in the national picture—and that he was a bit of a fascist, too, philosophically speaking. Malachi, who walks the middle road rigidly, maybe a bit to the left in spite of his money, disagreed mildly with his host. I admired the whiskey and the furnishings and yawned, and suddenly we broke up. It was just one and the extra hour had been: pleasant. I wondered if it was not because Della Carson and her Latin lover had left and I also wondered what the hell they had done with that hour.

We gathered Ilene and walked across the grounds, a couple of hundred yards to the hedge. Carson waved to us from his doorway and we went the rest of the way alone. Before we went through the gap in the hedge, the lights in the big house went out. There had been no lights upstairs, and Carson only had to throw a switch downstairs to turn off all the lights, leaving little phosphorescent buttons on the stairs to show him the way—a very cute arrangement.

We saw Ilene to her cabin and then Malachi and I went back to ours and got into bed.

We smoked a cigarette and Malachi said: "Carson's not bad at all. But why should he feud so with Beech? Ed is a very nice guy who never went in for chasing the chippies."

I said: "Porky doesn't look the type, either. But Bunny—"

"Bunny is a talker, not a doer," Malachi said positively. "There's something screwy about all this.

I said: "Something like Mrs. Della Carson…"

Then we heard the scream. The wind was our way and the scream was very loud anyhow. We both heard it plainly. It was a woman and it could only be the woman I had just so carelessly named. It gave me a bad feeling for a second, as though I had put the curse on her by mentioning her so contemptuously. In the next second we were pulling on shorts and canvas shoes and running down the path.

Ilene came out, fastening a halter around her neck, and she could run as fast as we could. Running is no longer my dish, nor Malachi's, but we made pretty good time. We cut through the hedge and the moon striped the sand with white and purple. Ed Beech was coming behind us, then passing us, calling: That's Della's voice!"

Well, hell, everyone knew that! The Carsons had a Negro couple who cooked, but it wasn't a colored woman who had screamed. You could tell, and somehow you could tell it was Della. As we ran toward the house, the lights suddenly came on. I saw Katz, sprinting from the direction of the powerhouse in the rear. He had a gun in his hand and was going faster than any of us. We were all terribly excited, of course. There is nothing in the world to raise the hackles on a man like a woman's scream in the night unless it is a banzai charge by a company of drunken Japs.

We all sort of barged into the living room together, I guess. Ed Beech had slowed up, as though he needed company before entering Carson's house. But he needn't have. Carson was past caring. He had gone to whatever heaven was reserved for munitions kings who walked with the great heads of states.

He was lying at the foot of the stairs. There was a scarf around his neck, a white, narrow silken scarf which his wife had been wearing earlier, and which I remembered seeing on the window seat behind her when we had been playing hearts. He was lying there, twisted and distorted and she was crouched on the steps, her blond hair disheveled, weeping as if her heart would break. Ricardo Perez was pawing her aimlessly, trying to quiet her and at the same time, keep from being sick to his stomach—a neat trick if he made it.

Malachi was leaning close to Carson when Ed Beech turned on his heel and abruptly walked past me toward the door. Katz, his gun pointed, snarled: "Stay right there, Beech! You an' yer joik frien's! Don't none of you start fer that gondola of yours."

Then I saw that Porky and Bunny also had arrived and were gaping from the veranda. Beech said shortly, "Don't be a damned fool, Katz!" and made as if to go on.

I saw in Katz's eyes that he was going to do it, and took off. I got him with a lateral block. The gun sounded very loud and sinister in that pleasant room. I nailed him to the wall and he tried to work me over with the gun muzzle. He was frantic with rage, and I think grief, too, as if Carson had been his friend as well as his employer. I slapped his wrist with a Marine Corps trick and he lost the gun. He tried to gouge and bite me and I had to clunk him one on the chin. He was still swinging when his lights went out.

ILENE HAD her handsome chin cupped in a calm hand. She said: "If he was strangled, why the blood?"

Malachi said without looking up: "He was knifed, too. There's a hole in his chest. Must have been a sharp knife—it sure cut his shirt neatly."

I said: "Katz was right. Don't any of you fellows go away right now."

Ed Beech said: "He—he would have shot me."

"Just in the leg," I guessed. "As a lesson to you. Never defy a man with a gun. It's not brave, it's silly."

The three of them stood awkwardly, watching. Sudden and violent death in circumspect surroundings is so incongruous that people are always overwhelmed by it, which is why fewer murderers are caught. Little things are over-looked. Malachi and Ilene and I are not detectives, but we've had experience with murder. Ilene loves scenes like the one we were having. She's as cold as iced tea—just stands, looking everyone over.

She said: "Ricardo, leave Mrs. Carson alone!"

The pretty Latin sulked, but he was shaking too hard to talk. His jaws were clenched. But his eyes were not fright-ened, not one whit. It was his nerves, not his nerve.

Ed Beech said: "Someone'll have to go for the sheriff. It's a cinch who killed him—if it wasn't Katz."

Ricardo Perez stopped shaking. He was girding himself to get the business, of course. He withdrew from Mrs. Carson a few steps, leaned against the wall and managed to light a cigarette.

Malachi said: "Get our camera, Tack. We'll have to move him, but we can take pictures."

Ed Beech said: "Hadn't I better go for the sheriff, Mala-chi?"

Katz sat up, rubbing his jaw. He mumbled: "I'll take 'im inna next roun', so he'p me!"

Malachi shook his head at Ed Beech. He said: "If you will see to it that Mrs. Carson is made comfortable, we'll start worrying about the law later. After all, the murderer couldn't possibly get away, except on your boat or Carson's. And if he tried that, he would automatically be aspiring to the hot squat."

Ed Beech said: "But it had to be Ricardo—or Katz."

"Did it?" asked Malachi quietly. "Where were you when Mrs. Carson screamed?"

"Why, on the beach, walking in the moonlight. Are you kidding, Malachi?"

I wheeled on Porky, who stood open-mouthed, listening. I said: "Where were you"

"Uh—in the bed, half asleep. She woke me up!"

Malachi was already on Bunny. "And you?"

"I was reading in our living room, so as not to disturb Porky," snapped Bunny.

"And you had all been doing just that for the previous hour, and can more or less alibi each other," added Malachi. "More or less! But any one of you could have slipped over here, waited for us to leave, then killed Carson. Any one of you could have!" He slammed it at them, and, coming from their old friend, it slayed them. They didn't even protest. They just wilted and took it.

I went out and over to our bungalow and got out the camera Malachi always carried, the good one with the gadgets I don't savvy. Then I drifted into the cabin shared by the three others just for the hell of it. There was no opened book in the living room. There was a shelf of books, but there was none lying around the room. I couldn't imagine Bunny pausing to replace a book in a shelf before racing to the scene of a crime.

I went into Porky's room, and the bed was mussed, but the cover hadn't been turned down. He may have been lying on the bed, but he was not in it for the night.

I went out on the beach and it was slick and smooth, the tide having just slid out. There were no footprints at all on it, and it was a narrow beach which would have showed footprints if Ed Beech had been walking on it. Then I went through the hedge and, on a hunch, I walked along the Carsons' beach. I did find prints there, and they could have been and probably were Beech's, but when I tried to trace them to the house I got lost in a maze of markings. Carson's beach was wider and the tide hadn't slicked it up that far, because his house was a hundred yards farther from the water than the bungalows. So I went back and handed the camera to Malachi and he took pictures.

That was when I first got a good look at Carson. His face was red, so he had been strangled before he had died. The knife wound had been fatal, but the murderer wanted no outcry and had used the scarf to make sure, I thought. It was a very thorough job of murder, one of the best I had ever seen. Carson had been caught at the bottom of the steps by someone above him, evidently. He was a sucker for it, that way.

It could have been anyone. It could, for instance, have been Della Carson. She wasn't weeping now. Her face was sullen and hard and she was over on a divan, her legs curled under her. She wore the sheerest of nighties and everyone pretended he wasn't looking at her because it wasn't decent with her husband lying there. But Malachi took a good look, all up and down her and into her face, and asked quietly, while Katz, the colored man, Beansy and Ed Beech carted the body upstairs to the front bedroom: "Do you want to tell me, or shall I call the law at once?"

She hesitated, then said: "It doesn't matter, does it? He's dead. What difference does it make?"

"The killer has a better chance every hour," Malachi said. "The sheriff is a dope. I know him. Tell me, and I'll give you the killer."

"I don't want him," she shuddered.

Malachi said: "I do. It could have been Tack or Ilene, or me, you know. I don't like that. We have no motive, but this sheriff we are going to have to call sooner or later is a complete no-good. I've been rattling the skeletons in his closet and he would love dearly to throw me in the pokey. That would be a calamity, as I need this vacation."

Ilene said conversationally: "Nothing like a vacation with murder."

Della Carson made an effort. She was game, I thought, after all. She said: "I heard you three leave. I saw the lights go out and knew Robert had thrown the switch."

Malachi said: "Just a moment… did Katz throw the switch?"

Katz was rubbing his bruises, re-entering the room. He said: "I was inna powerhouse, see? Gotta keep d't'ing erled and runnin' smooth. D' lights dey went out. Yeah, I guess he t'rew d' switch, huh?"

Malachi said: "If he did, he was in the dark, with the little phosphorescent buttons to guide him. He went to the foot of the stairs…"

Della Carson said steadily: "He did not mount the steps. It worried me, somehow. I got up and came into the hall. I thought I heard someone moving and called to Robert. A door—I think it was on the side, there—closed softly. I came down the stairs, groping a bit…"

"The murderer went out on the Gulf side," Malachi supplied, "as you were coming down the steps… Perez!"

The pretty boy jumped inside his skin, but his eyes were still calm. "Yes, sir. I was in my room. I cannot prove that. I could have gone out that door, around to the back, and upstairs."

"Thank you," said Malachi. "Ilene, Tack and I were all together until we put Ilene to bed. At the sound of Mrs. Carson's scream, Ilene came rushing out of her bungalow slightly undressed. That's our story and we know it is true. You can believe us or not. Now, Mrs. Carson, everyone has placed himself—"

Ilene muttered to me: " 'Slightly undressed!' I like that! Malachi never misses a thing—but I was *absolutely* undressed when I first hit the dirt."

Della Carson said: "There's nothing else to tell. I stepped on him—in my bare feet. I screamed, I guess, loudly."

"Then Perez came from above," Malachi said. "Katz and the rest of us came in the front."

"I was dazed," she said. "I don't really know."

Malachi said: "Do you have a strong sedative?"

"Yes," she said, naming a sleeping tablet sold too readily in drugstores.

Malachi said: "Come upstairs with me." He took her hand and she went with him like a child.

ED BEECH came across the room, hunched a little, staring at Perez. He said in a low voice: "You dirty louse, you killed him."

Perez fooled me. He came off his chair and punched Ed Beech right on the jaw. Porky flew into it. Katz just stared, rather pleased.

Bunny squealed: "He hit Ed! He hit him!" As though it was a miracle or something.

I stopped Porky first, because he was the most dangerous. He bounced off the wall and then Katz came alive and covered him with the gat he always had handy. I got between Beech and Perez and caught a couple of harmless wild swings. I got a hand on each and shook some sense into them.

They had manners. They recovered quickly, glaring at each other, but not resisting me. Perez said: "I did not kill Señor Carson. He was my patron. I had nothing to gain by killing him."

"You're after—" Beech shut up. His face regained its normal color. He said quietly: "I lost my head, Hinton. I'm sorry."

I said: "I suggest you guys go out now and cover the island. Make sure no rowboat or canoe docked in here. Take flashes and examine every foot of the shoreline. Then Malachi can get this thing straight."

Beech said: "If Perez didn't do it, I'll apologize. But it had to be him or—or—"

I said: "Uh-huh. You're beginning to get it."

Beech said: "Come on, men." He stalked out and the others trailed him.

Katz slid the gun into a holster he wore under the flapping blue shirt, next to his skin. He said to me: "I gotcha now. You was fullback onna Gi'nts."

"That was before Guadalcanal," I said. "Now be a good boy and give me that roscoe."

Katz backed away, shaking his head. "Somebody knocked off my boss. So maybe you're O.K., see? But I'm gettin' d' guy what done it. He's for me, huh? You can see how it is."

I said: "You want me to take it away from you, Katz, the hard way?"

"I do'wanna have you try it," he said. He backed up another step, which brought him to the stairs. Malachi, moving like a feather—bum leg, two hundred and thirty pounds and all—reached over and nailed him and lifted his gun.

Katz said disconsolately: "You joiks got too much onna ball. What if d' guy comes at me, now, huh?"

"What if you killed Carson?" Malachi asked him.

"Fer what?" asked Katz disgustedly. "I do'wanna mess with d'broad."

Ilene, who had found the Scotch during all this, said: "How impolite! Is she really a broad?"

Katz clammed up. He shook his head. He was the kind who could really go dumb on you and I gave Malachi the high-sign to lay off.

Malachi said: "I heard you send the boys off, Tack. That was good. Now we'll look around."

He turned on every light in the room. He found a magnifying glass and began going over the floor where the body had lain, down on his hands and knees, like Sherlock Holmes. Katz scratched his head idly, then muttered something about the power plant and went out.

Ilene said: "I see what you're at. It's undignified as hell, but nobody in shoes could walk on these polished floors and not leave a mark. Sand and shell from outdoors would be bound to come in with him."

I looked at the mat on the porch. It contained all kinds of traces. Malachi was drawing it a little fine. We'd all been rushing around the joint.

Malachi stopped, staring at a section of the floor where there was no sand at all. Then he got up, went into the kitchen and came back with some flour. He sprinkled it gently on the place, then blew it off, until only the faintest trace remained.

There was the outline of a bare foot, that is the outer part of a bare foot. It wasn't anything you could identify without those police measuring devices, but it was a bare footprint, all right.

I said: "All but one of us was wearing shoes when we came in here. Mrs. Carson had no slippers on when we found her. Nobody down here has got his feet toughened to the sharp shell yet, and everyone keeps rope-soled sandals or canvas sneakers handy all the time."

Malachi said: "I knew you'd be able to tell me. Now do you think Perez did it?"

"Why not?" I asked. "He comes down the back steps, out to the Gulf side door, walks in, barefooted and silent, stabs Carson, makes sure with the scarf, blows back—like he said."

Ilene said: "I got another idea. Carson turns out the lights, goes to the stairs. Mrs. Carson is waiting—with knife."

Malachi said: "I've looked for the knife. Let's look some more."

We looked. The three of us had got to be pretty good lookers for things. We looked very hard. Then Katz came in and his battered face was a bit ashen-hued. He had something in his hand, wrapped in a soiled handkerchief. He said: "Inna power plant. Onna shelf behind an erl can. If he shoved it another inch, it woulda dropped down behind a cab'net and never been found, huh?"

The knife was long and keen as a razor. It was of Spanish design, a poniard sort of thing. Someone had honed it. It was one of the nastiest weapons I had ever seen.

Malachi said: "Could Perez have made it out to the power plant as Katz rushed in, then got back upstairs and down behind Mrs. C?"

We thought about that. Katz said numbly: "I ain't got d' skull fer it."

Malachi said: "Don't let it worry you. I know who killed Carson."

Ilene said: "You're full of—of malarkey."

"Language, dear," said Malachi. He looked more like a blond Mephistopheles than ever. "Pass me the Scotch. And relax, all of you. I'm ready to take you to the mainland on Beech's boat. Then I'll call Washington, get the FBI and deliver the killer."

It sounded like a nice, safe deal. We all took a drink, even Katz, who needed it worse than any of us.

THE THREE men reported to Malachi at our cottage. Ilene was already asleep, like a baby, in our bed. Ed Beech said: "Nobody came on the island. Nobody has left it."

Bunny Drake and Porky Dunn corroborated this with nods. They were still stunned and very wide awake, although it was now almost four o'clock. Ed Beech kept talking about all the angles of the killing that he knew. He was not naturally a voluble fellow, I imagined, but he was full of words now.

Malachi said very little. I got sleepy and nodded in the chair. I awoke one time to hear Malachi saying: "You all have to get some sleep whether you want to or not. Tomorrow will be a busy day. I'm bringing the FBI down here via plane. Carson was a national figure and they'll want to know everything about his death. You all want to be sharp with your answers."

"The FBI?" Bunny said. "Malachi, they're tough. Why not just the sheriff?"

The little guy was worried. It was so evident that I almost came wide awake. He gnawed a thumb, like a spoiled and petulant child, and I wondered why the others liked him so well. I decided, as I drifted off to sleep again, that he was just a hangover from college days. They were used to him, they had always known him and he did not break too many of their rules of conduct. He was one of them, and that was part of the business with these well-to-do folks. To be ostracized you have to do something really bad—like committing a murder.

The next time I awoke it was because Malachi was shaking me. His face was pinched and he was practically standing on one foot. I knew his shattered knee ached and he was bone-weary, but his face was very much alive. I got up and he said: "Over to Carson's. Make it quiet and easy."

It was just four-fifteen and almost light. Fantastic pinks were mingling with the dull gray and a cloud bank was the only thing that kept the sun from giving us a dappled gold Florida sunrise. Deep purples predominated. We went out and slid along the spite hedge and Malachi talked.

He said, whispering: "There are too many motives. Della looms as the first bone of contention. But Carson's start in life was in Latin-American trade, where he swindled some people, I guess. He quarreled with Ed and the others. Katz looks like a gunsel who could be hired. Della was always rowing with him… Rage, revenge, jealousy and possible gain from his death—they're all present."

I said: "It was planned."

"So is the next one planned," said Malachi.

I came really wide awake then. "Huh?"

"Too many people snooping around at the time of the murder," Malachi said. "Someone besides me has figured out the killer."

"Then whose number is up?" I demanded.

"The killer's, or the possible witness?" Malachi said: "If I knew that, I'd act."

We entered the Carson grounds. Katz slept in a cottage to the rear of the big house. The servants were farther away and to the west. The long, low ranch-house lay humped and angled in stark isolation. I saw a figure moving. I said: "That's Drake!"

"Uh-huh," nodded Malachi.

"He's going in through the door the murderer used."

"Uh-huh. Run!" said Malachi.

That running was bad for us. But we got to the door Bunny had entered. It was dark inside the house. We stopped dead, listening. I wished Malachi hadn't left Katz's gun in our bungalow.

A moment later I wished it more devoutly. Because a gun went off. Again I heard Mrs. Della Carson scream, on a long note.

Malachi said: "Dammit! The fool!"

We went in and I snapped the master switch. Nothing happened. Malachi said: "Keep quiet and wait. Leave that switch on."

We crouched, waiting. Suddenly the lights flooded on. Malachi said. "Ah! I thought so."

Bunny lay at the foot of the stairs. He was on his side and his canny little face was quite blank. There was a slight odor of cordite and it did not take an expert to see that Bunny was dead, shot through the brain.

I went upstairs as quickly as I could. Mrs. Carson was in the hall, wearing the same sheer nightgown and I had to look away, as the light was behind her and I am not *that* war-weary and murder-sick. I grabbed at the door of Perez' room and he was coming off the bed, pulling a robe on, seemingly drugged with sleep.

He said: "I heard her scream and thought I was dreaming."

I said: "The shot didn't wake you up?"

His pretty face fell into hard lines. He said: "Ah! I see. The murderer struck again!"

I said: "Come down and take a look."

I led him downstairs. Mrs. Carson was alone in the room, staring at Bunny with eyes filled with loathing. "That nasty little man—what was he doing in my house?"

"Coming to consult you about your husband's death," I guessed. "He must have known who did it."

She looked at me and said stonily: "That got him killed?"

"Yeah," I said, wondering where Malachi had gone. Then I put two and two together. It was about time.

I said: "Holy Cow! Perez, stay right here. Don't let this woman out of your sight!"

THAT RUNNING in the sand was awful. I was struggling for wind when I got to the hedge. I staggered through, my bad lung practically collapsed, and headed for the bungalow. It was touch and go whether I'd make it or not. I kept cursing myself without expending any energy, just cursing inside.

I had sense enough not to burst in the door. I walked up quietly and heard Malachi say: "If you've hurt her badly, I'll take you apart slowly, worse than any Jap."

Then Ilene's voice came groggily: "Just a slight tap on the noggin, darling. Ignore me and try to figure how to get the gun."

Malachi said: "He's not going to do anything. Tack's still alive, and Perez and Della Carson and the others."

I had to go in. I went around back, walking in the sand, my shoes discarded. I went in through the kitchenette. There was a little foyer and I tiptoed across it.

There was a swinging door leading into the living room where they were. I hesitated, gathering my strength, trying to regain my wind. Then a thought struck me.

I heard Malachi's voice, lighter and easier now that he was facing danger. He was always good under fire. He was just talking along, and it must have been tough on the man with the gun. He was telling a few things he had guessed and that the FBI could prove.

I had managed to get my fingers in the door. If I crashed it, I would be going in blind against a loaded gun. I wanted to pull it to me, let Malachi know I was there and get some cooperation.

The door hinge squeaked. I jerked it open then, knowing I had failed in surprising them.

Ilene was on the couch. Malachi was against the wall, his bum leg crossed over his good one, lounging. Porky Dunn was standing directly in front of me. I hit him so hard he bounced all the way across the room and out onto the porch, taking a screen door with him.

Malachi came away from the wall, arms extended, seeking a hand grip. I tripped and almost followed Porky through the door as my feet skidded on the gleaming, polished floor.

Ilene came off the couch. She's a fiery-tempered young lady even in peaceful times. But now she had the empty Scotch bottle in her hand. I trimmed my sails, tried to carom off the wall and rebound into the middle of things, but I only succeeded in bumping Malachi.

There was one shot. Then there was a crunching, tinkling medley of sound. Ilene said: "All down. Set 'em up in the next alley. Damn you, Malachi, you were late in getting here!"

Malachi said: "Darling, I'm sorry."

"Well," she said. She looked at the neck of the bottle still in her hand. She said: "I shall keep this piece of glass forever as a memento of the time you apologized to me."

Malachi said: "I didn't think he'd go that far. He had all the motives for the first killing and one for the second, but none for attacking you—"

"The gun, you umpchay!" she said. "He'd got rid of the knife, and he needed something to kill Bunny with!"

Malachi said: "Bunny knew and you were wise to that?"

"Certainly," Ilene said. "Bunny was a nosey son. He was out walking, but he lied, trying to give Porky an alibi."

Porky crawled in, straightened up, stared at the man on the floor. He said abruptly: "I don't believe it. He couldn't have!"

Ed Beech was coming to. Malachi had the gun, wrapped in a cloth from the table top. Beech sat up, both hands in front of his face, his shoulders shaking. He was a handsome young man, slightly disheveled, but the kind of young man you can see in any high class bistro, sure of himself, drinking the best liquor, squiring the best gals.

He didn't look up at us. He kept his hands over his face and his jaw muscles worked. Porky said: "Ed! Tell them something—anything. Straighten us out, Ed. You can do it, old boy!"

There were footsteps on the porch. Della Carson came in. Perez was behind her, and then Katz. They looked at Ed Beech. They looked at Malachi.

I said: "Carson was partly right, partly wrong. He didn't like Bunny, he thought Porky was a dumb stooge, but he sort of thought Beech was O.K."

Malachi said: "That's right. Mrs. Carson, you can tell us something more. I assure you that Beech killed both your husband and Bunny Drake."

Beech never looked up, even then. Della Carson said: "He made love to me, if that's what you mean. Drake, Beech—but not Dunn. I don't know what's the matter with Dunn. Doesn't like girls, I imagine."

Porky said: "I'll be damned if—"

"Perfectly natural assumption," Malachi said. "Everyone else did—why not Porky? Well, I'll tell you—Porky is more like us. He has scruples. Small ones, but they're his. And he thought, in his own romantic way, that Della was unhappy and Ed Beech would eventually win her. He worshiped Ed Beech, always, even in school."

Della said: "I loved my husband. We quarreled often—but that was part of our life. We were both violently jealous. I was furious when he paid so much attention to Miss Carver."

Ilene murmured: "He never made one pass, darling. Just trying to get your goat."

MALACHI SAID: "Beech got us down here to cover him up. He had his scheme all planned. He knew how Carson turned out the lights himself, on that master switch. He went in as the lights went out, through the oceanside door, and did his killing. He went out the same way, doubled around the house, put the knife in the power-house while we were all running, ran along the hedge, followed us to the scene, then played his part in the aftermath.

"But Bunny was prowling. Bunny had a yen for Della also."

Della said: "He was—nasty."

Malachi nodded. "Just so. When I told him the FBI was coming, he became afraid and tried to tell you it was Ed. He knew it couldn't be anyone but Ed, because he'd snooped on everyone else. Porky was just wandering around at the north end of the beach. I found his footprints easily—there's a whole stretch of them. He was worried about Ed and Della—he's a very loyal and quite honest guy."

Porky blushed and actually shuffled his feet, like a schoolboy.

Ilene drawled: "So my friend here decides Ed will kill Bunny, but doesn't remember he needs to do it at long range. Beech comes in here and takes the gun. After he turns off the switch in the Carson house, to make sure nobody lights his second kill, he has to go back and throw the switch on again. He thinks Malachi and Tack are still asleep. He knows the scream will awaken them if the shot doesn't and doubles back to replace the gun after we all leave. But I wasn't quite out, so he slugs me from behind and by that time my big, dumb boy-friend realizes that I might be in danger—because the gun had to be purloined from here—and returns in time to get held up. Enter Hinton, the pride of the marines."

"And falls over his own feet," I said bitterly.

Ed Beech shuddered. He still hadn't uncovered his face. His hands relaxed, slid down. His features were contorted, the lips drawn back from white, even teeth. He slumped sideways and curled up, kicking a little.

Malachi said quietly: "He won't die in the chair."

"He's been chewing poison," Ilene said calmly.

Porky Dunn lurched outside, hand over his mouth.

Katz said: "So d'joik's dead. He kilt my boss, didn't he?"

Perez put out a hand to Della, then withdrew it. He was a game sport and he had lost and he knew it. Carson's death had finished him more than if Carson had lived to quarrel daily with his beauteous young wife. Already her face was stiffening into harder lines, and grief was etching its indelible mark on her.

She had loved Carson, all right.

Malachi said, to break the tension: "I tried to stall Ed off by dusting that bare footprint, which was not his. It didn't mean a thing—in fact, it could have been anyone's from earlier that day. I knew it was Ed because he had the most guts. He always had the guts and he was always cool. Talking about Carson, he showed his hatred to me. Talking about Della, he showed his infatuation. He lied about his whereabouts, he lied about everything. But it was lying with a motive and it would have stood up unless the FBI could have dug up more than I could learn."

Della Carson said: "I once read that you can only catch a clever murderer if you know all about him and his victim. You learned the other side, our side, in very short order."

Malachi looked at her with respect. The dead body of Ed Beech, his old friend, lay on the floor like an empty sack which no one particularly wanted to notice. Dunn was being sick somewhere but the rest of us were, I think, relieved.

Malachi said: "When I saw you first, going after your husband, perturbed, with Perez following you, offering you sympathy and understanding you did not want, your side of the picture was clear enough."

Ilene moved forward until she stood alongside Della Carson. Her figure overshadowed the lean lines of the blond woman which seemed to have hardened with her husband's death.

Ilene said: "Darling, you must go and put on something and take a rest."

She put her arm around the thin shoulders and led Della away. I caught her eye and she tipped me a deliberate big wink.

Leave it to Ilene to remove any woman upon whom Malachi looks with approbation and respect!

OBJECTIVE—MURDER!

GOING AGAINST TOM MULFORD'S KILLER WAS DESPERATE BUSINESS. THIS WAS NO BACKWOODS CRACKER AMATEUR, BUT A SMOOTH OPERATOR WHO KNEW HOW TO USE A KNIFE LIKE A BIG-TIME SHIV ARTIST, AND WHO PROVED IT—TWICE!

ILENE CARVER and I sat on the terrace of the Shoreland Hotel and looked at the Gulf of Mexico, which was busily changing hues under the coaxing of a midwinter sun. Ilene was wearing a brief bathing outfit and drinking a Martini, very dry, with a twist of lemon. Her red hair was caught up by a scarf and her greenish eyes were worried.

She said: "Malachi is almost never late, the rat."

"It's only four," I said. "He's messing around with a local cop who runs a small blackmail racket...."

"I know what he's doing," she said impatiently. "Butting into things that are none of his business. Just because he has seven or eight or twelve million dollars doesn't mean he should try to cure the world of its ills. I'm getting sick of this, Tack Hinton. I'm getting sick of hanging around waiting for Malachi."

"You just said he was rarely late," I pointed out.

She gave me a dirty look. There is no use trying to be logical with a woman, even one as smart as Ilene. The truth was that she and Malachi led a cat-and-dog existence with very few tender passages. There was nothing to keep them from marrying except their own independent temperaments.

Malachi's predilection for messing around with petty crooks in politics or public service had started when we first returned from the Pacific to lick our wounds, and had served to relieve tension and banish boredom. Malachi had the money and the brains and I was his guy. He still limped a bit and my lung lesions, though healed, were not sturdy. His money eased the path and besides I loved the big mugg.

We were at Shoreland because this cop, Andy Spesak, had given us a ticket on the highway when we were celebrating the return of gasoline, and then had offered to tear it up for twenty bucks. Malachi had preferred to accept the invitation to the court and pay his fine, then had blasted the cop. Spesak was a surly, black-thatched individual who deserved dismissal, but Malachi had run into a local situation and some former pals in the upper strata of Florida finance, and a storm was gathering. Ilene recognized the signs and was taut.

She said: "There come the weird foursome—Malachi's pals!"

"Not pals. Just acquaintances," I said.

THE WOMAN came first, wrapped in a gaudy Filipino sarong. She was shaped like a bureau with the upper drawer open—a waist you could span with your hands, and legs which made Grable worshipers gape and stare. She had flamboyant blond hair, dyed. She was about thirty and as ripe as a black olive. Her name was Dora Acton.

Her husband ambled behind, following the pot which was his tummy. He was bald, except for a fuzz over each ear, and pink all over—his face, his smooth, hairless body, his eyes. He was all curves, a round ball of a man, no taller than his wife.

Dave Acton had never done a lick of work in his life, owned almost as many shekels as Malachi, had been 4F in the war—and no wonder, the liquor he drank. Not that the booze showed any effects on him. He was a two-fisted guzzler, but liquor only made him more amiable and friendly. He never said a cross word, nor did a mean thought ever seem to cross his mind. He wasn't pretty, but he was kindly and people liked him.

Rem Cartright was a step closer to Dora Acton, which was symbolical. Cartright was Acton's age, but taller, slimmer, square-jawed and wide-shouldered, with much wavy hair on his rectangular head. The contrast between the two men was fantastic, and when you believed the gossip, that Cartright had always been in love with Dora Acton, had lost her to Acton's millions when he was a struggling young grove owner but had never given up, you had a queer combination indeed. The three were always together and Dora treated both men with amazing impartiality—at least in public.

I grabbed Spesak and used him as a shield against the bottles.

The fourth member of the group was young. He was tall and reedy, with a powerful, overdeveloped right arm. He wore only brief trunks and his bronzed body had the trim litheness of the trained athlete. I always stared at him, envying him, remembering my palmy days when I'd been in shape to go against the Bears or the Redskins at the Polo Grounds. This kid was Tom Mulford, a ranking tennis amateur. Acton, oddly enough, played a damned good game of doubles and Mulford was taking a free ride between seasons, serving as Acton's partner on the courts. They had creamed Malachi and me a couple of times with great ease, and it had rankled Malachi, who can't stand to lose at anything.

Ilene said: "If I have to listen to that woman martialing her lovers once more I'll bust her on the nose as sure as you're a big-eyed dope, Tack Hinton."

They came down to the beach where a Negro had unfolded umbrellas of brilliant hue and the woman gave orders in dulcet accents, but with decision. "Put the cocktails there... The blankets are wrinkled... Straighten them... Adjust that umbrella... All right, now, sit down... You pour, Tom, you don't spill so much... I'm dying for a drink..."

Somehow or other Dave Acton disengaged himself from the minor mêlée of settling down on the hot sand. He came waddling up to us, looking disturbed. He said: "Hiya, folks? I'm worried about Malachi. He got that policeman discharged... Political pressure was put on me... Spesak is tough. He swore to get Malachi in court... Where is Malachi?" Acton talked in bunches, like bananas.

Ilene said: "He's probably blasting the cop."

Acton said: "There's funny business... Got a hunch. Danger of some kind. Man named Joe Monk, cousin of

Spesak, a giant… Got the Crackers goin'… Talks like Huey Long… Ignorant, but virile. Get's 'em stirred up."

Ilene said: "You better hire guards for that feudal estate of yours. I hear you indulge in a bit of peonage yourself. With the colored folks, I mean." Ilene has little or no tact.

Acton batted his eyes. "Got to keep help… Dora gets very unhappy if they quit… They owe me for stuff… The sheriff is cooperative."

"Dave!" came a cool voice from under the umbrellas. "Bring Ilene and Tack down for a drink."

Ilene kicked me under the table with her wooden sabots and I said, wincing: "Got to meet Malachi. See you later."

We got up and went to our cabanas. Ilene said: "That damned woman. She makes me sick. Let's hurry and find Malachi."

I said: "Sure. You dress and get out the car." I went into the cabana and discovered I hadn't put my wallet in my pants, so I hurried upstairs in the hotel to get it.

The Shoreland is one of those sprawling, stuccoed, two-storied affairs for the idle rich. I opened the door to the suite I shared with Malachi and stood there, gaping.

Malachi was sprawled in a chair, his long legs thrust out before him. His blond head was back and his face was reddened and bruised. He held a towel against one eye and ice water ran down his arm. His hound's-tooth sports jacket was slung over a chair, soiled with swamp muck. His hair was tousled and he was quietly furious with rage.

I said: "Somebody finally chose you and won, huh?"

"Do I look like a winner?" he said. His voice was steady but I know him well enough to detect the underlying tenseness.

I said: "A guy named Joe?"

"So the word is already around?"

"No. But it couldn't be Spesak because you'd be ready for that palooka," I said. "This Joe Monk must have got you from behind, while you were looking at Spesak."

"Down at the edge of Frog Swamp," Malachi said, nodding. "I went down with Spesak, just we two. Monk must have followed."

"Blackjack?" I asked, peering at the bruises.

"Just his fists," said Malachi grimly. "He's rough. Mouthed a lot at me about the common man and my money getting Spesak fired. They have an organization. Agin everything—except themselves."

"You're going to have a mouse on that eye," I said from rich experience. I picked up the phone, called the desk and had a boy sent out to page Ilene. Malachi groaned.

I said: "She's got to see you sooner or later."

"I don't mind anyone else," he said. "But what she'll say can cause nothing but trouble—for both of us."

I picked up my coat and slid into it. I found the keys to Malachi's car and my wallet and pocketed them. I said: "Well, it'll be better if she doesn't have an audience…"

The door banged open and Ilene came in. She stopped, staring at Malachi. I tried to close my ears against the triumphant invective which I knew was coming.

Then I saw that Ilene was paler than I had ever expected to see her. She took one step forward and her voice was deep in her throat. She said: "Tack, go get the guy who did this. Get him and kill him, whoever he is."

I started for the door. Malachi just looked at Ilene with his one good eye, not moving. I know he was as startled and touched as I was. I went into the hall and closed the door very quietly.

I HURRIED because I was anxious to get away before Malachi could stop me. I am unable to see anyone hurt him without doing something about it, but I knew he would want to even up this score himself. As I headed for the car a thought struck me and I detoured to the beach.

Under the gay umbrella, Rem Cartright sat alone. The others disported themselves in the Gulf. The square-faced man looked thoughtfully at me and said: "Where is Malachi, Hinton?"

"In his room," I said. "Do you know a man named Monk?"

"The agitator? I know him only too well. Provoked a strike in the box factory," said Cartright. He had a heavy, precise voice. I'm strictly Bronx myself and I knew he chose his words carefully through lack of formal education. "He's a dangerous thug."

"Where could I most likely find him?"

Cartright said: "What could you possibly want with him?" Then his face hardened and I could see his mind leap. He said: "Ah! The Spesak case, eh? I warned Malachi. You'd better watch out. Monk always has a dozen tough Crackers at his beck and call."

"He sounds like a meatball," I said. "I love meatballs— without bread."

"You're tough, all right," Cartright said. "Dora keeps telling us you're a hard one. But Monk is something to worry about. He's like a gorilla. He's been attacked by many people—but never hurt."

"Where does he hang out?" I demanded.

"There's a joint called Manuel's Place," said Cartright reluctantly. "It has a back room. The Monk crowd meets there. You'd better take help, Hinton. How bad is Malachi hurt?"

"I didn't say he was hurt," I said. "See you later."

Dave Acton was coming out of the water, his trunks sagging below his tummy, a sorry sight. The brown-skinned tennis player and Dora were still in the water. I noted the look Cartright cast Gulfward, shivered and went my way. I got the long convertible out of the yard, found the road leading past the swamp where I remembered seeing a juke joint. Shoreland Beach was man-made, and a miasmal swamp lined the shell road to the east from town to the bridge which led to the key. The town of Shoreland was garishly new, built around the Acton estate and groves, and the Cartright box factory. These two also owned all the real estate—and the town, I reflected. Spesak had been an employee of the two men who had pioneered in this isolated section of West Coast Florida, yet they had seemed sympathetic to Malachi and his crusade, against Spesak and the whole city administration.

The winter twilight fell swiftly. I parked before a pine board shack of some proportions and went under the glaring neon sign to the door. The swamp was all around, but Manuel had hacked out a clearing a hundred yards square from the surrounding tangle of lush foliage.

I went in and stood at the rough, unpolished bar. The jukebox blared a hillbilly tune. There were a dozen men about—Cracker types, lantern-jawed, seamy-faced, slant-eyed, canny. Manuel was a Latin from Tampa, burly, scar-faced, swarthy.

I had a drink of bad bourbon and said: "Where's Monk?"

Manuel batted his eyes. "I dunno. He ain't here."

I had another drink. The Crackers regarded me slant-wise. I said: "I got a message for him."

The back room was cut off by a partition. The door opened and Spesak came swaggering into the bar. There was instant silence. Even the jukebox ceased its clamor.

Spesak stared at me through red-rimmed eyes, a gangling, spindly man, six feet tall, with large knobby hands and evidence of ringworm. He said hoarsely: "That there is Manatee's muscle. Y'all look out, now."

I said: "I want Monk. You're just a crumb. I want the meatball."

A Cracker growled: "He called Joe a meatball!"

"I'll make him a meatball, for spaghetti and sauce," I promised.

Someone moved behind me. It hadn't been smart of me to come here, but somehow, remembering Malachi's eye, I didn't feel like being smart. It was action I craved. I ducked and spun and a coke bottle sailed over my head. Someone yelled, "Git him!" and the riot was on.

I grabbed Spesak and used him as a shield against the bottles. But the Crackers had fruit knives, with long blades and springs in the handle. I threw Spesak at them but he crawled out of it, ran for the door and out into the gathering night.

I began using my hands, and the Crackers kept falling down. Finally they closed in on me and only by gouging and rabbit-punching could I get to the wall. Manuel had a blackjack and I was trying to get it away from him.

A big man came in with Spesak following him. I only got a glimpse of him, but he had shoulders wider than mine and was almost as tall as Malachi. He was bad. I could see it in his eyes and the scarred map of his face. He plunged through the futile mob and was at me.

I ducked and came up, knowing this was my meatball. I hit him four times in the face. He bled, but he hammered as though he loved it. My neck was paralyzed by a near-hit. He came in, trying to get close, using his fists like mauls, ignorant and glorying in it, just swinging and taking it. He was all man and a yard wide.

I took it. I got to his gut, and it was like iron. I slugged him in the groin and I swear he never felt it. I lifted one to his jaw and he went backward.

Instead of boxing him, I followed close, trying to kayo him. I got one to his jaw, but he gathered me in with his left hand and just held me. Then he slugged me on the jaw with his right.

I can take it on the potato. I tincanned, rubber-legged, but not out. I thought I still had a chance. I moved out of range, trying to box a little, now. Then someone shoved a leg between mine from behind and shoved me forward.

He was smart. He played my middle. Since that Jap bullet did things to my lung, I'm not so hot down there. A long fight is not for me and I know it. He got me and my blood turned to water. He shifted to the chin and not even Joe Louis could have taken three of those. I went out like a light. I heard them all yelling, sounding savagely happy, and then I was out.

IT WAS very dark. I turned over and shoved at the ground and it was oozy and wet. I slipped and my face went into the mud. I cursed as best I could through a swollen jaw. It was a nightmarish thing, but nothing seemed broken except maybe a couple of ribs. I rolled over and sat up. There was no moon and the swamp was all around me. I thought of rattlers and coral snakes, got hold of a vine and somehow pulled myself erect.

The next question was, how had I gotten out? There was no light. I had no sense of direction. I took a step and floundered. I clutched a mangrove root and stood ankle deep in the ooze trying to get myself together. A light appeared as though by magic and a calm voice called to me: "Tack? Can you come over here?"

I said: "Malachi! Where the hell are we?"

He said in the same flat voice: "Follow my flash."

I stumbled, making progress as my blood began to stir. My chest hurt and of course my face was a wreck, but my limbs seemed all right. I went past a thick vine and saw Malachi plainly in the reflection of his flashlight. He was standing straight and tall, staring downward.

I followed the ghostly glow of the torch. Someone was lying on his face, arms outstretched. He wore a light sports shirt. The back of it was slit and the edges of the tear were black with dark stain.

Malachi said: "Fifty yards. A quarter-mile player."

It was Tom Mulford, stabbed in the back, beneath the left shoulderblade, neatly and surely murdered.

"How far off the road are we?" I asked. "And how far from the juke joint?"

Malachi said: "Fifty yards. A quarter-mile from Manuel's."

"What time is it?"

"Eight o'clock. Manuel's was closed when I arrived. It was a job finding you. I went to town first. Cartright told me you were here."

I said: "Where was Acton?"

"With Cartright. They drove in on business, before dinner. Mulford was with Dora Acton at the hotel."

"How did he get here, then?" I asked.

"That's what we've got to find out," said Malachi. He turned the flash on me and grinned a little. "I see you met Monk."

"And I'll see that meatball again," I said. "Alone."

"Do you think the two of us could handle him?" Malachi asked seriously.

"Alone," I repeated. "When I'm not sore."

Malachi shook his head. "Maybe. But he's awful tough. Let's go back, Tack. Chief Owen will have to pick up this poor kid. Let's go to town and see if we can find Monk."

We trudged out of the swamp. We got into the car, which Malachi had picked up at the juke—we had separate keys—and drove toward Shoreland.

Manuel's was boarded up, deserted. I thought about the Crackers and their knives and the dead boy in the swamp. But it would not be as simple as that. There was that look Cartright had thrown at Mulford when Dora and he were swimming together in the Gulf. There were Acton's premonitions of disaster and violence. There was the labor situation and the forces of the rich pitted against Monk and his merry men.

I said: "Malachi, what about the Crackers? Are they underpaid by Cartright and Acton?"

Malachi said: "I don't know."

I said: "Spesak was a shakedown artist. Is Monk running a racket among the working people?"

"I don't know—yet," said Malachi.

"Chief Owen will never catch a murderer who has sense enough to take the weapon away and lose it in the swamp and leave his victim where he might not be found for weeks," I said.

"The buzzards would have found him," Malachi said. "You don't know Florida buzzards."

"I met a big one," I said.

WE DROVE into town. Chief Owen was a mild, innocent man who belonged to Acton and Cartright. He was completely upset by our report of the killing. He immediately called the sheriff of Shoreland County, another nonentity who happened to be in Tallahassee at a sheriffs' convention. Then he sent some hastily sworn-in officers out after Tom Mulford.

We went back to the hotel. Malachi thought I needed a doctor, but I was sure my ribs were O.K. We went up to the suite and Ilene opened the door, took one look at me, then gulped the remainder of a large Scotch and soda. Finally she said: "I'll take this Monk myself. Where's my gun?"

"He'd eat your pop-pistol," I told her.

"Save him for us when we get him alone."

Malachi said: "And try to remember anything you can about what Dora Acton, her husband and Cartright did this evening."

"On account of someone killed the tennis player," I added.

Ilene poured three big ones. We drank and she screwed up her lovely face and tried to remember. She said slowly: "Funny, I was sort of watching them. Dora was pitching woo at Mulford... How was he killed?"

We told her and she went on: "Mulford wasn't taking it too well. It seemed to me he was scared. As if he had been playing a game and suddenly it became serious, you know?"

Malachi said: "Then what?"

"Acton and Cartright went off before dinner. Dora chased Mulford down on the beach, but came back alone and furious." She considered. "That was about seven-thirty. They had eaten together."

"Did she stay in sight?"

"No. She took her coupé and drove off. I don't know why I noticed. She gets my goat." Ilene said eagerly: "She could have followed Mulford and killed him!"

"And carried him into a swamp?" Malachi shook his head. "I want to know how Mulford got out of here without a car."

"Walked. He was a great walker," said Ilene. "Tell me everything now, will you?"

I told about the fight. Malachi told about stumbling over the body while looking for me. He deduced that Monk had beaten me up and had searched the swamp for an hour before finding Mulford.

I said: "Say! How could I have been out that long from a slight beating?"

"Have you noticed your shirt?" Malachi said. "Whiskey stains on it. They poured something into you. A Michael Finn, no doubt, to keep you quiet until they could fold the joint."

I touched the stains with my fingers. My mouth felt funny and I remembered the trouble I had getting up when I had come to in the swamp. Things began to get screwy in my mind. Manuel's joint equipped with kayo drops and a brute like Monk, with brains enough to decamp when things were hot, leaving me to live or die by snakebite made a strange picture of a back country Cracker set-up to my mind.

There was a knock at the door and I opened it. Dave Acton and Cartright came in. Cartright said harshly: "What's this about Mulford? My God, this is awful!"

Acton mumbled unhappily: "Owen's goin' in circles... Don't make sense... Who could've killed him?... Dora's having hysterics..."

"How did he get mixed up with that gang at Manuel's?" Cartright asked. "Owen will never find a killer among that crowd. He's afraid of Joe Monk." He stared at me, said: "I see Monk got you, too. Can't anyone stop that man?"

"He's a brute," said Acton with owl-like solemnity. "A depraved brute. He killed Mulford."

Malachi finished his drink and poured more, limping about the room. When everyone's hand was filled, he said: "Monk had no motive to kill Mulford."

"Born killer," said Acton, his fat cheeks quivering. "Tom went down there after you and Hinton fought them. They figured he was in with you and attacked him."

Cartright said viciously: "If you could pin it on him, Malachi, you'd be doing a great public service. Monk has got to go!" His angular face was granite hard, his slanted, elliptical eyes shone with fury and hatred.

"Try it," Acton begged. "Get him. Do anything for you, Malachi. Can't pay you in money—you got enough. Do anything you say, though."

They stared at him, waiting, two frightened rich men.

Ilene drawled: "Would you arbitrate your labor disputes? If Malachi finds the killer, will you let us act as a board— Tack, Malachi and me?"

They scowled at her. Cartright said: "We want Monk out of the way. I know he must have killed Tom—or had him killed."

Ilene said: "Malachi doesn't frame people."

They swallowed that, then got up, put their glasses down half full.

Acton said: "Think it over, Malachi. Do anything for you. Not what Miss Carver asks. Silly. But anything else." He went out and Cartright followed.

Before the door closed a wail came from down the hall and a soothing nurse's voice cut into it, but the petulant weeping went on and on. That would be Dora Acton and I pitied her husband.

There was nothing to do but go to bed and lick our wounds.

WE WERE up early, for a change. My face was worse than Malachi's, Ilene said, as we ate breakfast together. "It certainly is a change to have you beaten up instead of the other fellow," she added.

I said: "The question is, who murdered that simple, unfortunate kid? And how did they get him into the swamp? If it was Monk, he wouldn't have left the body near the spot where they dumped me."

"Not knowing you were merely drugged," agreed Malachi.

Ilene said: "I vote for Dora. Those curved jobs will do anything when spurned."

Malachi said: "What made you put in that crack last night about arbitrating the labor trouble here, Ilene? Since when are you a bleeding heart for the underprivileged?"

"I'm not," she said calmly. "I just knew it would annoy those two characters. I'm not fond of Acton or Cartright. I'm not enamored of Shoreland. I don't even care who killed the tennis player. I would merely like for you two to get hunk with Joe Monk. That's our slogan, Get Hunk With Monk. To hell with all else!"

Malachi said: "It's a nice little set-up. Assault, murder. I'll look around. You hire a car and examine the labor situation since you're so interested, darling. Tack will stick with the threesome you abhor."

"I'm not crazy about them, either," I said. "And suppose you meet Monk in your travels today?"

Malachi stood up, all six feet-four of him. He said: "You think you can take him, everything even. What makes you think I can't do the same?"

I had nothing to say to that. Malachi had a bad gam, but we didn't talk about it and, anyway, he had more endurance than was left in me. So we watched him go, with that limp which gave him the common touch, a dash of humility in what would otherwise have been perfection.

Ilene said: "The fool. We could gang up on Monk and continue our vacation. But he has to mess into things. Cartright and Acton *are* exploiting the Crackers."

I said: "Check all the way through. But take your gun."

"If Monk tackles me," she promised, "it'll be the last assault he ever makes." She thought a moment, then asked brightly: "Is he good looking?"

"Like Gargantua."

"Oh," she said. "Well, maybe I'll go to work on him, at that."

"That I'd like to see," I told her. She went off, her hips on oiled bearings, having the same effect on every male who saw her.

I put some salve on my face and went down to let the sun heal my scars. There was a commotion a few yards away on the sand and I heard the voice of Dora Acton. It had not altered one bit. She was giving orders.

"Dave, you've simply got to see Malachi... Rem, those trunks are unbecoming... Now be careful with the drinks... The sand will blow on us if you don't change that umbrella… Where is that red-headed vixen?… I don't trust that woman… Oh, is that Hinton? Well, what are you waiting for?… Get him… I want him."

It was Acton who came over. He said apologetically: "Wife's upset. Wants to talk. Thought a lot of Mulford, y' know? C'mon over. Have a drink."

I went over. Dora looked at me boldly, her black sloe eyes going up and down appraisingly. She said in a come-hither voice: "Sit down, darling. By me."

I sat down, said: "I'm sorry about your friend. When did you see him last, Mrs. Acton?"

It was a stunt the way she shut out Cartright and Acton. She spoke to me and suddenly we were all alone on a sandy island. It was sex at its peak. "Call me Dora… You're very strong. How did that awful man beat you?"

"With his fists," I assured her. "Did you drive Mulford into town yesterday afternoon?

"Why, no," she said. "He walked in. He loved walking. I went to the beauty parlor. Do you like my hair?"

She had it rolled up, some new way, I suppose. I said: "It's very nice… Then you didn't see Mulford in town?"

For a moment the curtain rolled back and I could see Acton and Cartright. There is a stunt—split vision, they call it—which is highly developed in football players. Without looking, you can take in what is going on in an area ten feet either side of you. By shifting on the sand, I could see Acton staring at his wife, his thick lips parted, while Cartright glared straight at me. They were frightened. I had known that last night and now I saw they had not recovered.

The woman said: "I saw him… at a distance… talking to a man."

I said: "You don't know the man?"

"No," she said slowly. "I don't know the man."

The silence was thicker than the Shoreland Hotel fish chowder. A lie had been spoken. The two men relaxed, and I knew Mulford had been speaking with one or both of them, and that they both were afraid to have it known.

I let the rest of the afternoon slip by. We drank quite a lot of Acton's cocktails from the thermos and had sandwiches sent down. It was late when Malachi drove in. Ilene followed him a few moments later and Dora stiffened and lost interest in me, or anything else, watching Ilene swing into the hotel. I didn't blame her. Ilene was like a race horse, Dora like a milch cow.

I unfolded myself and said: "One more dip. The water's pretty cold, but it's good for my bruises."

Cartright said: "I'll go with you."

We went down to the water. As we swam through the gentle rollers Cartright edged over, threshing a bit, for he was not an expert swimmer, and floated on his back. He said: "Hinton, take a tip from me. Don't mix into our business here. I mean the factory."

"Who, me?" I laughed. "Forget it."

He said: "Miss Carver was doing it today." I wondered how he knew, but I didn't dare ask. He had been at the hotel all day, and if he got a phone call, I hadn't known it. I said: "Miss Carver is a free agent. You might speak to her."

"I'd rather you did," he said drily. "Miss Carver is—sudden."

We parted and I swam in. His voice had been different, harder, more decisive than I had ever heard it before. He gave the impression of strength withheld, and I realized I had been viewing him as the hanger-on of the Actons, particularly Dora, instead of the tycoon of Shoreland. He was a determined man—and he could be a killer.

I DRESSED and went up to the suite. Ilene and Malachi were drinking Martinis which Ilene had made—four parts gin to one vermouth. I stuck to bourbon and listened to their talk. Malachi had traced the movements of Acton and Cartright in town and discovered that they'd been together all afternoon and evening. If they had seen Mulford he had not been able to obtain a witness to the meeting. Dora, he ascertained, had visited the beauty parlor—but briefly. There was much time, around dusk, unaccounted for, and no one had seen any of the trio eating dinner.

"So any of them could have killed Mulford," mused Ilene. "I learned he went to Manuel's. Walked there from town, they said."

"Who said?" Malachi asked.

"Joe Monk," said Ilene, grinning at us. "I tackled him in a tavern on the edge of town. He thought I was a reporter from a Yankee paper. He gave me the hoopla on Cartright and Acton, how they owned this county and ran it like Hitlers. No liberty for nobody, he said in his elegant manner."

Malachi said: "Did he make a pass at you, darling?" His voice was light, but there were undertones of danger which Ilene recognized; but did not choose to fear.

She said: "What do you think? He's a man, isn't he? A good enough man to take you and Tack on the same day."

"Sure he's a man," I said. "A hell of a tough meatball. And he also had the opportunity to kill Mulford."

"But no motive," said Malachi. He scowled, wrinkling his brow.

"Unless—but that's fantastic…"

For once Ilene didn't interrupt or ask any questions. Malachi was limping up and down the room. We drank and they finished another pitcher of those dynamic Martinis. Suppertime came, and Malachi ordered it sent up. Ilene played the radio. I sat, deep in thought.

It was nine o'clock and the radio was giving out with music from Oklahoma. From down the hall, at the far end, came a sudden, piercing scream.

Malachi was nearest the door and got into the hall first, but I passed him on the carpet. I hit the door of the rooms occupied by the Actons and it flew open. Dora Acton was standing in the exact center of the large, high-ceilinged room and emitting horrible noises at the top of her voice.

Dave Acton lay on the rug. He was deflated, like a balloon which has been ruptured. Someone had stabbed Dave Acton in his fleshy back. There was the same slit in his shirt, the same stains as those which had been on the shirt of Tom Mulford. Acton's mouth was open, his eyes staring pathetically at nothing. He had been dead more than a few moments because the blood was already drying.

Ilene swung in close behind Malachi, took a look, turned to the livid, hysterical Dora. She said, "This will hurt you more than it does me," and swung with her left. Her hand slapped hard against Dora's cheek, her right hand followed the left.

Dora stopped making noises and gasped, the color returning to the slapped parts. Outside, the manager was rushing up. Malachi bent close, his nose almost touching the wound in Acton's back. He murmured: "A quick, expert thrust, no slashing. Just like Mulford. The same spot, the same stroke. An expert operator, this character."

The manager came in and began moaning hysterically. Malachi went to the window, which was open, and looked out. Then he beckoned and I left the room with him and went out and around to the spot where the murderer had obviously jumped. It was a fairish drop and the imprints were deep, but they were also marred by hasty scratching. Malachi had brought a flashlight. The tracks led to the shell driveway.

A frightened Negro boy said a small car had left a half hour before, but he had not seen the occupant. Neither had anyone else.

Malachi said softly: "Well, this about tears it. Poor Dave—he was afraid of it."

"Cartright is afraid, too," I said. "This afternoon they were both afraid when they thought Dora might reveal something about a man who was seen talking to Mulford yesterday afternoon. I could tell they were scared. And Cartright is worried about Ilene investigating his labor situation."

Malachi said: "It adds up—almost too obviously. There's more in it than I can be sure of, but I think we can go ahead with what we have. The shape of the wound, the opportunity for killing, and the motive. No proof, actually, yet. But how often do we get court proof of a murder? That's for the big police departments with laboratories and sleuths galore and a little room downstairs where they can beat the tar out of people. I think we can move in."

I said: "I want Joe Monk."

Malachi didn't answer that. He was striding around the corner of the hotel, and Ilene was sauntering toward us, a coat over her arm. A car started, heading away from Shoreland. Ilene said: "That's Dora. I thought we ought to follow her."

"I'll lay four, two and even we can join her later without trailing her," said Malachi. He had something wrapped in his hand. We got into his car and rode to town, taking our time.

IT WAS about ten when we got to the edge of Frog Swamp. Malachi parked the car beneath some pines and we walked the rest of the way, Ilene between us. Going against a killer and a man like Joe Monk may be duck soup for heroes, but to us it was a desperate business. Actually, this was none of our business, except as citizens, and how many citizens deal themselves into murder mysteries? It was Malachi who did that to us.

There were no lights in front of Manuel's juke joint, but in the rear a sickly gleam struck across the clearing to the swamp edge. We crept close and found there was a window. I took a peek, and nodded. They were all there. Malachi went to the back. Ilene remained at the window, her gun in hand. I went to the front and set up a clamor.

That was to cover Malachi. After a moment I bashed in a window, removed the glass, climbed over the sill. There was a great deal of confusion in the back room, so I knew Malachi was already in.

From outside, Ilene's voice called, strong and clear: "Settle down. I've got you all covered and I'll shoot the eyes out of the first guy who gets tough."

Then I crashed into the back room. Malachi was standing just inside the door, his eyebrows like inverted V's, his mouth thin and harsh. I closed the door and put my back against it.

Dora Acton was sitting on a chair, tense with fear and excitement. She didn't look like the woman who had vented her grief over her husband's death in loud piercing accents. She looked like one of those operatic babes who lust for revenge, or something.

Cartright was standing, crouched a little, and again I saw him as a hard, capable man. He was calm, glaring at

Malachi, then at me, then at the window where Ilene held the gun on them.

Joe Monk was on a chair, huge even when sitting. His face was sneering, calculating. He let his pig eyes slide around calculatingly. Manuel stood behind him and there were a couple of others. One was Spesak, the ex-cop, and the other was a gaunt, hard-bitten Cracker.

Malachi said: "A little meeting of the clan. More plans— for murder, perhaps?"

Cartright said: "You'd better get out, Manatee."

"There are a couple of corpses," Malachi explained. "And a pair of beatings, dealt out by Monk."

"I've killed no one," said Cartright. "This is private business. You've no right here."

Malachi said: "No, you didn't wield the knife. You and Frankenstein!"

Cartright said: "I'm trying to find out who stabbed Dave and straighten out this mess with the men. Dora came here on her own. There's nothing to do with murder in this meeting."

Malachi shifted his gaze to Monk. He said: "A simple Cracker boy who uses knockout drops… Who stabs upward beneath the left shoulder blade, professionally, like a big-time shiv artist. You're no hillbilly, Monk, in spite of your drawl."

Monk grinned. "O.K., I've been places. But I don't stab people inna back, see?"

"Cartright was anxious to prove you did," said Malachi.

Monk shrugged. The power in him was obvious to all. He was absolutely without fear, I saw.

Cartright said harshly: "I find he did not kill Mulford— or Dave. We merely wished to get together…"

Malachi said to Monk: "They dumped the corpse of the tennis player within fifty feet of the place you left Tack. Dave was getting onto it, feared for his own life. So he got it next."

Monk shrugged. "I din't even know the guys."

Ilene suddenly screamed. The gun disappeared. Ilene was shoved violently away from the window. I was sorry it had to be that way, but I had been waiting for it, and I guess Malachi had been waiting for it, too. Manuel produced a knife, and so did the Cracker and Spesak, the ex-cop. I dove right across the room and landed in front of Monk. He got up like a lion.

There was a single shot outdoors, and for a moment I froze, but then Ilene's voice came through. "Try it on me, will you?" Then I knew she hadn't been overcome by the attack. Ilene was plenty tough.

Monk was trying to take me first. Malachi went past me and began doing things to people in the way the Marines had taught him. He had a pair of brass knuckles and a blackjack and he used them often and well. Men began falling like chicken heads in a kosher poultry market on a Friday afternoon.

Monk missed me eight times. I just went close and let him try. He hammered down with a rabbit punch and I slipped aside. Then I let him have the full treatment. The fingers in the eyes, the stiffened palm against his nose, the punch at the base of his ear. He gave back, trying to kick me. I grabbed his heel and lifted and he went over backwards. His head hit the baseboard and he didn't move for a moment.

I turned around and Spesak was behind Malachi, on his knees. He had the spring-bladed fruit knife in his hand, thumb along the blade. He was trying to stab upwards.

Manuel was down, the Cracker was sprawled over a chair. Cartright was dragging at a gun in his pocket which had caught in the lining.

In a corner, Dora stood watching, her eyes narrowed, a wild excitement in complete command of her. She was actually enjoying herself!

I reached out and took hold of Spesak and removed the knife from his grasp. I broke his wrist doing so. He screamed, and Malachi lashed out with the blackjack. Cartright went down on his knees and stayed there, like a stunned bull.

THERE WAS another shot and Ilene said triumphantly: "That got the bum!" Then she came in, swaggering a little, the gun still smoking. "Blew a small hole in him. I'm afraid not fatally."

Malachi was wheeling. Monk came off the floor, still brave, still swinging. Malachi slipped the knuckle off his hand, threw the blackjack to me. He let Monk get all the way up and then started. He struck out his left and threw the right in behind it. That was good punching, with Malachi's six feet-four leveling in a perfect pivot behind the right hand. He got it on Monk's chin. It was like felling a tree.

There was a crash and Monk hit the floor, flopped over and lay still. Ilene dramatically raised her arm and began to count: "One, two, three…" She could have made it a hundred.

Cartright was holding onto a chair, shaking his head.

Malachi turned, said to him: "You hired Monk to come down here and stir up trouble. You wanted turmoil so you could get rid of Dave Acton. You wanted Dave's groves and you wanted his wife. It was an old hatred, the kind that festers. It came to a head and you planned to have Dave killed and blame it on Monk."

Cartright didn't speak. Malachi went on: "You hired Spesak, a cop, as the assassin. You figured that was a cunning angle. Then I had Spesak fired and you couldn't do anything about that without tipping your hand. So you had Monk on your hands, a killer already in disgrace. Then Mulford became a problem, as your lady love fell for him. You lost your head, Cartright."

Spesak moaned. I said to him: "I'll twist that busted wrist for you if you don't talk." He moaned some more, pleading dumbly with Cartright for protection.

Malachi said: "I can place you on the road where Mulford was killed, Spesak. When Monk awakens and finds out the truth, he'll testify."

"He killed Dave Acton, too," said Ilene. "He must have."

"No!" mumbled Spesak. "I didn't. I never did."

Cartright said: "You're right, Manatee. I give up. Spesak killed them both. He wanted to kill you, too…"

Again there was silence in the room. Malachi turned and looked around at the shambles, taking his time. Dora Acton had not moved from her corner, the others lay about in broken attitudes. Monk stirred, turned over, sat up, rubbing his jaw. His eyes went to Malachi and a look of the utmost respect came into them.

Malachi said softly: "You'll confess, Cartright?"

"I'll go in and give myself up right now," said the square-faced man doggedly.

Malachi said: "You're all right, in your own way, I guess… Mrs. Acton, would you let him admit to the crimes?"

She said, a bit hoarsely: "He—he—says he had them killed."

"But he didn't," said Malachi gently. "He wanted to. He would have, if we weren't here, probably. He was a bit insane. Mulford was the worst. He was used to Dave, but Mulford was new, and young. He didn't realize that Mulford had spurned you and had walked to town prepared to take the bus and leave the whole deal. Dave knew it, because Dave was the man who talked to Mulford in town and gave him the money to go away."

She said: "You're crazy—Rem admits he did it."

"Because Rem Cartright knows you stabbed Mulford and hired Spesak to dump him in the swamp. Spesak wasn't present when Tack was left there, and took the easiest road in. You killed Mulford because he had refused to play with you and had run away." Malachi's voice was like thunder. "You stabbed him with a stiletto which is entirely different from the fruit knife weapons of this country, a weapon I saw in your room tonight, after your husband was killed. The police here may be rural, but they have that much sense. Chief Owen has that stiletto right now, testing it for bloodstains in Tampa. Maybe he won't find Mulford's blood on it, but poor Dave's gore will be fresh enough to trace!"

Dora Acton opened her mouth, but no scream came forth. She sat there, panting, her eyes wild.

Cartright tried to go to her, but Malachi shoved him aside. He said: "Owen is on his way out here now. You can buy a police department for petty, local stuff, but didn't you know you couldn't get away with murder? When Dave accused you of stabbing Mulford, why did you also kill him? Cartright would have done that for you, sooner or later, and maybe without leaving any evidence."

She leaped at him, clawing. "You lousy son! You couldn't know these things…"

Chief Owen came in then, with three cops, and took her. Cartright stood, white and stony-faced, while they added him as a material witness. The Chief said heavily: "I listened. You got a case, Mr. Manatee, if Spesak and Monk will talk."

Monk was on his feet. One hand went to his jaw. He said thickly: "Any guy that can kayo me with one punch… I couldn't handle that trick stuff Hinton gave me, but I never thought a punk could nail me with a reg'lar wallop… I'll talk, Manatee. I didn't contrack for no murders. Cartright wanted to upset Acton's apple cart. That's all I knew. I ain't no killer."

"Of course, you're not," Ilene said briskly. "Take them away, Chief. And watch out, I think the fat babe is about to pass out on you!"

They took them away. We relaxed a bit and I found a bottle of pretty good whiskey behind Manuel's bar. We had a drink. Ilene said: "I was right all the time. The bosomy job did it."

"Uh-huh," said Malachi. "Both times in a passion. She was so scared when she killed her husband that she ran to Cartright. He made her wait a while, then drove out so that people would think it was an outside job. He thought he had her for himself, then, with Mulford and Dave both dead. He really loves her."

"He was willing to take the rap for her," I said nodding.

Ilene poured another drink, said: "I'd like to see either of you in a spot like that. I've got a big steel engraving of you taking my crimes on your shoulders! Huh! Those plump babes heave around and roll their eyes and men fall like ten-pins for them. It makes me sick!"

"You don't do so bad yourself," said Malachi maliciously. "You sure had Monk going for a while."

"The meatball," I said.

"Meatball, is he?" she cried. "It took the two of you, one after the other, to knock him out. He could lick either one of you in a fair fight."

Malachi said: "What is a fair fight? Who makes the rules? Let's argue."

We did. Manuel's was open very late that night. We drank up a lot of whiskey and settled nothing. But it relieved our nerves, and we had a lot of fun.

And Monk wasn't a meatball, I privately conceded. He was a very tough racketeer, but he was no meatball.

DEATH WINS AN OSCAR

THIRTY YEARS IN STOCK HAD
SO HAMMED SIMON CHESTER
HE NEEDED EGGS NOW TO
LOOK NATURAL. IN FACT THIS
ENTIRE MOVIE MOB MALACHI
WAS RUNNING AROUND WITH
WERE STRICTLY PHONY.
EVERYTHING ABOUT THEM
WAS FAKE—EXCEPT THE
JACK-KNIFE THAT HAD
FINISHED OFF TWO OF
THE CAST. THAT WAS REAL
ENOUGH. TOO REAL FOR
COMFORT.

WE **WERE** in Bay City, on the west coast of Florida—Ilene Carver, Malachi Manatee and me—when Atomic Films sent the company down to shoot the outdoor scenes of *Cracker Boy*, an opus dealing with the rise of a southern politician to national power, riches and, of course, love. Malachi was intensely interested in anything new and immediately exerted his charm to become acquainted with the folks from Hollywood.

"And Malachi *has* charm, the big baboon," said Ilene Carver. "I admit it." Ilene is the most beautiful redhead in the world. Why Malachi does not marry her is one of life's major mysteries. We were sitting in the Bay City House lobby and she was wearing a sweater and— It doesn't really matter what else she was wearing since nobody would notice, except that there were no stockings on her slim, gorgeous gams.

Roland Mansard, who played the Cracker in the picture, kept strolling by, giving with the profile and George Outlaw, the slightly simian looking director, kept glowering at Mansard, whom he hated. Ilene said, loudly enough for them to hear: "Although why he bothers with these dimwits from Hollywood I cannot fathom. They're the dumbest bunch of hamdonnies the world ever saw. They exude ego. They have no conversation. They are unquestionably impotent, impudent and thoroughly impossible."

I said: "Leave us go into the bar and have a drink."

Mansard was as red as a turkey cock. He walked to the elevators and disappeared. Outlaw, however, grinned and hung around. He was a pretty tough monkey, I thought. He ruled his little bunch of actors with an iron hand, and seemed to have as little respect for them as Ilene.

Ilene said: "Why can't we go to New York and see some high-class bums, if we have to hang around bums? Anyone connected with the motion picture industry is low-class. There's not a brain in the business."

Outlaw gave up and followed Mansard to the elevators. Ilene said grimly: "That disposes of those two. Do you suppose Malachi is really romancing Ada Chester?"

At that moment there was a flurry of excitement. Bellhops ran, desk clerks stood at attention. Doors swung and

The knife wound was in Outlaw's chest. He was already dead by the time we reached him.

a gale swept into the lobby. Malachi Manatee actually held open the portals.

Malachi is six feet-four, blond, and satanically handsome. The slight limp caused by a Jap bullet becomes him. His face is extremely alive and intelligent and his smile is enigmatic, which women love. The woman swept in, paused to thank him with her eyelashes.

She was not tall, but she seemed tall. She had whatever it takes to make people stop and stare. She was deeply brunet this season and sun-tanned to play the part of Mansard's hometown sweetie in Atomic Films' current epic. She was Ada Chester—an actress, it was alleged.

In her train was her uncle, Simon Chester, a fat man, a heavy. He tried very hard to simulate the sinister suavity of Sydney Greenstreet, but thirty years in stock had hammed him until he needed eggs to look natural. He used his eyebrows a lot, but they just flapped like window shades. His role in the picture was the small-town politician who started Mansard on his way up, then was cast aside. This was a very serious picture.

Behind Simon came Ozzie Putnam, the assistant director, the man who did the real work of organizing the job in hand. He was a lanky, sandy-haired young man with a furrowed brow, and very homely. He adored Ada Chester with the blind love of a puppy for a boy. When she was around he was always stumbling over things and getting magnificent tongue-lashings from George Outlaw.

Desirée Trebble completed the party. They had been juking, I knew, with Malachi as guide. It was almost midnight and Desirée looked it. She had been a bigger star than Ada Chester in her day. Now she played the slatternly sister—elder, of course—and was comic, in spots. There were lines in her once classic features which only a hard life could account for. Her figure, once the toast of millions of morons, had begun a general surge toward terra firma. She clung to Ozzie's arm and the poor guy looked sunk.

Ada Chester said in her famed, husky voice: "That Mike Dugan! Really, I mean, so tough! And his giant Negro—what was his name?"

Malachi said politely: "Dugan is not a native. He came down from New York ten years ago, opened the joint and knew enough to buy police protection. Hobey, the Negro, is authentic—part Seminole Indian…"

Ilene said viciously: "Malachi the tourists' guide—the big jerk!"

They came closer and Ada Chester said: "I'm going out there again, but not with a crowd. There's danger in that place. It's positively sinister—the lights dimmed, the big Negro padding about, the couples with their heads close together in the unlighted booths, the splendid isolation—"

Ilene said: "Hell's fire, it's only a corny juke joint where high school kids hang out. The woman's slap-happy!"

Ada Chester fluttered her eyelashes at Ilene. "Miss Carver! Did we escape you? I mean, we thought you and Mr. Hinton would join us."

Ilene unfolded from the low chair. She was four inches taller than the movie queen and seven times handsomer and she knew it. She said: "Miss Chester, I'd have to be dead before I'd go juking in doubtful company. After all this is my home."

Desirée Trebble laughed gently. "Ilene, you're a card. Always making with the jokes. Let's all have a decent drink, shall we?" She linked arms with Ilene and bravely put her haggard remains of beauty against Ilene's fresh loveliness. Ilene liked Desirée and gave in. We went into the bar and took a corner for ourselves.

MALACHI SAID: "Dugan's Bar-B-Q stand is not vicious, merely slightly disorderly. The Moonlight Grill is the gambler's hangout. Dope is peddled in almost all of these places, and marihuana smoked as a matter of course. The city police are disinterested because the joints are off town limits…"

But Ada Chester had lost interest in Florida jukes. She was saying: "Where is that tiresome George? And Roland? Simon, do go and see."

Her uncle caressed his third chin and hooped his eyebrows. "Send Ozzie. I'm weary. All this carousing about…" He seemed to doze off.

Ozzie was already on his feet. The waitress brought our drinks and announced that this was the last round as it was midnight. We sipped Scotch and soda. Ilene was getting very restless. Ada Chester began talking about the shots they had made that day—they were putrid, she announced, and she knew it. George Outlaw was a tyrant, his reputation exceeding his talents, she hinted, in hushed accents, as though imparting a great secret. The whole thing was very boring.

I couldn't get Malachi's angle. Since the war we had been barging about Florida, looking for excitement and finding enough to keep us busy. Now that the restlessness engendered by action under fire was wearing off, he had shown signs of getting ready to settle down. This movie stuff was bad for him.

He had millions, but these are not times to let money stagnate. Pretty soon no money, I figured. It was time to go into business and be busy and progressive. Florida, the land of opportunity! Ilene and I both wanted Malachi to get into something which would keep him occupied.

Failing that, Ilene wanted to go to New York and start something up there. "The Big Time," she said, "is the place for Malachi. Besides, I know a bar where they make the best Daiquiris in the world. A girl can always amuse herself in New York."

But Malachi was a Floridian and he had been investigating fruit concentrates, cattle, oil, the fishing industry. He had even considered politics, since his deepest interest lay in cleaning up government in its relation to crime. But he lacked the pomposity so necessary to running for office in the South.

Me, I'm just a mugg who goes where Malachi goes. When they got Malachi in the left leg, they got me through the lungs, and the resulting scar tissue had not healed. I may look like an ex-tackle on the Giants, but inside I am not so hot, except for brief moments. I just tag along, wishing Ilene were in love with me, and wonder if she is really in love with Malachi, or if he is only a habit, like the cigarettes she constantly smokes.

Ada Chester was saying: "One drink isn't enough. I have a bottle or two in my suite. Let's go up and have a small party. I mean, it's too early to quit. At home we never stop early on Saturday. It *is* Saturday, isn't it, darling?"

She was addressing Malachi. Ilene batted her eyes once, and I said: "Down here we go to bed and get up early for church on Sunday." Ilene tilted her chin. "I'm for a party. I love parties, especially with brilliant people."

"Oh, you're such a card, darling," cried Desirée Trebble.

We straggled to the elevators. One of the doors opened and Ozzie Putnam stumbled out. Grabbing Ada's arm, he whispered, too loudly: "Roland and George are fighting. Hurry!"

We shot up to the seventh floor. We all fell into the hall and ran after Ozzie, to Room 702. He banged open the door and Malachi was in first despite his bad leg. Malachi dearly loves a fight.

Outlaw had Mansard against the wall. He was holding him by the collar and saying: "I won't spoil your face because I need it. But I'm going to punch out your guts, if you have any, you silly saphead." He shot a fist into the leading man's middle that sunk up to his wrist.

Mansard turned green but his knee came up and his foot shot out. He got Outlaw in the groin and sent him reeling away, to fall over a chair.

Malachi stepped between them. As Outlaw came raging back, Malachi put out one long arm and stopped him cold. He said: "I pronounce this bout a draw. Go to your corners."

Outlaw actually tried to hit Malachi with a swinging right. I saw Mansard reach for a heavy ashtray and slid over, giving him the rush to the wall again, taking it away from him. He slapped at me like a hysterical girl and I had to handcuff him and throw him on a couch. His eyes were red as fire and he said to me: "I'll kill him. Before God, I'll kill him!"

When he saw who I was, he relaxed and sat there, holding his belly. But he kept repeating, like a litany: "I'll kill him."

Ada Chester had taken charge. She said to Outlaw: "George, if you don't quiet down immediately, I shall wire Goldshaw... Roland, stop mumbling and begin thinking about your contract. You two have got to make these shots down here. Do you hear me?" Her voice was tough, incisive. Artifice was laid aside, she was a businesswoman talking to subordinates. She was cooler than ice and her jaw was hard.

Outlaw stopped trying to get past Malachi. Mansard stopped repeating his threat. Ada Chester said: "Now cool off. George, go to your room, take a shower and come to my suite for a drink. You all go on over. I want to talk to Roland. Hurry!"

We went. Even Ilene recognized Ada's authority and good sense. We went down to the corner suite overlooking Bay City's business center and stood awkwardly around the way people do after a fracas. Desirée found whiskey for us, said: "You see why Ada is a star? She's got it, kids. Like her or not—she's got it."

Simon Chester said sharply: "She was always a virago."

"She's a great woman," said Ozzie hotly. "She knows they were fighting over her and she doesn't love either of them."

"Love?" Simon whinnied like an old horse. Desirée said: "She's too clever to love. That's what kills." The lines in her face were like canals beneath the make-up. Her eyes were dead. Ilene put an arm around her and raised her glass.

"To love," said Ilene. "And the hell with the consequences."

Desirée relaxed and grinned clownishly. "Darling, you've got the right idea. There are always character parts—in life or pictures!"

The door opened. Outlaw came in, his monkey face calm. Mansard followed, urbane, smiling as though nothing had happened. Ada Chester said: "This won't do—this standing around. Let's all go out. I want to go back to Dugan's Bar-B-Q. Malachi said it gets rough after twelve. Come on, gang! Let's go on the town."

Well, that was smart, too, busting up a set scene, taking them out and putting everyone in motion. So we went.

DUGAN'S BAR-B-Q was on a side road leading off the main highway north of Bay City. A small neon sign proclaimed its location and we piled out of the two cars, Malachi's and the hired sedan. Ada Chester had brought along a couple of bottles and everyone was a little tight, a natural development under the circumstances. Mansard was in our car, with Ada and Simon Chester and Malachi and me. I heard him whispering to Chester, but paid no attention since Ada, sitting in the front seat between Malachi and me, was carrying on about Hollywood and how Malachi could make a million out there.

As they all went toward the juke, Ozzie Putnam lagged behind, dragging at my elbow like an importunate street urchin. He said: "Hinton, you've got more sense than the others. Watch Mansard, will you? Outlaw swears Mansard tried to kill him. Mansard thinks Outlaw is deliberately making bad shots of Ada to ruin her because Ada turned him down. Outlaw says Mansard is a neurotic cokey."

"Does Mansard really hit the dope?" I asked.

"He got cured," said Ozzie. He was the kind who always had a good word for everyone, I had found. Naturally, he was doomed to assistant directorship forever in Hollywood. "He's all right now. He really loves Ada—I think."

"Guys like Mansard love their mirrors," I said.

"Well, Simon stirs up Mansard. Then he runs to Outlaw. Simon's the real troublemaker," said Ozzie, frowning. "Ada's wonderful. She's a great actress. But her uncle—I can't understand him."

"Hollywood politics don't interest me," I told him. "I'm here only under protest. Malachi picks up the damnedest people. You're the only decent one in the crowd, for my money."

He blushed and fell over his feet and we went inside. It was just a Florida joint—a bare, barnlike structure with a bar at the side, a nickel-grabbing jukebox which played the worst records of the day, some tables with scarred tops and uncomfortable wire chairs. A huge Negro put the party together, a scar-faced black boy with muscles like a wrestler. His name was Hobey and he had chaingang scars on his ankles.

Mike Dugan came out. His face was a pie plate with hair growing down over the edge and a slit for a mouth. He was a wide man, but thin through the middle. He was past forty and none of his years had been fruitful. He knew Malachi and was respectful, but there was a cautious watchfulness about him. He said: "There's some tough Crackers in here tonight. I'd sorta take it easy, pals. You know how it is."

Ada Chester said: "My good man, bring us Scotch. And soda."

Dugan's pale eyes rested on her for a moment, then he went away. He spoke to Hobey and moved toward the opposite corner. Some giggling girls in short sleazy frocks with bruised bare legs giggled and stared. Tow-headed Crackers leered at Ada and Ilene and sneered openly at Mansard and Malachi. It was not a nice place.

The juke played and the Crackers danced, their own variety of jitterbug, very athletic and sweat-making. Ada Chester applauded, then insisted on joining in. Mansard obliged, and he was good. Desirée danced with Ozzie. Ilene glowered and drank Scotch. Malachi talked to Outlaw and Simon Chester.

Suddenly Mansard bumped into a Cracker. Hot words came to my half-closed ears. In a moment Dugan, Hobey and I were on the floor. A knife flashed. Mansard swore and tried to hit a Cracker.

Everyone became involved. Dugan used a blackjack he had hauled from his pocket. Ada Chester bawled for the police. Ilene slapped her, shutting her up for the moment. I hit a Cracker and he collapsed.

Then the lights went out. We were practically in the middle of a field, miles from the city and there was no moon. It was very dark.

I grabbed Ilene and swept her away from the crowd. She said: "This is a hell of a note, bub. Someone is going to get hurt."

There's nothing like flat darkness to cure combativeness. The sounds of brawling grew dimmer. Ilene rested against my chest and said: "I hope Malachi is the one who gets it." Dugan was swearing and demanding to know who had turned the lights out. I thought he had ordered it done himself.

The lights went on again and I saw that the master switch was just in back of our table, in a box which Dugan had never bothered to cover. Hobey had his hand on the switch and was blinking toward the middle of the floor.

George Outlaw lay on his back. His mouth was open as though in protest. His arms were outstretched and he had the look of violence, which is a thing you get to know about if you hang around such characters as Malachi Manatee. It is a definite, special thing, and it spells trouble. I stepped in front of Ilene.

Malachi was already bending over Outlaw. He didn't touch the fallen director, but just looked. I came close and said: "Got him, huh?"

"Didn't miss," grunted Malachi.

The knife wound was in Outlaw's chest, right under the left breast. It was a stab wound, shrewdly delivered. He was already dead when we reached him.

Dugan said: "A hell of a thing! They'll close me up for a mont'."

"You'll be paid," said Malachi. "Just take it easy."

Dugan said: "I don't even know them Crackers."

I realized then that the Crackers were gone. They had fled, each and every one. Whence they came, no one knew, and where they went was a mystery no man could solve. Their automobiles were creaking on the highways, going over swamp roads none could follow. They were just people—like any other folks—and we could never identify them.

Malachi said: "He must have run into the one with the knife."

"Yeah," nodded Dugan. "You know him?"

Malachi said: "Call the sheriff. We'll stand by." He got a cloth from somewhere and put it over Outlaw.

We all sat around and acted the way people act when a tragedy has occurred. Ada Chester looked frightened, for once. Desirée wept a little. Simon Chester looked the way he always did, only paler. Ozzie jittered. Mansard tried not to look too pleased beneath his shock.

Malachi looked thoughtful. So did Ilene. After a moment or two, I began to think, too.

Outlaw had been anything but popular. Mansard, for one, had threatened to kill him. I got up and drifted away from the table. I walked outdoors and found I could see inside through the long, open windows of the pike. Everyone seemed so absorbed in his or her own private thoughts and emotions that I was sure I was unobserved. I walked all the way around the juke and when I came to a deep shadow on the corner something grabbed me.

It was like being snared by an octopus. I was nearly crushed in the first second. I twisted, got an elbow working and slapped the edge of my hand against whoever held me. The old Marine trick worked and I staggered loose. Immediately I kicked out and a low moan was my reward. Something fell to the earth.

I picked it up. It was a knife—a large knife. The man who had grabbed me turned and ran into the darkness, but I knew it was Hobey. No one else around there was that strong.

I took the knife around to the front, under the neon light. It was not a Cracker knife. It was horn-handled and had only one strong blade. It was the kind I had seen in hock-shops down on the Bowery in New York. Normal, every-day people do not carry knives like that. There was fresh blood near the folding edge of the blade....

DUGAN CAME out of the juke and looked at the weapon, then at me. He said: "Uh-huh. You gonna turn it in?"

"What do you think?"

"Them Crackers made for the door when the lights went out," said Dugan. "They was all gone when the gee got his. I been around, pal. I keep track of things inna dark."

I said: "The sheriff will be glad to hear that."

"I ain't talkin' to no law," said Dugan composedly. "You duck the shiv an' some Cracker done it in the fight. Thas-sall there is to it?"

"Except maybe a little blackmail," I suggested.

"That's no skin off your elbow," said Dugan. "I ain't tacklin' you or Mr. Manatee. What's moom pitcher people to you?"

"Less than nothing," I said. "Is that the sheriff?"

Cars came down the side road. I folded the knife on impulse and put it in my pocket. I knew Tatum, the sheriff.

He was all right in his way, but he was a politician. There was no use worrying him with a detail like the murder knife—he wouldn't know how to handle it. He was taking orders from Dugan, of course, and I didn't like Dugan. A blackmail rap would be a nice thing to hang on the juke operator. I went inside, then Tatum came with his deputies and a lot of hoopy scoopy went on in which I took as little part as possible.

I kept watching the people in our party. I saw Ada Chester open up all the stops and play her part of grief. I saw Simon, slick and oily, go through his paces. Mansard was cool, dignified, the hero of the fight. Desirée alone seemed deeply grieved. Ozzie was suffering from shock and was useless.

But I knew each and every one of them, except Ozzie, was faking. Anyone but Sheriff Tatum would have known that at once. That worthy sent his deputies post-haste after the departed Crackers and vowed to find the murderer within hours.

We finally gave our names, got into our cars and departed. We drove to the Bay City House, and the movie people got out. Ilene, Malachi and I left instantly and went to the little house we had managed to build out on Mavis Isles, a suburb of Bay City situated over a bridge in the bay, but adjacent to town. We used this house for headquarters and had an old housekeeper of ebony hue named Hattie who ran it and chaperoned us, in a way. Not that Ilene cared about chaperones....

We sat in the living room and had a drink, which we needed. Malachi said: "All right, Tack, give."

He had seen me outside, as he saw everything. I told him about it. I gave him the knife and he opened it. The blood had dried, but the stain was apparent. Malachi snapped the big blade shut and put the weapon in the little safe in the wall where we kept such oddities. There was a painting of Ilene over the place where the safe was built in—not really to conceal anything, just to cover the hole in the wall.

Ilene said: "Who's your candidate, gents? Mansard? Simon? Desirée? The great Ada herself? Surely not poor Ozzie!"

Malachi said: "Dugan and Hobey were milling around."

"Oh, sure," said Ilene sarcastically. "Plenty motive they had for killing a movie director."

"They could be bought," said Malachi. "Cheap."

"Who'd have them?" Ilene shrugged. "You know better than that. Those movie characters were seething beneath the surface. They all have reasons for hating each other. Even Desirée—and I like her—was once Mansard's girl-friend. She started him to stardom, then lost the last of her looks."

"Who tells you these things?" Malachi asked interest-edly.

"Desirée," said Ilene. "She says Ada will have you chunk-ing dough into the independent producing company she's trying to start, within a week. She's seen Ada work before. Outlaw gave her her chance, years ago. But she double-crossed him, and Desirée thinks he *was* making bad angle shots on her in this picture. Mansard had something there."

Malachi said: "Go on. You're the gossip kid. You're terrific." He was angry about the crack Desirée had made, but he was curious, too.

"Simon is a gambler and was once a hophead, like Mansard. They were in the sanitarium together. Simon hates Ada because she got out from under his thumb when she made a hit in pictures. He warns Mansard daily that she is a bloodsucking leech—and I double that. In spades!"

Malachi said: "Did Simon hate Outlaw?"

"Simon doesn't love anyone," said Ilene. "You can see that with your eyes shut. Outlaw despised him. In fact, he despised them all, except Ada. Her he had—like a disease."

"A nice lot," I said, finishing my drink. "But Dugan shouldn't be allowed to blackmail them. We can take Dugan, anyway. Maybe the murderer will turn up if we keep on Dugan—and that Hobey. Chaingang Negroes are unpleasant critters and Hobey is tough, believe me. He and Dugan make a fine pair of nothing."

Malachi said: "We'll keep on it, all right. Tatum will go around in circles. I'll bet Atomic Films is in a dither right now. You'd think they would let a good, efficient kid like Ozzie take over and finish up here. But they won't. They'll have another big name director here in a day or so."

Ilene said: "Meantime, during the delay, you can commiserate with the colossal Ada. Have fun, darling. Because I'm going to." She winked at me and went off to bed.

Malachi said: "Ilene can never understand that I don't get romantic about other women."

"How could she?" I started for our room, yawning. "You're never that way with her, you dummy. I'll bet she's beginning to wonder about your war wound. Are you sure it was your *knee?*"

He cursed me fluently, but I was already in bed. I was asleep before he came in and tumbled into the extra-length couch upon which he preferred to sleep.

IN THE morning I had a bad taste in my mouth and Ilene's picture hung askew on the wall. Malachi still slept. Ilene came out and saw me standing with the safe door open. She said: "Good morning, Tack. Did someone steal the deadly weapon?"

"Yeah," I said. "I always knew that safe was made of tin. There was a mess of stuff in there, too. It's all gone."

She said: "Two old guns, used in murders, a blackjack that cracked you on the head one time, Malachi's football and basketball medals, three pictures of me as a baby—horrible ones Malachi kept to tease me, as if I cared—and what else?"

"Oh, junk," I said vaguely. "And some money. I wonder why Malachi put the knife in there?"

"So it would be stolen, simple," said Ilene. She was wearing a thin robe and when she moved between me and the light I decided to get breakfast. They either ought to make more girls like Ilene or stop making any. She followed me into the kitchen and said: "You know how it is. Always letting people put themselves on the spot. Like a big spider. Scramble the eggs, darling, will you? And remind me to stop saying 'darling'—like that damned movie actress."

Malachi was up. I saw him over Ilene's shoulder, going to the safe. He closed it, hung the portrait back with care. He stood in the center of the room in his shorts, a lean wolf, sniffing the air for a trail to follow.

First he examined the windows. He found one which seemed to suit him, then ran back into the bedroom and put on pants and a T shirt. He came back, climbed out the window he had selected and began to circle the patio, which was tiled. The eggs were cooked before he came back inside.

He said: "That was a smart cookie. Came in through the patio, wore gloves—or wiped up after himself."

"How did the thief know the combination of the safe?"

"I left it open," shrugged Malachi. "No use having it busted. It'll be interesting to find the knife. Whoever has it is the murderer—or knows who killed Outlaw."

"Very, very clever," said Ilene. "I vote for Ada Chesty Chester. Did you know she wears deceivers?"

Malachi said: "After breakfast we'll go down to the hotel and look over the suspects. Then we'll drop in on Dugan."

"Such wonderful ways of spending the days," said Ilene. "Malachi thinks of nothing but our fun."

We dressed and went down to the hotel. The newspapers blared the story of the director's death. A mysterious gang of hoodlums was blamed. Sheriff Tatum had a posse out after them.

The important members of the company were gathered in Ada Chester's suite. She greeted Malachi with open arms. "Darling! So good of you to come early. The company is sending out Donald Proshka. He'll be here tomorrow. Meantime, Ozzie is carrying on. We go on location today. The show must go on, and all that…"

In the hubbub, I managed to speak to Ozzie, who seemed somewhat confused. "Where do you locate?"

"George had arranged to shoot some juke scenes at Dugan's," he fretted. "Do you think that's—decent? Shouldn't we get another place? Or could we go ahead and just not—er—mention that it was the place where George was—where George died?"

I said: "If time is of the essence, you'd better go ahead. It'll look better for you."

"I was just thinking of the company," he said. He would never be a Hollywood success, I know.

I said: "What kind of a guy was George, really?"

"Regular," he said emphatically. "Tough, but fair. Except he did take strange shots of Ada… But I ran some rushes this morning and, do you know, they were good. Shadows, lighting, everything was different. But good. He made Ada look—like someone else. Someone sincere…" Ozzie broke off sharp. He had been talking half to himself, I realized, thinking about the pictures he had seen. His eyes slid around to see how I was taking it. I played dumb.

He went on: "It's a funny racket, Tack. George is forgotten already. They're worrying about the picture and the new director. He's a good one, but they're afraid he'll change George's idea of the story."

They were all jabbering at a great rate. I saw Ilene draw Desirée Trebble aside. Malachi seemed to be drifting aimlessly among them, but I knew he was asking questions far from irrelevant. There was a general movement toward the door and I let myself go with it.

Simon Chester was talking in a low voice to Mansard as they passed me in the hall. I heard the fat man say: "There's no profit in it. Keep your mouth closed. You threatened him, you know…"

Mansard was grim-faced. He answered Chester angrily, but I couldn't hear what he said. Ada had Malachi's arm and Ilene fell in beside me. We got into the cars. I drove Malachi's new four-door convertible and Ilene rode with me. We ran out to Dugan's clearing and stopped. The truck with the sound camera came behind us.

Hobey was there, opening the doors. He had cleaned up the previous night's mess and one spot on the floor was cleaner than the rest of it. Even Ada Chester shivered a little at that glaring space of floor. Then the cameramen came in and a big discussion ensued with Ozzie being very stubborn about something.

A make-up guy with very long hair and a lisp set up shop and began dabbing at the faces of the actors. Ozzie won his point, it seemed, and the camera was set up so that the boom came in through the biggest of the windows which lined the side of the juke.

We all sat on chairs and watched. Dugan came over and said in my ear: "They closed me up, all right. This is a break. I'll make enough outa this to pay me back."

"And the blackmail?" I asked.

"Nix," said Dugan virtuously. "It ain't kosher, chum. I ain't buckin' Manatee an' you. I heard about youse guys."

Ozzie called: "Quiet, please... Now this is the scene where the Cracker realizes he has fallen in love with the girl—Miss Chester. We don't need the dance shots— they'll be dubbed in as montage. Mansard, you play this big, then drift away. Your scene comes when you are alone, wrestling with your ambition as opposed to your love for this simple country girl... Miss Chester, we will stay on you with the camera. You're pretty sure he loves you and you have always loved him. He has gone away and returned and you sit there and register happiness—youthful, unthinking happiness... You know your parts. Ready, please..."

Mansard and Ada went to the booth and sat beneath the long arm of the sound camera. There was some arranging with lights and stuff. Ilene and Malachi stood against the wall, lounging, watching, and even Ilene showed interest.

Mansard wore made-to-order city clothes—he had just been elected to the legislature from the back-country district where the scene of the story was laid. Ada Chester was in a plain frock and somehow she had shed years and sophistication with her Hollywood garments. She was appealing, she was shy. She was damned good, I thought. Mansard was good, too, going into his *Cracker Boy* part.

They talked a little, but mostly they made with the eyes, then with the hands.

The scene was re-shot several times before Ozzie was satisfied, and it was a funny thing, the way Ozzie took over. The fumbling, nervous youth was gone, and a sharp, incisive man had taken his place. He bullied them, cajoled them coaxed them. He enacted each part, showing them what he wanted. He was terrific—and they took it from him like lambs.

At last he straightened, looked about, making sure all was right. His voice mounted: "Silence… Silence, please… Camera ready?"

Stillness fell. No one seemed to breathe. Ozzie's voice came firmly! "Roll 'em!"

Mansard spoke. His voice was the voice of the Cracker boy. Ada murmured, and she was the country girl, the simple soul. The concentration was intense. It was the real thing. There was something about it. These people, who seemed such silly folk, were damned competent. It was amazing how really good they were.

Mansard rose abruptly, making an excuse. He was wrestling with himself, just short of a declaration of love. Without words, he conveyed it to us. He went out the back way, through a door. The camera remained upon Ada Chester.

She sat there. She was tender, she was confident. She smiled at the door through which Mansard had passed. The scene ran on—they would cut it, of course, but they were taking all she could give, now. She played with a paper napkin, her lips and eyes doing the work, but with restraint, with artistry. People moved in the background but we outsiders were held tight in our places by her superb performance….

"Cut!… That's it, Miss Chester," Ozzie said at last. Time had flown.

Ada Chester got up and said: "Damn it, this joint is afire. I'm sweating like a stuck pig."

Ilene sighed. "And just when I was believing it," she said. "I take it all back. That witch is an actress in spots, and that was one of her spots."

Ozzie said: "Let's get outside with the camera and take those shots of Mansard among the pines. I want that Spanish moss heavy in this scene."

The technicians scurried to gather the gray-bearded moss and hang it along an avenue of trees which didn't have enough foliage. The company was re-forming, and I realized that they had been paying little attention to the shooting of the scene. Simon Chester came out of the woods. Desirée seemed to have been in the little girls' room. Ozzie went out back to look for Mansard. Ada went to the place Desirée had just left. More time passed, then Ozzie came back to the front of the juke and said: "Where the hell is that ham, Mansard?"

From the back came a dry—"Ozzie… *Ozzie*." It was urgent enough to send us all running. A property man was standing behind the juke, staring at a heap of rubbish. There were old tin cans, worn-out tires, rags and whatnot piled against an incinerator made of wire.

A man's foot protruded awkwardly. I recognized the cuff of the ready-made trousers immediately. Malachi and I arrived at the junk heap together.

Mansard was wearing the huge horn-handled jackknife for a boutonnierre. It was on the left side and it was jabbed through the cheap cloth and through his shirt and skin and into his heart. He was a dead man on a trash heap.

SHERIFF TATUM was annoyed. He said: "This here'll git me talked about. After all, I got a position t' maintain in this county."

Malachi said for the tenth time: "Any one of a dozen people could have stabbed Mansard. There is no way to tell within half an hour how long he was dead when we found him. You can't arrest them all. Leave it to me, Tatum."

"I gotta, Mr. Manatee," said the sheriff. He had the knife in his hand. He said: "This ain't no Cracker knife. You better be careful of them people, Mr. Manatee. They is sho' a murderer amongst 'em."

He went away, finally, muttering to himself.

Ada Chester was in hysterics, and the entire company was now completely disorganized. Ozzie had already sent frantic wires to Hollywood and was rushing to town to put in a telephone call to Goldshaw, the Big Mogul. Desirée was pale and seemed thinner. Simon Chester kept picking at his lips, his eyes rolling.

Mike Dugan and Hobey were sullen. They denied knowing anything about either killing, swore they had not been within a hundred yards of either victim at any time, which was untrue, of course.

Ilene was suspiciously quiet. She stayed with Desirée mostly, but she had the gift of being everywhere unobtrusively when she chose. We finally got Desirée into our car and the four of us started for home. It was getting toward evening when we arrived at our house.

Desirée said: "I can't put you out like this. I ought to go to the hotel with the others." She looked terrible. There were circles beneath her eyes and her mouth would not remain still.

Ilene said: "You wouldn't make a cute corpse today, dear. We want to talk to you—and to think."

I was mixing drinks when the phone rang. Malachi answered it, then came into the kitchen and closed the door. He said: "That was Tatum. Someone stole the murder knife from him. He doesn't even know when."

I added soda to the ice and Scotch. I said: "There *is* a pattern to the business, then."

"Motive," said Malachi. "Who had a motive for killing them both?"

I said: "It was nice of you to provide the knife for Mansard."

He winced. "I'm not proud of that."

"This character acts too quickly for us," I said. "How about inviting all the people out here tonight and watching over them?"

"They can't all sleep here," Malachi scowled. He looks more like the Devil than ever when he is perturbed. He was angry, deep down inside, I could see. "If I only knew which was next on the list…"

"Sure," I said. "That would be ducky. These people are screwy, pal. Mansard, Outlaw, all of them. Simon was a hop-head. If you ask me, Desirée hasn't been a lily either. And what about Ada? She was close enough to both the dead men to have killed them."

Malachi said: "I know it. Anyone in the company could have pulled both killings. Or Dugan or Hobey could have been hired to do the job."

"If we get that knife again, we can send it to the FBI and learn some things," I said.

"I have no desire to pull that knife out of anyone else's hide." Malachi snapped. "Let's have a drink."

We went inside. Ilene was making Desirée comfortable on a couch, and a breeze was coming in across the patio.

I handed the drinks around and took a deep pull at mine. Malachi went to the phone, called the hotel and got Ada Chester. He almost ordered her to bring the others over after dinner.

Hattie appeared and served us fried chicken, rice and gravy and a fine salad. We ate. People die and are buried, but we eat. We drank some wine, and had a brandy. Malachi brooded. He's a great one for thinking. My head hurts when I think, so I didn't bother. I just worried about who was going to get killed next with the knife we should not have let the murderer steal from us.

Malachi was limping up and down when they arrived. It was dark and they were fretful. Malachi greeted them, brought them into the long living room, fed them the drinks I mixed.

Ada was not so much frightened as she was angry. Her picture was ruined. She kept saying: "They'll put it on the shelf. They can't replace Mansard. It would cost a fortune to start over."

"Mr. Goldshaw didn't say that," Ozzie protested. He looked years older than the kid of the previous night. "I talked with him. He's coming on himself."

Desirée said: "They'll make it, because it's sure-fire. I'm not worried about that." But she was worried. She was near to breaking, hiding it under a rigid, unnatural calm.

Simon was unperturbed and, as I served him a drink, I knew why. Simon, under pressure, had resorted to his old habit—drugs. He was high as a kite, I could see it in him. He sat like a fat Buddha, the drink in his hand, his face evil and blank.

They all quieted down and Malachi kept limping the length of the room. When he had them all watching him, he began talking—an old trick of his. He talked quietly, without particular emphasis and he held them. He had a bit of ham in him, too, and they recognized and respected it, I suppose.

"Two men have been killed by the same weapon. Without having the slightest idea who killed them, we can assume that it was the same person, as the weapon and the wounds are identical. That is, someone possessing a large knife who knows how to use it."

Simon Chester sneered: "Sounds like the corny shamus in a shaky B."

Malachi ignored the fat man. "Outlaw got killed by a coincidence. There was a fight and someone turned out the lights. But Mansard—the one who stabbed him knew the script of *Cracker Boy*."

"Who doesn't?" said Simon Chester sleepily. "The damn thing haunts my dreams."

"Also, we can take for granted that the killer was a person who hated *both* Outlaw and Mansard," said Malachi calmly.

Desirée, nearest the window to the patio, said sharply: "There's someone outside!"

"I'm not surprised," said Malachi. "Please don't notice them… Tack will handle the situation."

I drifted into the kitchen and rattled the icebox door. Then I shook ice into a glass. I heard Malachi say: "Having had a little experience with murder, I would like to get your reactions. Of course, I am aware that one of you is guilty…"

I ALMOST chuckled aloud, sneaking out the back door and going fast around the edge of the house, a blackjack swinging in my right hand. That last crack would hold them, I thought.

Mike Dugan backed away, saying sharply: "Now look out, Hinton."

Hobey came out of the shadows. He was big, tough and nimble. I led with a left, holding the sap in reserve. It was a good thing I did, because he grabbed me as I landed on his face and just swung me. I did a neat parabola, lighting on top of the patio wall, a low, wide affair.

I did a flying swan right back. He was following me and didn't quite expect this. I swung the blackjack and got him on the side of the head. He went down. Dugan was coming, now, reluctantly but of necessity. I kicked him low, then slammed him against the wall with my left. He groaned and tried to duck away but I needed him around, so I had to let him have it with the blackjack. He collapsed, face down.

Hobey was up, and he had something in his hand. I let him come to me, this time. He sliced the air with a shining thing and, since I am very unfond of knives, I retreated cautiously with the blackjack dangling. He came again, encouraged by my retreat.

I let go with a long one. It caught his elbow and the lead in the end of the sap bit at the bone. He groaned a little and his arm went down. I kicked him very hard in the shins. He yelped with pain and I slung the blackjack in an uppercut to his jaw. He, too, fell on his face.

I picked up the knife. It was the same one, all right. I went to the window and said: "Malachi, here it is."

Malachi opened the screen and I handed him the knife. I said: "It was on Hobey."

"Thanks," said Malachi. "Did they give you any trouble?"

"Oh, no, they were little gents," I said. "I'll get some rope and tie them where they lay. They're too bulky for me to be carrying them about."

After they were tied, I went back into the house. The knife lay on a coffee table, the blade open. It looked wicked.

Everyone was trying not to look at it, but all eyes came back as to a lodestone.

"I always did think knives were dirty instruments," drawled Ilene. "A bullet is much cleaner. What do you think, Miss Chester?"

"Shut up, you damned redhead," Ada Chester almost screamed.

Simon Chester was in the second stages of dope now, jittery. "Why don't you call the sheriff and have those two hellions jailed?"

"In good time," said Malachi. "They came in to work a little blackmail, of course. Hobey is deft with the fingers—he lifted the knife from the sheriff. I wonder how he knows to whom it belonged?"

"Maybe he didn't," suggested Ilene. "Maybe they came in to find out that very thing. It would fit conveniently into Miss Chester's handbag, wouldn't it?"

Everyone looked at the big bag the picture star always carried. For a moment I thought Ada would burst. Then she said: "I'll sue you for defamation of character! I'll have you in court the rest of your life, you redheaded—"

"Defamation of *what?*" demanded Ilene. "Hell, you can't kill a dead dog, you know."

Malachi's voice stilled them. "It's apparent that neither Dugan nor Hobey did the killings of course."

"What? Why not?" demanded Simon Chester. "They had the weapon. They had the opportunity."

Malachi said: "I mentioned before—the killer *hated* Mansard and Outlaw. Outlaw got it in a hurry, but Mansard was left dead on a trash heap. There is only one motive for both these murders—hatred. Oh, other details enter into it. But a good hater did the jobs because he loved doing them."

Ozzie muttered: "Someone who knew the script. Someone who hated them both. Someone with a knife and knowledge of how to use it."

"Exactly," Malachi nodded. "Someone who stabbed Outlaw, then threw the knife out of the window, where it could be recaptured later. Only it was found—by Hobey. Then Tack got hold of it. And then someone stole it from this room!"

They all stared then. Malachi had them. He stood near the door to the kitchen and smiled satanically at them. Then he took one step and I knew he could reach the light switch. I got ready. His bellow was so sudden and so unexpected after the softness of his former speech that even I froze with fear for a moment. Then the lights went out.

You have to know Malachi and know how he works to get along with him. He never tips you off if the occasion doesn't warrant it. He had said it all, right in the open, and left the ramifications to sink in. His shriek of horror in the kitchen was designed to galvanize tortured nerves into action. My cue had to be picked from the context of his talk.

It was simple enough. I dived over Desirée on the couch, and crouched near the window. Furniture went upside-down, drinks crashed to the floor. Hattie would hate us for this, I thought irrelevently, waiting by the window leading onto the patio. Then someone plunged over the divan for the window.

I followed, hurdling the low sill, then dropping low. A voice said: "Dugan—Hobey—where are you? You've got to get me out of here, hide me. That devil knows too much."

I saw the knife flash. That knife—it was everywhere. I moved out and said: "It won't do, you know. The Everglades are far from here. You can't hide."

With a low cry he sprang at me. He knew how to use a knife. He held a thumb along the blade and swung it up, for my guts. He had reach and strength and agility. I moved back and said reproachfully: "I always liked you, too, Ozzie. Shame on you."

He came at me again, trying a feint. The clumsiness was all gone. He sidestepped, weaving, and I moved backwards again. Suddenly a giant hand seized my ankle. I went down and my stomach turned over twice. Ozzie had had time to set Hobey loose.

I kicked, but Hobey had his grip. I was helpless. I thrashed around and footsteps came nearer. Dugan was swearing and saying: "Turn me loose. Let me get the hell outa here, too."

I had to go for Hobey. I hit him on the jaw with my fist. My bones scrunched in my hand, but I hit him again and again. Then I leaped away, leaving him limp.

I saw the knife and lowered my head, ready to go whichever way seemed best. Malachi's voice said: "It's all right, Tack. When he saw me coming he did a hara kari."

IT WAS Malachi who held the knife. Ozzie lay on his back, arms outspread. The moon was out, and it shone on his face. There was nothing evil there, only youthful longing and sadness. I stared at him. I couldn't look away.

Malachi said: "If you'll re-tie that big ape, we'll go inside."

I saw then that the lights were on and that people were peering through the window at us. The screen made them look as though they were in a big cell, somehow. I got more rope and bound Hobey securely. Then I took a last look at poor Ozzie and went indoors.

Malachi said: "I'm about to call the sheriff. But first I want to say that I thought it was Ozzie all along. He was the only one with nerve enough to take action. You all hated Mansard and Outlaw, but not one of you had the guts to do anything about it.

"Outlaw was a bully. Ozzie, as good a director as he was, had to take things from him no man could swallow and like. Then, when Outlaw tried to blackmail Ada Chester into marrying him by bringing up that old business about dope…"

"That's a lie!" Ada Chester said quickly.

"It's not," said Desirée. "You and Roland and Simon and I—we were all in it. Roland told Outlaw, in a fit of pique. Then when Outlaw taunted him with it, they fought. Simon was a part of it, too. We're a rotten crew."

"Ozzie loved Ada Chester, therefore he hated the men who meant no good by her." Malachi's voice was cold, angry. "He was a nice enough kid, a whittler. But Ozzie carried banners, as well as a knife, for his beautiful lady love. She wouldn't look at him, but he would serve her. If it had to be murder that was all right with Ozzie."

Ilene interrupted: "Now wait, Malachi. You're not going to tell us Ozzie turned out the lights in the juke, then ran over and killed Outlaw. That doesn't make sense."

"No, it doesn't," said Malachi. "Someone not in the mêlée turned off the lights."

"I wonder who that could have been?" asked Ilene. Her eyes were shining. "A nice little accessory before the fact."

"And I wonder who distracted attention while Ozzie followed Mansard behind the juke, stabbed him, then came back innocently looking for him?" asked Malachi.

"Whoever was in on the blackmail plot," said Ilene promptly.

"Just a question of making Dugan and Hobey talk," said Malachi, shrugging his broad shoulders. "They were coached in blackmail. They haven't the brains for something like this. If they keep him off the stuff long enough, Simon will confess. Won't you, Simon?"

Ada Chester stood up. Her face was white, but the contortions of rage were gone. She said: "Evil genius. That's it. All my life he has been my worst enemy. He stole from me when I was a kid. He carried tales every day. He made Ozzie a murderer."

She started across the room like a hurricane. I grabbed her midway, and for a moment it took all my strength to hold her. Then she collapsed.

Ilene followed me into the kitchen. We had a big straight one. Ilene said: "Well, she's human after all. I never would have believed it. Poor Ozzie."

I choked a little on my drink. But what the hell, she is Malachi's girl and what's a guy going to do about a thing like that? I had another straight one.

GAME, SET AND MURDER

ALL MALACHI MANATEE WANTED WAS A LITTLE GOOD, CLEAN TENNIS. BUT FROM THE MOMENT HIS GIRL STARTED FLIRTING WITH A SAILOR AND LANDED IN JAIL, HE WAS BUSY GETTING HER OUT OF TROUBLE—AND HIMSELF NECK-DEEP INTO IT. INTRIGUE, MURDER, SMUGGLING—HE PLOWED RIGHT IN—AND NEARLY GOT HIMSELF PLOWED UNDER IN THE PROCESS.

CHAPTER ONE
AND SUDDEN DEATH

WE HAD to be in Bay City on some sort of business having to do with Malachi Manatee's millions, and since our wounds from the late, almost forgotten war were healing a bit, we played some tennis at the Bay City Club, and that is where I met Bud Harrison. Malachi and I only play doubles and Harrison represented Dunson Sporting Goods Corporation, which meant he was pretty good, and we couldn't beat him and Sam Gold but it was fun.

We showered after the match and sat on the club verandah and enjoyed the Florida West Coast evening breeze and drank Scotch and soda. There was no Scotch for sale anywhere, but Harrison had brought some from New York, he said. He was a tall, blond, easygoing guy I had known when I played tackle for the Giants. This Sam Gold, a quiet-spoken character, black-haired and tanned, was also from New York. It was nice to relax and drink and let Harrison brag about his easy life and his women and the liquor he could get anywhere, any time, because he knew all the big shots. Bud was a harmless joker who could boast without giving offense.

Malachi, who is six feet four and somewhat sardonic, stretched his bad leg and said: "I'll take one brunette and a case of bourbon... but right now where are Ilene and Lily?"

Ilene Carver was the most beautiful redhead in the world and Lily Clay was a girl of doubtful antecedents but glorious physiognomy who had taken a fancy to us around the tennis club. They had borrowed Malachi's 1942 Cad for an excursion to the beach that afternoon.

Sam Gold glanced at his wrist watch and said: "They are late." Sam was not an original conversationalist, he seemed just an ordinary New York guy, maybe a cloak-and-suiter in a big way, well-dressed, loaded with money.

Harrison said: "Maybe they picked up a couple of swifties over at the beach. Those babes don't appreciate us

There was a flat, whining sound.
Culpepper jerked back as
though a bee had stung him.

broken-down athletes beating out our brains on the tennis
courts." He hefted one of the three rackets he carried as
samples. They were good bats all right—little as I knew
about the game I could tell that. "Did I tell you about the
time we were playin' mixed doubles at Forest Hills with J.
Donald...."

He always had a story, which is part of a salesman's
business, I reckon. My business was staying with Malachi
Manatee and helping him do nothing, so I did not have to
listen. I went inside the clubhouse to ask if there was a call

for Malachi. At that moment the clerk turned from the telephone and said: "Mr. Hinton—for you."

I took the instrument and said: "Hello, hag."

It was Ilene, all right. She snarled: "Get Malachi and come downtown. And make it snappy."

I said: "Downtown where, beautiful? To the pokey, maybe?"

"You think not?" Her voice was a scream. "These damn cops have got us down here and are about to give us the works. Drunk driving. Soliciting. God knows what. Well— are you going to gape in that phone or come down here?"

I said: "O.K., baby, O.K.! Hold everything." I hung up as she began telling me what I could hold and how she felt about the whole thing. I went outside, saw Malachi comfortable and half asleep and thought about how he hated cops and the tremendous excitement he would create downtown when he heard the news. I tiptoed back and put in a call to Pop Gilmore. The old alderman was influential in Bay City. When he answered, I suggested that I pick him up or he pick me up and we hurry. He said he would come for me and I went out on the porch to the front of the clubhouse. Sam Gold came from the verandah, which was on the rear, facing the courts, and smiled at me in his cool way.

"Harrison is really wound up. I don't think your pal is listening," he said. He had Harrison's three rackets and was going toward the phone to call a cab.

I said: "Wait a minute and we'll take you downtown."

"O.K.," he said. "You going alone? Without the gals?"

I said: "Keep this quiet, but they're in trouble. I've got to spring them. The vice squad picked them up, it seems."

Gold said: "Is that a gag?"

"You don't know Manny Silvestriano," I told him. "Bay City's wart. The sergeant of detectives in charge of vice. A rough little guy—on women and kids and colored folks."

Sam Gold said: "Silvestriano? Yeah. I know him."

Pop Gilmore came driving in at that moment. He is an old, windy guy with a mouth full of loose false teeth. He boomed: "Get in, son. Anything to oblige a friend, son. I haven't had the pleasure of knowin' this otheh gent'man, have I, son?"

I introduced Sam and we got in. Gilmore drove his jalopy with the aplomb of a race track driver, but at eight miles per hour. I was beginning to get nervous, thinking what might be happening at headquarters—to the cops, not Ilene. I said: "Which hotel you at, Sam?"

"I'll go with you," he said quietly. "I'm interested."

Gilmore was rumbling along about a lot of things, including a big, fat apology if anything was really wrong which Malachi would resent. Gilmore was one of the old-timers who remembered always that Malachi was worth six or ten millions of dollars and that it paid not to cross that much dough. We got to the station house at last and there was Malachi's car, parked in front.

I got out of the crate and looked at the old, dingy police station-jail-headquarters, and I began to get angry on my own hook. I led the way indoors, and when a cop was slow getting from under foot, I gave him the shoulder and spun him through a door. Inside the room off the corridor sat Lily Clay. She was a small girl, but curvacious like mad, with a mop of chestnut hair and large blue eyes, round and deceptively innocent. She did not seem at all perturbed.

Ilene was walking up and down, her red hair immaculate, her slacks creased razor sharp, her slim body almost boyish, if you did not look close enough. There was a runty little guy with pig eyes and a lascivious mouth, wetlipped, behind the desk, and a gorilla-like plain clothes cop stood in a corner. The ape-man was Obie Culpepper, a Cracker. The shrimp was Manny Silvestriano, a potent political figure despite his unsavoriness I knew. I snapped at him: "You looking for it, Manny?"

Pop Gilmore shoved past me, huffing and puffing. He intoned: "Now, boys, let us not get essited. Good evenin' ladies. Good evenin', Sergeant. Now, folks, there may have been a leetle mistake. To err is human, yawl know...."

Manny had a voice like a steel rasp. "No mistakes. These women were drinkin' whiskey an' coke at Jolley's Jook an' flirtin' with a couple sailors. We watched 'em for half an hour. Just when they was puttin' the gobs inna car we picked 'em up."

Ilene said: "You dirty little pig. You filthy little bum. They were two cute boys, that's all. We were going to give them a lift downtown. You stinking little jerk." Her voice was quite low. She drove the words at Manny, but the detective had a hide like leather.

"I'm holdin' them for fifty apiece," he smirked at Gilmore. "You can't pull no politics on me, Pop. I know what I kin do."

I HAD the hundred out before Pop could say more than: "Now, Manuel, you know I ain't askin' for anything ain't right. The inalienable rights and privileges of the Ammurrican citizen...."

I had forgotten Sam Gold. I was trying to get Ilene out of there before she went over the desk and clipped Manny. Gold went past me and picked up the hundred dollars. He said in his ordinary, gentle voice: "You've made a mistake. You did not book these girls. You brought them in here and

harangued them. Now you want to prefer a charge. Well—
do it, smart cop, before you ask for dough."

Silvestriano got to his feet. He said shrilly: "I'm doin' it,
ain't I? I'm goin' in now and do it. You got no right to butt
in here."

But he was scared. I saw Gold follow him outside and I
saw that Gold had something on him. It tickled me, and
after I had got Ilene into the hall and Lily with her, and had
realized that Lily was pretty plastered, at that, I waited just
a moment. Pop Gilmore kept moaning low about nothing
and Ilene told him to shut his big trap. Lily smiled mist-
ily at everyone, without saying a word. Culpepper, the big
dope, came out and stared at me.

Gold came back. He handed me the hundred and said:
"That jerk. He decided not to press the charge because
he forgot to pick up the sailors. He's yellow all the way
through."

Ilene said: "I'll catch him sometime. I'll fix his dirty little
hide. If it wasn't for that big Culpepper, I'd have let him
have it today."

I herded them all in the cars. I said: "Ilene is tough—
but she figures the angles. Culpepper would clip her as
soon as he would me. Those two should be thrown off the
force, Pop."

Gilmore said: "I shall speak to the Chief about it, son.
Yaas, indeed…."

There was more of that, but we finally got to the club.
Gold still had the rackets under his arm. He said: "I bought
these damn things and now I'm carrying them around. Can
I leave them in your locker?"

I said: "Sure. Here's the key. We'll have one drink in the
bar and then we'll take you downtown, huh?"

He said: "All right. Don't mention anything about the deal with Manny, huh, Hinton? I hate to be thanked and all that stuff."

"O.K.," I said gratefully. I followed Ilene to the verandah and Harrison was still talking. Malachi opened his eyes and I knew he had been dozing. I said: "The girls had a little trouble downtown. They only tried to solicit a little, but the coppers said nix. It's all fixed now, though."

Harrison gaped, but Malachi just nodded. "Ilene will have her fun. Let us eat, children. Shall we all eat together? How about Spanish bean soup and cold little green peas all over a salad, very lousy but Latin?"

Harrison said: "Lily! You got arrested?"

"It was fun," Lily said dreamily. "You should have heard Ilene. She can swear worse than you, darling!"

Harrison managed to get his mouth closed and we went to dinner. We dropped Sam Gold at the Topper Hotel and I thanked him with a wink and then we ate.

MALACHI HAD a house out on Mavis Isles, not a large house, built sprawling, with wings. Ilene stayed in one wing with Hattie, an ancient colored woman who cooked like a dark angel. Malachi and I lived in the other. It would have been a lot more convenient if Ilene and Malachi would get married, but that was another story and there was nothing I could do about that.

I had a room at the extreme rear of the left wing, which gave me a heap of privacy. I had shelves of books and a phonograph and a small but powerful radio—all gifts from Malachi, who was strong on making presents but sometimes thoughtless about providing cash for his employees. Still, it was a better life than I was used to before Malachi and I had been Marines.

At midnight I played some new blues recordings by old-timer Eddie Condon and drank a brandy in memory of Nick's in the Village and was about to turn in. Malachi and Ilene were somewhere in the house, but it was Hattie's night out, which was why we had eaten at the Spanish place. My light was very dim. There was a tapping at my window.

I doused the lamp and grabbed for the blackjack which always hangs at the head of my bed. Anyone could come through those first-story windows. I slid to the wall out of range and said: "What's the score, bub?"

A hoarse, unmistakably southern voice said: "I gotta talk to ye, Mist' Hinton. K'n yo' come outdoahs? I got somethin' foah ya."

I said: "Who are you, Santa Claus?"

"I'm Culpeppeh, the cop," said the voice apologetically. "I mean t' do right, Mist' Hinton."

Culpepper was slimy Manny Silvestriano's partner. At least they were paired off in vice squad work in Bay City. Due to Malachi's insistent interest in all local politics, I knew that their activities were unsavory. It was their practice to pick up couples in automobiles and shake them down. Failing this, to put them on the blotter for such charges as "indecent exposure," charges which they did not dare answer in court for fear of publicity. Innocence was no protection against such attacks as these, of course, and Silvestriano had piled up a huge sum in estreated bonds—which endeared him to certain city politicians. But Culpepper was not the instigator of these machinations, I knew, he was merely attached to the squad's boss.

I said: "Get away from that window and stand where I can see you. I'm going to put on a light and I want you in it. Then I'll come out."

I pulled on my pants and slid the blackjack into the pocket. I stepped aside and yanked up the Venetian blinds. Then I jerked on a light and scrammed into the hall, out through the kitchen and into the back yard.

He was standing there, a hulking, stooped figure, peering into my room, whence the light limned him. He had a patient, stupid look about him, and there was puzzlement in him, I thought, and fear too. I paused and crouched in the shadow of a large hibiscus. I called: "Culpepper!"

He turned toward my voice, took a step. There was a flat, whining sound. Culpepper jerked back, as though a bee had stung him.

I went out of that bush faster than a pack of wild rabbits. I hit the corner of the house as lead clipped stucco closer to my head than I liked. Inside I lammed for my room on all eight. I clicked off the light first, then dived for the bureau where my gun lay. I cursed myself all this while as if repeating a litany, for not having the gun in the first place. The blackjack had seemed sufficient against poor Culpepper, but I should have had more brains.

Manatee's voice came crisply from in front. "What were those shots, Tack?"

"The yard. Someone shot Culpepper out back." I was already ploughing my way out, my gun cocked. I hit the yard and there was the big cop, a dark blot on the grass, unmoving. I went the only way the murderer could have gone, to the rear of the property. The lot backed up on the waterway which led to the bay. I thought I heard the putt-putt of a motor going into open water. I made a complete circle and did not find a trace of anyone.

I came back, humiliated. Malachi and Ilene stood over the prone policeman. Malachi had some papers in his hand and while Ilene held a flashlight he went through them.

"Routine stuff," he muttered. He bent and put them back in Culpepper's coat pocket. "What's the story, Tack?"

I said: "He called to me that he had something for me. I went out with a mace in my jeans to listen to him. But I put him in the light—made a target of him. He never got to tell me a word of what he had in mind."

Ilene said: "The big bum's dead. Ugh!"

"I put him right on it for them," I said. I hated that part of it. No matter what he was like, I hated having spotted him. "Malachi, he must have had something important to spill. Killing coppers is no joke, even down here."

Malachi said: "I'll call Homicide, while you mix a drink. You'll need one. Don't feel too bad about it. They must have been onto him to have followed him here. The best that could have happened was that they got him after he spilled his guts… and they might have got you."

I said: "I heard a boat going out."

"Sure." Malachi nodded. "That's the only smart way to get away from here. Let's leave him and go inside."

I got the bourbon bottle. My hands were shaking. Malachi used the phone and Ilene chipped ice. We made drinks and sucked on them and pretty soon the cops came. Manny Silvestriano was with them and I braced myself for a tough time.

But they were amazingly nonchalant about it. They toted Culpepper's body off in surprisingly short time. They asked a thousand questions but they were almost polite. A gray-haired lieutenant named Mose Mosely seemed almost smart. Manny made horrible faces at us and I expected we would all be arrested but Mosely merely admonished us not to leave town.

As they were leaving, the lieutenant lingered. He waited until the last cop, even Silvestriano, was in the car, then said: "Mr. Manatee, there's been some funny stuff goin' on. Culpepper was in it. I donno what it is, but we don't want no trouble with you. If you and the lady could jest keep kinda quiet until we can straighten this out and find out who done it to Culpepper, I think I kin guarantee you won't get no bad publicity."

Malachi said: "If I feared publicity, I would certainly mind my own business, although I certainly could never restrain Miss Carver. Keeping quiet is not any part of my intention. This man was killed in my back yard. I intend investigating."

Mosely said: "I jest wanted to warn ya, Mr. Manatee." He departed, not without dignity.

THE THREE of us had another drink and looked at each other. I said: "Ilene, what was the gag this afternoon? You'll have to tell us, now."

Malachi said: "Yes, darling, who were you leching at? I was going to skip it, but now it looks suspicious."

Ilene said: "We were in this jook—Jolley's Jook—it's really a sort of bar and drive-in. Lily went to play the organ and this sailor grinned at her. We'd had a couple and Lily gave him the old eye."

"Lily, Lily, always Lily," said Malachi. "You were just drinking a coke!"

"Shut up, you big stiff," said Ilene. "I'm getting to me. Not that I'd tell you if it wasn't for this murder—you and your tennis at your age in this weather. There were two sailors. Lily got friendly with this one and the other came over. I had just ordered a drink—we were in a booth for four—when the cops jumped us."

"Sounds cozy," said Malachi. "Were these sailors drunk?"

"No. The one who flirted with Lily was only a boy and reckless. It was in his eye. The other was older, harder—and handsomer," said Ilene.

Malachi considered. Bay City was a port and many ships docked there from every land. He said: "You wouldn't know what boat they were from?"

"No," said Ilene. "I wasn't going aboard their ship. One was dark and the other was darker—almost swarthy. I think he was a Latin—the one I had."

"The one I had," echoed Malachi. "You sound more like Lily every day."

"Sometimes I wish I was like Lily," said Ilene. "Look at the fun that girl has had. The stories she can tell! What do I get hanging around with a couple of amateur Sherlocks like you? You're not even the Nick Charles type."

Malachi said: "You get bonded bourbon when everyone else is drinking sixty-five percent neutral spirits or worse."

"Nuts," said Ilene. "My sailor said he could get rum for two bucks per bottle. They're bringing it in all the time. It's cheaper and it's pure. He was a very interesting sailor and I wish I could see him again."

"Smuggling," nodded Malachi. "They were probably a couple of smugglers." He scowled, rubbing his chin. His eyebrows, like inverted blond Vs, went up and down. He said: "Those sailors… Culpepper… smuggling… If we only knew what Culpepper wanted to tell Tack. And why."

I said: "I'm a damned fool. I should have let him inside, under a gun."

Malachi said: "He evidently wanted to remain outside, or he wouldn't have tapped on your window—he'd have used the door. We'll have to work backwards. I'll interview Silvestriano. He'll be hanging around Headquarters."

He had his jacket on before we could stop him. It was two o'clock, but the Cad roared out of the driveway and Ilene and I drank another bourbon. There was no stopping Malachi when he got started on something like this. The corpse had obligingly come to him this time.

She said glumly: "There goes all the fun I had planned. That Lily—she's out of this world. I was going to scandalize Bay City society by taking her to the Yacht Club dance and turning her loose. Now it'll be all serious business with Malachi sleuthing around like Warren William in a shaky B."

I said: "Malachi is plenty burned up about your escapade. He'll blast Silvestriano."

"Malachi is a big jerk and I am going to bed," said Ilene bitterly. She made a face at me and went across and into the wing where she stayed. The ball bearings they had put in her hips were certainly celestial. Maybe it was the drinks, but she looked better to me than seven angels on gold pedestals. If she did not marry Malachi pretty soon, I wondered if I could restrain myself. The scar tissue our little brown brothers had put on my lung was about healed and I was beginning to feel like a complete man again, or at least so I imagined....

The phone rang. I put down my drink and answered it. A booming voice said: "Malachi, old boy?... Say, I shah am sorry, son, to heah youall had trouble agin. Culpeppeh shall be missed—an honest officeh, son. Now look heah, Malachi, jest lay low awhile, will yo', son? Some things goin' on around town we cain't jest talk about right now. Pow'ful lot of smugglin' and stuff you wouldn't be interested in, son..."

I said: "This is Hinton, Alderman."

"Oh..." There was silence. Then Pop Gilmore said: "Waal, son, jest tell Malachi.... Lay off this business." His voice was not so hearty and some of the bombast was gone and it sounded threatening to me, but of course I had been drinking a lot. That old goat could not be threatening, I thought, hanging up on him.

I went back to the bedroom and turned on my light. I put down the blind and lay on the bed. The gun was on my night table alongside the blackjack and they looked pretty useless lying there. I turned on the radio, and pulled in Los Angeles, where it was only midnight. There was a band and it sounded sad and lonely and I could not help thinking about Culpepper and how I had put him on the spot for the killer.

Sometimes a guy's life telescopes down on him and he finds himself in the dark and not liking what he sees. This was one of those times for me. It was extremely unpleasant looked at from the angle which presented itself. I was a high class bum, and if it were not for Malachi's money I would be a low class bum, I suppose. I toiled not, neither did I spin. I just got myself and other people into trouble and now a man was killed, right outside my bedroom window where I lay and looked out, and it was my fault for not trusting him and telling him to come inside. No matter what Malachi said, if I had asked him in, he might have escaped them later. He must have known he was in danger and he was a big enough guy to take care of himself.

If I only knew what he was trying to tell me. I remembered how he had stared at me at Headquarters, as if he recognized me. I knew he had played football one time and maybe that was it—he recognized another dumb linesman and meant to confide in me.

I finally went to sleep, but it was a bad night.

CHAPTER TWO
WHAT PRICE
HOMICIDE?

WE HAD a date to play tennis with Harrison and Gold the next afternoon and there seemed to be no reason why we should break it. Lily was on the verandah when we drove up, already sucking on a Tom Collins. She smiled vaguely and said: "Have a drink. Have a flock of drinks. This is my third. Isn't the weather but wonderful? Bud and Sam are in the locker room."

Ilene said: "I'll have a stinger. Can we borrow the car, Malachi?"

"Use your judgment," said Malachi sweetly. "If you like murders, go ahead and start another train of circumstances."

Lily said: "Murders? I read them all the time. Do you like short ones, or books? Books sometimes give me a headache. But I enjoy any murder."

Malachi said: "She's a beautiful ghoul."

I kept looking at Lily. She did not look that dumb to me, somehow or other. Voluptuous, yes, and maybe too much on the easy side, but not so utterly stupid. She must have seen the morning paper, with the account of the murder and our names splashed all over the first page. But Malachi just shrugged and led the way to the dressing rooms.

But Harrison was already in shorts. He had long, brown legs, very muscular and well-shaped. Gold was naked, a hairy, brown man, not at all good-looking. Harrison said loudly: "Aha! Cop-killers, huh? Hell of a thing. Just because a couple of snoopers bother your girl, you shoot one of them!"

Two or three other people in the locker room laughed half-heartedly and Gold said: "Shut up, Bud. Killin' a cop is not funny."

"Poop," said Bud jeeringly. "Why in New York you eat cops—"

"Shut up, damn you," Gold growled at him. He was not fooling and Bud flushed, but he shut up.

Malachi said: "The whole deal was peculiar, but let's not talk about it. Have you got a racket for me, Bud?"

"Had it strung yesterday," said Harrison, half sulkily. "It's in your locker."

Malachi said: "But it isn't—"

I looked in my locker, which was adjacent to Malachi's and there were four new bats in it. I took one out—they were identical—and handed it to Malachi and said: "The boy made a mistake. These other three are Sam's."

Gold said: "I'll take them now." He put them in his case. He had one of those suitcases which are made to carry tennis rackets and balls and athletic equipment, very swank. He had a slightly used bat, of the same make.

I said: "You believe in keeping rackets on hand."

"I'm going to Cuba," he explained. "Can't get my favorite down there. But can't seem to keep the man stocked. When I get used to a weapon, I like to have one all the time."

I said: "You play a good game, all right. Where'd you learn?"

"New York," he said, evasively, I thought. I let it go at that. He did play well—he and Bud had won about a hundred from us. Malachi fancied himself at doubles, but I was no good. I couldn't get the rhythm, and the old boxing and football muscles were not adapted to tennis. Of course my reflexes were pretty good, and I could sock the volleys, but I had no finesse.

We went out and started to play and the girls were gone and so was the Cad. Malachi was out of humor, but he played better because of it, and Gold was a bit erratic. We won three out of four sets at twenty-five apiece and Malachi felt fine. He loved to win, always.

We dressed and sat on the verandah and drank Scotch out of Harrison's private bottle. He told us a lot of stories, some of which I am sure were true. Gold drank more than usual and seemed impatient of Harrison's yarns for once. My mind kept going to Culpepper, dead in our back yard.

Malachi finished his third drink and stood up. He said: "We're playing in Clearwater tomorrow, so we'd better get our stuff."

I said: "Sure. You start calling Ilene."

He went to the phone and I went in and put our rackets in presses, two each, making sure Malachi's new one was among them, and shoved a dozen new balls into the bag. It was just an ordinary flat suit-case, not a fancy deal like Gold's—although I had seen Malachi eyeing Gold's and knew we would have one as soon as Abercrombie & Fitch could handle the order. I carried the bag out to the lobby of the club and Malachi came from the phone booth and said morosely: "She was back at that Jolley's Jook. I thought she would be. Looking for those two sailors."

"Some day she'll get hurt that way," I said worriedly.

"Not likely! But *someone* is bound to get hurt." Malachi was restless. He said: "I saw Silvestriano last night. He doesn't know anything about Culpepper's death."

I said: "I didn't think he did it."

"Culpepper was his partner, but he has no idea why Culpepper came to us." Malachi shook his head. "That's plain strange. Culpepper was certainly not the subtle sort, yet I have a feeling Silvestriano was telling the truth. I gave him some money and threatened him."

"Did you sock him?" I asked hopefully.

"Not yet," said Malachi. "I am saving him."

"O.K.," I said. "I want a piece of that myself. I don't like slimy little cops."

Malachi said: "Mosely knows something, but he won't confide in me. We are going to have to go ahead and work independently of the police."

"Something new, something different—not." I was depressed, for some reason. The girls drove up in the car and Ilene honked, which meant she had stuck to stingers and too many of them. Lily got out and her legs were slightly rubbery, but she smiled that dreamy smile and made the verandah.

She said: "No sailors today. Just sweet old men with beards." She wobbled past to join Harrison and Gold.

Malachi said: "One of the finest bums I ever met. No men living are evil in her category."

Ilene slid over and let Malachi take the wheel. She said: "Jolley never saw the sailors before. They didn't come back... Maybe the cops scared them. You know what, Malachi? That Lily is promiscuous. There were a couple of old goats out there slugging themselves in an attempt to get young again and she picked them up."

Malachi said: "You don't say? But if they were young sailors, then it was cute."

Ilene said: "I hate old men. Ugh!"

Malachi said: "Hattie has steak for dinner. Let's calm down and not drink too much and think about stuff—like why someone should kill a cop in our yard."

Ilene was subdued, for once in her life. We ate and played some records on the big phonograph and then I went back to my room and played some low down gut bucket for myself. I tried to read but that was no good. Then, contrariwise, although it was only about ten o'clock, I got sleepy. I undressed quickly and got in the bed—it wasn't often I could get a good night's sleep.

I GUESS I awoke about two in the morning. It was very quiet in the house. It was too quiet. There is a thing in the night which everyone knows—his own house should make certain noises. If those noises are absent, the quiet is as oppressive as the lull before a hurricane. It was like that now.

I got out of bed and this time I took the blackjack and the gun also. I slid out of my room as quietly as possible and went up the hall toward the front, making the turn of the L and not wasting any time. The distinct sound of someone breathing came as I paused on the threshold of the large living room.

I closed my eyes tightly, trying to get them accustomed to the darkness, and then opened them and tried to line up on the windows at the rear. These windows led to a patio, which was rimmed by a low wall. Culpepper had been killed back of this, of course, but on the other side of the patio wall a lawn led down to the canal, or waterway. I thought I saw someone leaning over an object on the floor and said sharply: "Who's there and hold it!"

Something exploded to my right and I knew there were two of them and I had muffed it again. I fired twice, I think, but I was blinded by the explosion of the gun, which was too close to me. I went down and things faded, and my last conscious thought was that I was a damned dummy and deserved to be killed.

When I awoke the room blazed with light. Ilene was holding my head and pouring bourbon down my throat. There was a bandage around my skull and I said: "You could be an angel in heaven, but I didn't lead that kind of a life, so I must be alive. Did Malachi get them?"

She said: "No. They scrammed in a boat, like last night. What do you suppose is the big idea?"

"What were they after?" I asked. My head was spinning and I had no desire to move.

She said: "They nearly got you, Tack. You bled like a pig. They were bending over your old suitcase with your rackets and sports clothes in it. Evidently they didn't know what they wanted."

Malachi came back through the windows. He had my gun in his hand and was very angry. He said: "This has damn well got to stop. I don't even know what it is all about. There has to be some reason for all this."

I said: "If I wasn't such a sap, we'd have found out. If we could only get our hands on one of the characters who are acting up and who got away in that boat, we would learn about things."

Malachi stared at our suitcase. I managed to get my head up exerting all my will power, and saw that the case was wide open, but the contents seemed undisturbed. It certainly did not make sense. Malachi took out each article, handling it carefully and thoughtfully, then replaced everything as it had been, closing the bag. He said: "There are footprints outside, but I don't want to call in the cops on this. We either ought to be real detectives or quit messing around."

I said: "Who's messing around? I stuck my dumb head in here and some louse tried to shoot it off. Is that messing around? What should I do when I heard burglars, holler cop?"

"Don't get sore," Malachi said mildly. "Have a drink."

Ilene said: "That's the whole trouble. You wouldn't let us drink tonight and none of us could think straight."

"You were sopping up stingers all afternoon, wasn't that enough? You and your sailors and your old men!" Malachi was riled.

Ilene said with dignity: "I already told you I hate old men. Now pour some whiskey and let's think about who is doing what to whom and who is going to get paid."

Malachi got out the whiskey. I stood up and had to hold onto a chair for a moment. The bullet had creased my skull and I began bleeding again, but Malachi got out the old first aid kit and re-bandaged it. We learned a lot of that stuff on Tarawa, believe me, and the wound I had was nothing. The bullet had crashed into the wall after it glanced off my thick skull and Ilene was trying to gouge it out with a kitchen knife.

Malachi finished with my head and said, somewhat mollified: "You're being constructive, Ilene. If we ever do find the gun, we can get the FBI to check that bullet."

Ilene said: "I was going to keep it for a souvenir."

Malachi said: "This thing has no pattern. I'm trying to put it together in my head, but it won't jell. The trouble is, we don't belong in this. We got into it by accident—whatever it is. The question is—where did we accidentally cross the trail of some very rough characters?"

"My sailor was tough. He was tattooed from his ear to his elbow," said Ilene complacently. Then her green eyes widened. She said: "The sailors! But of course, Malachi— Tack!" The bullet fell into her hand and she tossed it to me. It was a .44 and I shivered to think what it might have done to my brains. Ilene said: "Sailors—cops—police station—it all ties up. Could it be smuggling? Like they said rum was only two bucks?"

Malachi said slowly: "It's an angle. We'll work it. Tomorrow we find those sailors, if we have to send you and Lily soliciting again."

"Oh, goody," said Ilene satirically. "Another trip to jail!"

"Better that than another shot at Tack," said Malachi. "I can't afford to lose him."

We went to bed. I was happy Malachi felt that way about me. I was beginning to believe privately that I wasn't worth shooting. Two failures in two nights on my own home grounds seemed par for the course to me.

OF COURSE, we couldn't go to Clearwater. My head spun around whenever I took a quick step. I hung around the house and gloomed and ate aspirin, while Malachi scoured the town for sailors and Ilene drove Lily on the same errand. But Lily only got high as a kite again and at five Ilene brought her home to sober up. I had quit the aspirin and was working on the whiskey myself by that hour.

Malachi came in at six. Ilene said: "You didn't learn anything?"

"Maybe I'm getting stupid," said Malachi. "I learned nothing."

Lily said: "You're not stupid, darling. You're terrific. Everyone knows how terrific you are." She said with semi-drunken logic: "And besides, you're so damned rich!"

Malachi said: "Bud is down at the hotel screaming for your company. I'll take you down there as soon as I have a drink."

"Anywhere with you," nodded Lily solemnly. "I think you're wonderful. Have you really got six million bucks?"

Ilene said: "He's got eight million but no sex appeal. Lay off him, Lil." She gave me the wink and I managed to struggle to my feet. I was feeling better at that. I got out the car and Lily came out amicably, her arm around Ilene. Malachi was walking up and down the living room like a detective and I wondered if he had learned anything. Lily got into the car and snuggled up close to me, and went asleep.

At the hotel she awoke and said: "You're a nice, comfortable big guy, but you haven't got eight million bucks, have you?"

"I haven't got a dime," I replied. "Furthermore, Bud is coming out of the hotel right now, blood in his eye."

She said: "Blood he has got—but only in his eye. So long, nice guy. I wish you had all that money. Ilene has got Malachi all tied up in knots. Too bad she drinks."

She got out of the car, walking far too rigidly straight, and as Bud grabbed her arm she said: "Where have you been? I've been waiting at Malachi's for you. I thought you were going to call..."

It was wonderful—the same old story, a good attack to offset the fact that she was lying. He protested and I drove away without speaking to him. I saw Sam Gold sitting in a chair in the lobby, just sitting and looking without expression and it occurred to me that Bud was making a nice thing out of his association with Sam, who had plenty of money. And then I wondered how Bud managed to keep hold of Lily. Sam was the type to take her away.

Then I wondered over some other angles of that set-up, like how did Bud ever get a high-priced gal like Lily to begin with. As a sporting goods salesman, even with his Cuban tie-up, he did not rate in that company. The more I thought about it, the stranger it seemed. If my head had not begun to ache again, I would have thought hard about it.

When I got home I told Malachi what I had just been pondering and he said: "That's right. And do you notice something wrong with Lily?"

I was about to deny that there was anything fundamentally wrong with that sleekly upholstered babe when Ilene came into the room and said: "She doesn't drink enough to get as high as she gets."

"That's screwy," I said. "She's always a little stinko."

Malachi said: "Not on liquor."

The moment he said it I knew he was right. I had put in a brief spell as a private detective once during my New York career and had seen enough to know that I should have spotted it long ago. I said: "You're right! Snow!"

Ilene said: "Now wait. Remember me? I've become pretty steeped in crime since travelling with you, but this one has me whipped. What makes?"

"Dope," said Malachi. "And it begins to make sense. Sailors—a meeting you thought casual. You said Lil picked up the sailors. I thought it was your line...."

Ilene said: "She did pick them up. Not flagrantly—"

"She is a very high class babe," said Malachi. "But when they are taken off the junk, they crack. I read that somewhere in a book, I think."

"Can you have her arrested?" I asked.

"Not and keep her from getting heroin," said Malachi grimly. "Not with Silvestriano and his ilk running the police department. The trusties are all peddlers. While Silvestriano looks for car-neckers, the jailbirds sniff dope."

"We'll have to take her ourselves," said Ilene. "How about the beach place? We could hold her there."

Malachi said: "You could get her there. The rest would be easy. She must be connected with some dope ring. The sailors bring it in, give it to her, and she passes it on."

"You read that in a book, too," I accused him.

"Well, something like it," said Malachi carelessly. "Culpepper must have had something to do with it. Maybe he got wise to Lily when they were bringing you in. She may have had a fresh charge in the ladies' room at Jolley's Jook, and he recognized it. So he came here to talk to us about our lady friend taking dope—Culpepper probably saw some advancement for himself if he handled it that way—and whoever is in on the dope ring shot him."

I said: "You have really got an imagination. A dope ring, now!"

"There is always a dope ring, very sinister people," said Malachi. "Dope is a thing which I do not like at all." He was very cheerful and his limp was pronounced as he walked up and down again, only more rapidly. "Silvestriano could be in on it. It would be fine if he was in on it."

I said: "You're doing a lot of guessing. And you haven't explained the attempted robbery last night and who shot me in the skull."

"That needn't have anything to do with it," Malachi said blithely. "The main thing is to get Lily over to the beach and hold her there without her dosage of dope and see if she will talk."

I said: "But you're really only guessing about Lil and heroin."

"You said so yourself," Malachi cried.

"I was guessing. You don't think they'd take my word in court, do you?"

Ilene said slowly: "I think Malachi is right. At any rate, tomorrow we can go to the beach—and take Lil. There's tennis for you at Clearwater, if Tack's able to play. Harrison and Gold will fall for it. We can watch Lily all the time—at least I can."

"We'll do it," said Malachi decisively. "Let's all get a good night's sleep for a change…"

I said: "Last night I tried that and got shot. I'm going to stay up and read a good book."

"If you play those Mound City Blues Blower records, play them soft," Ilene said. "They send me!"

I went back to my room and took off the bandage around my head. The place where the bullet had glanced was a little raw and Malachi had shaved off some hair. No stitches had been necessary but I taped it as neatly as possible. I heard the phone ring, but as Ilene and Malachi were in the living room I did not pick up the extension in my room.

The first I knew there was trouble was when Malachi began bawling my name, very irate. I grabbed my gun and blackjack and ran for the center of the house. Malachi was waving his arms and swearing. Ilene was quite pale and for once subdued, as though something had hurt her.

Ilene said: "That was Mosely. They just found Lily. In the courtyard of the hotel… She fell out of the eighth floor window."

MALACHI HAD stopped cursing and was on the phone. He dialed a number and said sharply into it: "That you, Doc Cone?... Manatee... There's been a death and the coroner will call it something-or-other, but I want an autopsy... Yes, a woman, name of Lily Clay... I'll have Gilmore on it... He'll call you."

He hung up, worked the dial again. He said into the phone: "Pop Gilmore? Get down to Headquarters and insist upon an autopsy upon Lily Clay... Certainly she's dead." He pronged the hook, listened into the phone. For a moment there was silence. I was thinking about Lily when I dropped her off at the hotel, the way she slurred her syllables when she called me a nice, comfortable guy and the way she had looked at me as she got out of the car. I guess Ilene was thinking about the light-hearted fun she had with Lily, because she remained subdued.

Malachi said: "Pop! What's the matter with you?... Oh, you dropped your teeth? Well, you call Doc Cone and tell him to make an autopsy and then you call Mosely and put the works to the cops. And get the state's attorney on it, too. I'll tell you why later."

He hung up and wiped his brow. His handsome face was taut and hard-looking, the way it got when something was taken away from him. Much as I loved that man, he was not a very pretty sight when he was crossed. Sometimes I thought Ilene did not bother to make him marry her because of this. He was accustomed to having everything millions can buy and he was tough enough to go after the other things—the ones it is alleged millions cannot buy. He got them. The only thing about which he had been able to do nothing was what happened in the Pacific, when we were in the Marines, and that was why he had me around. I had been part of that and it was a thing he valued, perversely, because it had been tough and had left him with a bum knee and a restlessness which he took out in such cases as we were now mulling over in our minds.

Ilene said: "I feel as though I ought to be with the poor girl, but that's no good. She's not there, is she?"

Malachi growled: "If I could only put my hands on those sailors."

The doctor would be able to ascertain whether she had been taking dope, I knew. Malachi was getting ahead of himself, it seemed. But he had the itch for action and it was ravishing him. He looked older, and his V-shaped brows kept folding and unfolding.

I said: "Maybe we had ought to check with Bud and Sam, at that." It was something to do. Malachi needed to move out of the house.

Ilene said: "Get the car, Tack. You're right, as always, pal."

It was still quite early—only eleven o'clock. I drove us down to the hotel and parked the car in the garage in the rear. We bribed a freight elevator operator and got a ride up to the eighth floor. Sam and Bud had a big double suite at one end of the corridor and at the other Lily had a single bedroom suite. We went down toward the mens' rooms.

Mosely opened the door for us. Silvestriano was in there and I heard him say accusingly: "Everybody knows you were that babe's sugar man."

"What a dirty mind," Malachi murmured. "Can't you shut him up?"

Mosely said: "It's a kind of sickening third degree. These two men alibi each other. They claim they were playing gin rummy in here when she went out the window down the hall. If Manny can make them mad enough maybe they'll tell the truth."

"What's the truth?" asked Malachi. I stood beside Ilene, between Malachi and the corridor door. I could see Sam

Gold, his knees crossed, smoking a cigarette and looking expressionlessly at Silvestriano. But Bud was on his feet, hunched a little, pale as a ghost and ready to spring at the cop. Silvestriano had his hand on his blackjack and there were two big dumb coppers standing by, but I knew Bud would get him for at least one punch and it looked good to me.

Mosely said: "The people in the next room heard a man's voice. Then they heard her yell as she went out the window. Then they swear the door opened and closed as though someone came out of the apartment. They were the ones who went in and saw that she was gone, and called the desk. She fell into the deserted courtyard and we might not have found her right away. They seem the kind who tell the truth."

Malachi said: "Make sure there's a p.m. on the woman."

Just then Silvestriano said something nastier than before and Bud jumped. Gold hardly moved—he just stuck out his foot and tripped one of the big cops. I managed to get the heel of the other with my toe, which made him fall into the one Sam Gold had tripped. While they floundered around, Bud hit Silvestriano four clips in the puss. Manny got out his blackjack, but by that time Mosely, swearing like a trooper, got in there and parted them, shoving Bud into a chair and tossing Manny to us.

Malachi hit Manny so hard in the ribs he knocked him clear into the hall. The two detectives were up by then, but they were so dumb they thought Malachi was just pushing Silvestriano to safety and thanked him with grunts. They hesitated, but Mosely and I shoved them after Silvestriano and closed the door.

Sam Gold said: "Hello, fellas. How about some tennis tomorrow? Say about three?"

Malachi said: "Sure, Sam. And don't worry about these local cops. Mosely will look up a couple of sailors and this thing will be solved."

Mosely said: "What in hell you talkin' about?"

So Malachi told him his theory, and when he was through, Mosely looked relieved and quite certain of himself. He apologized to Gold and Harrison and took off like a man in a hurry.

Harrison said feelingly: "Thanks, Malachi. You sure got them off my back. I'd have killed that scum. I was fond of Lily… man… the idea of her all smashed to bits. They kept saying Sam and I killed her. What for? Why should we kill a good kid like that?"

Malachi said: "We'll clear it up. See you tomorrow, gentlemen. Come on, kids, let's take a look for ourselves."

Ilene held my arm tight going out of the hotel. Malachi insisted on combing the jooks and the dockside places, but we found no sailors that night. We went home and it was still depressing, thinking about Lily. I had never known Ilene to be so quiet.

I did not play any records. Somehow I had no spirit for it. Culpepper and Lily both walked my thoughts. Death in the Pacific was one thing—having it walk around Bay City, its wings flapping too close for comfort, was strictly another, and one for which I could not go.

CHAPTER THREE
PURE AS SNOW

IN THE morning the telephone was ringing and I awoke and heard Malachi answering. I went into the bathroom and when I came out Malachi was calling me. I went into the living room. He was stalking the floor again. He said quite calmly: "I'm not as smart as I thought. The girl was taking dope, all right. Sniffing heroin. But Doc Cone and Mosely had to fight Gilmore on the autopsy. It seems our alderman didn't want any part of it and tried very hard to get in touch with relatives up north to prevent us marring Lily's remains."

I said: "Then Pop Gilmore is not pure as the driven snow." I remembered the phone call and told Malachi about it. "He's been wanting you off of this from the start. The old windbag is mixed into some graft."

Malachi said: "If I could only find those sailors. The key to the thing lies in their meeting with Ilene and Lily."

I said: "Maybe, but you're guessing about it."

"There were two men who tried to rob us...." Malachi said vaguely. "Two men... house burglars don't work that way... nor carry guns... especially .44s. I know I'm right." He darted into his room and I went to see if Hattie had coffee. She did, and some eggs and bacon. Ilene came out, dressed in a light suit, ready for the street.

Ilene ate four eggs and a half pound of bacon. She would never talk until she had slupped up that longshoreman's meal. When she was finished I said: "Malachi's all excited."

"He is taking everything in the old suitcase apart again," she said. "He must think those burglars left something in there instead of stealing anything."

We smoked a moment and Malachi came in and roared for breakfast. He ate even more than Ilene. Then he said: "Maybe we can do better by staying out of this for the present. Let's just take a ride around and meet the guys at the club at three and play tennis like nothing had happened."

I said: "Poor Bud Harrison won't feel like playing."

"I'll call him," said Malachi carelessly. "Let's get the car out and slide over and get a swim, huh?"

It did not seem exactly the thing to do, but we all three got into the Cad and drove twenty miles to the beach cottage and opened it for a change and a couple of hours in the Gulf of Mexico. It was extremely pleasant and we had a bottle of bourbon. We could not get any more Scotch and were running very low and the bourbon which Malachi's father had thoughtfully provided before Prohibition and the earlier World War was still ten cases high in the storage warehouse where Malachi kept it, so we had taken to much bourbon-quaffing. It was good, too, but dizzy-making.

We left in time to catch the tennis club at three. But for once Malachi had neglected to reserve a good court and we had to sign for one on the far side, behind the clubhouse and far from the verandah. We went over and hit a few, awaiting the others, and Ilene drifted around with a chair and put it under a lone pine. This court was an afterthought and cut off completely from the others. In a little while Sam Gold and Bud Harrison approached, carrying a couple of rackets apiece and looking none the worse for the bad night they must have had.

Sam Gold said: "I knew you'd show up. Told Bud you would."

"It's better to do something," Malachi said sympathetically to Bud. "Takes your mind off things."

"I guess so," said Bud. He seemed very quiet and different, but he was not distraught. He spoke to Ilene and we all took off our sweaters and got ready to play.

Sam Gold said: "I'll be leaving soon—how about twenty-five bucks per set, we play three? That'll give you a chance to get even."

"O.K.," said Malachi with satisfaction. "Let's start."

We picked up our rackets and went onto the court. Malachi was using the new one, the Dunson that Bud had strung up for him. I had a good bat he had sold me earlier in the month. We broke out new balls and rallied, and then we began to play. Ilene watched and Malachi was all over the place with his slightly gimpy gait. Sam played his usual game, but Bud was a bit off and we won the first set, 6-3. Sam spoke sharply to Bud as we changed courts.

Malachi said to me under his breath. "Keep on top of them. We can cop all three today."

We did win the next set also. Ilene said: "I think you are being taken because you had a worse night than my heroes, Bud."

He said: "Thanks... but they're really improved. 'Specially Malachi."

"Yeah," said Sam. "Malachi's playin' a hell of a good game."

We took a rest, by mutual consent, throwing our sweaters over our shoulders and drinking some water from a nearby fountain. There were some pine trees, just a little grove, and a few small palms between us and the gravel road which led to the club. On the other side of the trees was the water of the bay. The weather was warm, the sun brilliant and there was not enough breeze to interfere with the tennis, but plenty to cool us off.

Sam was opening a set of new balls. Malachi picked up a racket. I started to say: "That's Sam's bat," But Malachi was giving me one of those looks.

Bud came from the fountain and said: "Should we start playing again?"

Malachi said: "Yeah. I'm ready."

Sam picked up his racket, which was really Malachi's. I was sure of that. We went out on the court. They were all the same type bats, of course, painted the same color. Bud had sold us all alike—it was a new, post-war wooden frame, really whippy and yet solid, a nice weapon. But Sam hefted his, scowling down at it, as we began playing.

We began the third set and Sam was really off. He began looking critically at his racket as he knocked an easy fore-hand out of court. He walked over as though he were going to change, then shook his head and went back, his dark features very thoughtful. We won four games straight.

Now it was Bud who spoke sarcastically to Sam. They exchanged a heated word where we could not quite over-hear. Sam made a gesture and Bud said loudly: "You're crazy!"

Sam lifted his racket high over his head, as though stretching. The score was four—love, our favor, with Malachi serving. The set was as good as in the bag for us. Malachi served, Sam took it on forehand and knocked it wide of the alley. I watched it, turned around to say: "Out, Sam." Two men walked out of the trees behind Ilene and stood silently, staring. They had large revolvers in their hands.

Ilene sensed someone was behind her and turned. She said brightly: "Well, Joe, whaddayaknow?"

The two men wore clothing which smacked of ships. The taller, darker, older of the two said: "Hello, babe. It's nice seein' yuh." He was a Latin, all right, and he looked very tough indeed.

Sam was working the end of the racket, his hands strong and brown. His eyes kept going to Malachi. He said: "This is the one that got mixed up in the locker. Tack's locker."

The dark sailor said: "The cops keep lookin' for us, and they are gettin' close. We better scramola."

Gold wrenched the leather tab off the butt of the handle of the tennis racket. These handles are built hollow, with a little wooden plug in the end, then they are covered with the leather of the handle, and a finishing piece over the plug. He took off the finishing tab and the plug fell out. He looked at it for a moment, replaced the plug carefully, replaced the tab, smoothing it out with his fingers.

Sam said: "This is too bad, Malachi."

"The heroin is at my house," said Malachi helpfully. "When you didn't manage to get it before Tack interrupted you the other night, it just stayed in the racket handle until I got some sense about me this morning and remembered a whole heap of things."

Sam said quite sadly: "That's the trouble in this world. People have to go and get too smart."

I WAS beginning to sweat a little. These sailor fellows looked very capable to me and they both had guns.

Malachi said: "It's the little things you have to remember. Like Scotch which you guys always had. I remembered that there was no United States revenue label, which meant it was not brought down from New York, but imported from some foreign land. Why should Bud lie about that?"

"Bud talks too much," said Sam. "I always knew that."

"The cops," said the sailor, fingering his gun, "will be chasing the little boat down here. How about it, Sam? Do we knock off the babe, too? I kinda like the babe. She can really drink whiskey!"

Sam said: "Take it easy. These bums are friends of mine!"

Malachi said: "Thank you, Sam, I like you, too, in a way. Silvestriano gave you back the hundred dollars Tack advanced because you didn't want us in this, and I know you never meant to start us. But Culpepper, the big dummy, was on to Lil. He knew she was on the stuff."

"Lil was bad medicine," said Sam. "I kept telling Bud."

"Damn you!" Bud Harrison was suddenly sweating and white. His hands shook like aspen leaves in a breeze. "Damn you, Sam. You—I alibied you, but you killed her. You went in there and pushed her... pushed her out that window! You told me you were paying off Gilmore..."

Malachi said: "You see? It all comes out. Pop Gilmore, Silvestriano, taking bribes to let you handle the stuff around Bay City. The racket handles to fool the customs inspectors—and that was a honey. But when you admitted that you could not buy Dunson rackets in Havana—and we knew that Bud made the trip four times per year—that was not smart of you, Sam! Eventually, when I found the dope in the racket handle, it meant Bud was bringing back too many bats from his excursions to Cuba!"

Sam said steadily: "So. That is one time I was dumb."

Bud Harrison almost screamed: "You did kill her! You did! Damn your soul, you killed my girl!" He sounded like a man in the utmost agony.

The sailor said: "Boss, if this gee keeps yapping and the cops are around, there will be mucho trouble, huh?" The other sailor said nothing, but kept his gun at the proper level. It was easy to spot them for ex-soldiers, familiar with side-arms and calm under fire. There was no sign of cops that I could see. Malachi was not even trying to edge into position. Ilene never moved nor spoke. I knew she would not make a bad move—she never did, not when there was danger. Her green eyes kept going to the sailor and then to Bud.

Sam said apologetically: "We can't let you turn us in. Our boat don't travel that fast. If there was room, I'd take you along and maroon you some place. What the hell, I hate killin' people."

"You mean Lily wasn't people?" asked Malachi pleasantly.

Sam made a gesture. It was a sweep of his hand, the most contemptuous dismissal, a degradation without the curl of his lip. "Junky babes! A dime a dozen. No, they ain't people. They pass the stuff, but sooner or later—blooie, they go for some heel."

Malachi stepped aside then, but without haste. He has such long arms and legs that often he does not appear in a hurry when he is moving fast indeed. At the same moment Ilene smiled at the dark sailor and threw her chair at the other one, a combination of actions which seemed to confuse everyone.

I went right past Sam Gold. The younger sailor was tangled in the chair. The other fired, but Bud Harrison had spoiled his party.

Bud went in when Malachi stepped aside. Bud hit Sam Gold like a flock of furies. He was screaming like a woman, now, yelling obscenities and repeating time and again:

"She was better than you, you damned murderer! Better than you!"

I got to the littler sailor as Malachi and Ilene hit the other. Malachi hit him first, kicking the revolver out of his hand. Then Ilene hit him with the edge of her hand as we had taught her. It was a nice one, behind the ear, at the base of the neck, and the amazed Latin sailor fell forward to where Malachi belted him out with a short uppercut.

I got the gun carefully away from the smaller sailor and backheeled him against a palm tree, which would keep him out of it for a while, and then looked around for Sam. He was in a fix. Bud was sitting on his chest, whaling away with both hands. But even as I watched Sam reached coolly into a pocket and hauled out a pen-knife. He was going to try, right to the end. I didn't have the heart to shoot him. I handed Ilene the gun and went over and picked Bud loose. Malachi took Bud and I jerked Sam to his feet. He tried for me with the little blade, at that. He was one of those city kids and he didn't know any other way to go but game. I slapped him out almost with regret.

Then I said: "Malachi, where are the cops? This is the most dangerous, silliest thing you ever pulled. You don't tip us off, you come out here where Sam can signal his torpedomen, you leave us at their mercy while you play Sherlock Holmes. Dammit, you might have got Ilene hurt!"

Malachi put a hammerlock on Bud and said injuredly: "Well, I wasn't even sure they knew what was in the racket handles, was I? It might have been someone working a switch without their knowledge, mightn't it? How did I know they would be all ready and have this court fixed for us to get ours on?"

I said: "Sam is twice as smart as you, at that."

Sam did not say anything. Bud quit struggling and said dully: "I'll put them all in a noose. Gilmore, Silvestriano— Culpepper was on the level. Joe, that sailor, and his pal killed him when he went to you. They burgled your house, too, but Tack scared them off. Sam arranged today's date with some idea of either finding the racket or fixing you. I was too sick to object. I thought Lil had taken too much dope and had fallen out of the window. She was some-times—vague…"

Malachi said: "The Cuban ship due tomorrow is the one?"

"Sam has this little, fast boat. They arrange a pick-up when they have to. Sam is a big shot, Malachi. Millions go through his hands. He paid me off big. Sporting goods— hell, the president of my company never saw the money Sam paid me!"

I turned away, to make sure of my murdering sailors. To the end, all people remained alike, I thought. Bud could not help bragging, shooting the stuff when faced with the rope. He made more money than the president of his company! And he wound up where?

Ilene said: "I still insist he is handsome."

I lifted the Latin to his feet. There was no time for fool-ing around, so I tied him with his belt, did the same to the other. Ilene said: "They'll lose their pants."

"You might go call the police instead of staring," I said sourly. She went away, laughing like an angel. I would not get over being sore at Malachi for weeks. He might have got her hurt, at that, damn him….